Tales of Little Egypt

For Angelina.
An enduring friendship

Tales of Little Egypt

JAMES GILBERT

atmosphere press

Published by Atmosphere Press

Cover design by Josep Lledó

Library of Congress Control Number
2020909198

Tales of Little Egypt
2020, James Gilbert

atmospherepress.com

Contents

Introduction

Marion, Illinois sits on the north edge of Little Egypt, where the two great American rivers, the Mississippi and the Ohio entwine before plunging into the deep South. At the center of Williamson County, this small town is renowned for the violence of its marauding bands of Union and Confederate sympathizers and its warring armies of bootleggers in the 1920s. A countryside of farms, coal mines and small villages, crisscrossed by railroads and spinning in the competing orbits of Chicago and St. Louis, it was populated by English, German, African-American, Italian, Irish, and Polish immigrants, each group, in turn, drawn into the area by the shifting economic opportunities of field and farm and extractive industry. The accents of its people anticipate the broad drawl of its Southern neighbors (Kentucky and Missouri), but pronounced with a dash of Northern impatience.

Away from the booming Midwest cities, Marion grew at a more leisurely pace, and many of its sons and daughters, bored or frustrated, and fearing failure within the narrow limits of the futures it offered, fled west or north to the big cities that gleamed beyond its restricted horizons. Yet, such places as this occupy a privileged space in the collective memories of many Americans, even those who have never lived or visited there, for they epitomize the world of small towns that we imagine to be the places where our civilization is most authentic.

Between the end of the Civil War and the great influenza plague that swept through America in 1918 with the return of soldiers from the killing fields of Flanders, the area gradually filled with the settlers who determined its special character. The sketches in this collection document their lives—not, of course by portraying real persons, but rather their imaginary selves and experiences. If a town such as this could tell its real history, it might well speak through such stories as these.

The slow pace of life and the absence of anonymous urban crowds creates the impression of familiarity and intimacy among individuals. Family and community ties certainly bound its population together and to the accumulation of shared pasts. However, these connections could also narrow and constrain their lives. The geography of a few blocks and squares—extending along streets named for local trees like Chestnut, Cherry, Walnut, Beech, Elm, Dogwood, and Pine or on avenues named for the Presidents and prominent citizens—defined their prospects. Their lives inevitably intersected, creating a pattern like a map of the town itself. One life was a fragment in another until all the pieces together constitute the story of a whole.

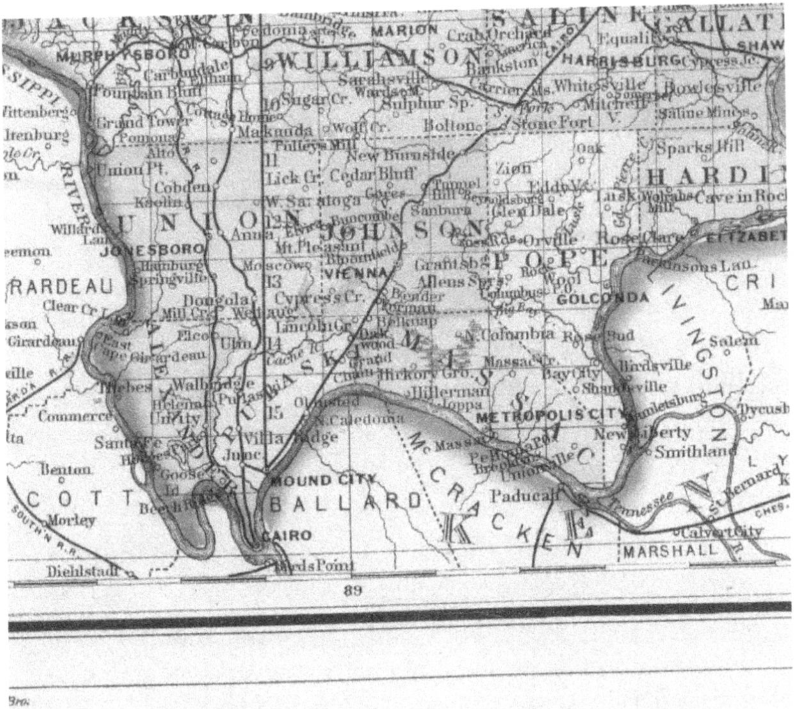

Map of Little Egypt in 1890

Doc Watson

Young David Watson pulled open the limp flap securing the entrance to the makeshift hospital set on a high ridge near Springfield, Missouri and ducked inside. The battle at Wilson's Creek had just ended, and teams of nurses were unloading cartloads of wounded Union soldiers. Quickly making a decision between hopeless and hope, they left those with no chance of survival on the hard earth outside; those with lesser wounds they carried in and laid onto soiled and bloody canvas cots. A chorus of low moans and the smell of death assailed Watson as he entered. He saw the low cloud of smoke that had ascended to the top of the tent from the hot irons used to cauterize bloody injuries and amputations. He always hesitated for a moment, not only to adjust his eyes to the murky atmosphere, but also to swallow back the nausea that rose in him. Over one shoulder, he had slung his bag of simple physician's tools: steel pincers and probes to extract the lead shards from soft tissue and a set of handsaws to remove shattered arms and legs. In his right hand, he carried a large bottle of spirits to deaden pain.

Only a doctor's assistant, Watson had quickly learned all of the desperate measures to ease the wounded into death or repair bodies for a return engagement with the fates of battle. How many times—he couldn't count—had he seen the same soldiers return, the fear of death in their eyes again; the familiar plea for hope. As a boy, he had thrilled to read of Napoleon's great armies—the majesty and symmetry of maneuvers, the heroic deeds of individual soldiers, the dash of cavalry, and tides of battles turned by genius. But this war was nothing like that fiction and he had relinquished all such illusions.

"If you want to be a doctor, young man," the head surgeon had instructed him, "then you've got to face up to the dying, be instructed by their pain; learn the colors of flesh as it rots; and know the look of fevers coming on."

Inside the tent, Watson received his assignment to attend the bed side of one of the twice-wounded, a boy of about his age who had suffered a severe stomach wound during a minor skirmish with Quantrill's Raiders. Apparently, he was fully conscious, but very seriously hurt, probably dying, and wanting to talk to someone.

Leaving his tools behind, Watson approached the cot where he lay, leaned over, and touched his face.

"What's your name, soldier?"

"Elbert Campbell, Doctor," he mumbled softly. A trickle of blood dribbled from the side of his mouth. "I know I'm dying, sir. I know I'm beyond helping. I got the coldness comin' on. And they tell me that's the sign."

"Can't be sure yet. We have to wait a spell to know."

"I gotta talk to someone. Just can't depart without sayin' what I got to say."

Watson was sure he knew what was coming. How many times had he held the hand of a dying soldier as he talked about home, his family and plans for the future—the girl waiting for him? How many times had he made a promise that he couldn't keep to send off a special letter or convey those pleading last words in person? How many times had he betrayed those last wishes entrusted to him?

"Promise me, doctor, you'll write to my girl back home."

"Where do you come from Elbert?"

"Marion, Illinois, just across the river." He paused, and Watson thought he could see a wave of pain pass across his face.

"Beautiful little town, farms, and my girl. You got to tell her—Delia." He paused and closed his eyes. "Got a picture of her in my pocket and a ring. You take them both. Only thing I have."

He tried to reach into his pocket, but his arm fell limp across the mass of bloody bandages. Watson reached over, unbuttoned his shirt and pulled out a crumpled picture and a simple brass ring.

"Tell her I love her. I'm sorry."

He coughed violently and spat out a large clot of black blood.

"Tell her...our life..."

Watson looked carefully at him and saw that the life had passed out of his eyes. He felt for a pulse and found none. Walking back toward the entrance where there was a set-aside area for doctors and nurses, he informed the person who kept records that Elbert Campbell had just died. Then he sat down on for a moment on a wooden stool in the corner. He felt an overwhelming sadness and guilt—

something he often experienced when he witnessed a death and a passing that he could do nothing to prevent or ease.

Opening up the folded daguerreotype, he stared intently at the picture of the girl. Despite the age of the paper, her luminous and silvery face stood out from the dark background. She was wearing a high-necked ruffled collar, her light-colored hair swept back. Watson thought that he had never seen such an image, almost sad and yearning, as if she already knew the fate of her beau. He folded it again and put it in his pocket and then he thought of the ring, the ring that held the dead soldier's promise. Taking it in his finger, he rubbed it gently. Perhaps this time, yes, when this terrible war was over, and when his job of nursing the wounded and dying was accomplished, he would keep this promise. It was only one promise; he could never undo all of the destruction and slaughter that he had attended; never cancel all the lies he told to those without hope. But this was what he wanted: to bring some solace to someone: to Elbert's family and his girl. Not that he even knew her last name or where she lived. He had the photo of her face and he knew enough of Elbert's history—and his name. In a small town, he was sure he could find the Campbell family. Better a mission when this terrible scourge ended: to keep one promise.

Although the fighting finally ended in April, Watson's work at the army hospital only gradually diminished. The gravely ill died quickly. The carts bearing the wounded stopped arriving. There was still work to be done, however: teaching those who were still mending how to watch for signs of fever and infection. There were always serious cases of dysentery to be treated. The winding down of his service was gradual, then, but it left him increasing time to think of the future and dream about the unknown. With his experience, he thought he might set up a practice in a town such as Marion. Perhaps he would even find a short medical course to take somewhere. He did not intend to enroll in the St. Louis University School of Medicine where he would have to compete against the best graduates from the East—even if he knew far more than they ever could fathom of a practical nature. Once he was done here in Missouri, he would travel across the river to southern Illinois. He might stop at Marion, deliver the message to the Campbells and Delia, and if the town seemed suitable, set up a practice there. Maybe.

In mid-summer of 1865, when the Army hospital finally shut down and the remaining wounded had dispersed, young Doc Watson, now 20, set off by train to St. Louis. After crossing the Mississippi, he traveled near Marion by wagon and then on foot the remaining distance. By the time he arrived, he was dusty and dirty and exhausted, and doubtful too when he saw the tall green cornfields that encroached right up to the first houses of the small community. As he walked along its few blocks of clapboard houses (a few of them fine and pretentious) he entered the modest central square. It seemed very much like the small town in southern Missouri where he had been born and similar, probably, to a thousand small towns across the country that clustered around a riverbank, a railhead, or a coalmine, or a market crossing where the up and coming dreamed of a metropolis. The same smell of horse manure on the streets, the same raised-up wooden sidewalks; there was the same jumble of old sheds and shacks side by side along new brick and stone buildings facing toward an ambitious future. If this border area in 1865 was anything like what he knew of Missouri, there would be a constant commotion of people, settling and unsettling such places. But how many of these small towns, he wondered, would already have a doctor, a lawyer, an undertaker, or even a banker? Not many. He could only be sure of a preacher's presence, for he had yet to encounter any village without at least one humble steeple, or sometimes, if the crops were plentiful and the trade brisk, a stone or brick church and attached graveyard set just off Main Street or on a corner of the town square.

When Watson arrived in Marion on that sultry August afternoon, the town seemed asleep under a heavy blanket of humidity. He entered the square, carrying his valise and a small case of medical tools—he called them "tools" and not instruments, because of their similarity to implements of other trades. Around the hard-packed, open ground, there was an assortment of stores and what looked like a bank. Several buildings had wooden hitching posts in front. One large wooden structure with a front porch announced it was a hotel. Watson was fairly certain that it held both a saloon and a boarding house of sorts that might serve meals along with accommodation. In the middle of the opposite side, he saw a dry goods store that looked as if it might be open. Although he could see no customers inside, there was a lone man with skin the color of untanned leather sitting on a wooden bench in front of the open door, sucking on a pipe. A spotted hunting dog, stretched out on the ground at his side, raised a lazy paw to swat a swarm of flies worrying his head.

Watson approached, full of questions, but hesitated for

a moment to ask. The man stirred and his dog opened a wary eye.

"What is it, lad?" he asked, shifting the cap on his head to get a better glimpse of the boy standing in front of him.

"Is there a doctor in the town?"

"Be you sick then?" The man straightened himself on the bench and moved slightly away.

"Oh no, not at all, sir. I'm in the best of health, thank you."

"Well then that's good to hear 'cause the nearest doctor is in West Frankfurt, up the road quite a piece. Only visit him when we have to and then there's Widow Daly, the midwife, but you won't be needin' her services, will you?" This last thought brought up a sudden, rough laugh, something between a snort and a cough, which ended almost as soon as it began. He spat a long stream of tobacco juice onto the ground beside him.

"Well, that's good to know," replied Watson, ignoring the puzzled look on the man's face. "And one more question if I might. Do you know the Campbell family and where they might live? I have a message for them from their son."

"Easy enough to find them, laddie. Just walk on west out of town 'til you get past the second farm. You'll reco'nize it for the metal windmill he put up f'r drawin' water up f'r his cattle and pigs. Yes, sir, Ed Campbell is forever tryin' out new contraptions; makes him an easy mark for any salesman what's passing through town. Got him a pretty piece of land, though, but a right shame that he ain't got no son to work it when he's gone. But, I reckon you must know all 'bout that if you're acquainted with the family."

Having delivered this long soliloquy, the man pulled his cap back over his eyes, touched his dog's head with his index finger, and fell silent.

"Good day and thank you, sir."

Watson was sure he would get nothing more, and so decided to ask in the dry goods store about lodgings, should he decide to stay. The only light he observed as he stepped inside seeped through the grimy front windows, but he could make out bolts of material laid out on shelves and a few ready-made dresses on metal forms standing like headless serving girls. In one corner, a row of bonnets and hats hung on wooden hooks. The air inside held a cloud of suspended dust particles that gave an amber glow to the goods on display. As he looked around, an elderly woman pushed through a muslin curtain that must have hidden a back sewing room. She stood before him and looked him over, head to toe. She was certainly no fashion plate herself, or advertisement for any elaborate costume that she might sew, but then, thought Watson, the only fancy dress needed in this town was for weddings, church and burials. Almost certainly, hers would be an entirely practical trade.

"Sorry to bother you ma'am," he began, trying to sound reassuring. "I'm new to town and looking for a hotel or rooming house. Do you know of one?"

She was silent while she finished her appraisal.

"Why yes, young man. I do. There is the hotel, across the way. But maybe you aren't the sort to be stayin' there. Kinda rough place for a young man like you. But my sister takes in boarders if you're interested. She's over on West Cherry St, just two blocks down. You can't miss it. It's a white house with a round window in the front door, like a ship's porthole we always say. But what's a ship doin' in Marion I can't tell you. Are you staying long in town? Business?"

"Thank you, ma'am, I'm obliged. And yes, I have business with the Campbell family."

"So sad about their son," she broke in. "They really don't have anyone else now. They were fixing on a wedding right after the war. Him and Delia. Almost started on her dress, did I; got her measure already. And to be lost so late, when most of the fighting was already accomplished."

"Yes, sad...Well thank you. I'll head over now to your sister's and then out to see the Campbells." Watson turned, picked up his battered leather satchel and medical tools and exited the store. The man on the bench and his dog remained immobile as he walked by them, without even a nod, or a half-opened eye or the twitch of a tail.

He easily found his way. West Cherry St was an assemblage of wood-frame houses, each with an expanse of front porch and brick sidewalks set back from the street. The neighborhood had been established long enough for several thin elm trees to grow up over the front lawns to cast a dappled black shade that allowed spotlights of sun to shine on the flowerbeds that edged several of the houses. There were even three or four lush looking rose gardens and several mounds of pink and red peonies. In the middle of the second block, before the road and houses gave out to spotty patches of prairie grass and irregular clumps of hickory and cottonwood trees several hundred yards beyond, he found the house with the peculiar front door. As he turned up the brick sidewalk to the whitewashed house, he thought it almost a principle that such small towns seemed tidy and settled until you reached the edges. That was where the road would give out into a dirt path waiting to be paved over and a patch of unkempt countryside waiting to be filled with houses like these and plantings of shade trees following the next pulse of expansion.

Up on the brick landing, he twisted the dark green metal doorbell and immediately heard a rasping clatter within. After a moment, the curtain over the portal window moved slightly, a pause, and then a woman of almost identical size and shape as her sister in the dry goods store opened the door. She wore a print housedress with an elaborate lace collar. Watson wondered for a moment if this was the work of the emporium and sewing business.

"Yes, young man?" she inquired, holding one hand securely on the doorknob.

"I've come about a room. Sent to you by your sister at the shop up the road. I'm planning to stay for a few days...depending. You see, I knew the Campbell boy over in Missouri and I'm here to deliver a message from him."

"You're welcome then, to stay here. I'll charge you by the week if you remain that long. And you can have your meals if you like. Mr. and Mrs. Campbell have been grieving something awful; and poor Delia too. She's almost like a daughter to them. Maybe it'll be a comfort to know something more. They only just got a letter from the government...like several families round about. But you'll want to see the room," she interrupted herself.

"Yes, if I might." It was the marvel of small town gossip, he thought, that everyone he met was acquainted with the Campbells and their grieving.

He followed the woman inside and up a curved staircase into a simple, neat room at the back of the house, furnished with an iron bedstead, covered by a pink and blue fan quilt, a chair, and a table on which sat a tin washbasin. In one corner, an open door revealed a small closet. In the other, a small, covered bedpan rested on a low stool. A square rag rug occupied the space in front of the bed. When he glanced out the window through the lace curtains, he could see a white outhouse set discreetly off at the end of the back yard and partially blocked from view by a large bush. A small barn or shed stood on the other side.

"It'll be fine," he said. "I'm obliged." He placed his valise and medical kit down carefully next to the bed.

She looked at him cautiously, and then smiled. "Would you be wanting a cup of tea? Just come down to the parlor and sit while I make it."

"Thank you very much, Mrs.?"

"It's only Miss, if you please. Miss Adams. And your name?"

"I'm Watson. David Watson."

"Well just make yourself to home." She turned and led him downstairs. She showed him into a bright parlor and pointed to a dark green upholstered chair.

"Sit there, young man, in the guest chair."

Most of the furniture in the room, the tables, a love seat and a breakfront holding dishes and several figurines, were of dark, heavy wood. The walls had been papered in a design of green and pale yellow stripes. Without the large western window, it would have been dreary, but the strong August light gave everything a warm aura. As he settled back, Watson felt entirely at home feeling confident that if he might like to settle down in just such a house.

After he drank his tea and settled up for a week's stay, and answering enough questions for Miss Adams to know most of his history, he headed out of the built-up area. He had first washed his face and hands and changed into his one clean shirt, because he wanted to make a good impression on the Campbells. He strolled along a dusty dirt road, past a hay field where a red-winged blackbird rose angrily to warn him away. The late afternoon sun gave off undiminished heat and the breeze only fanned the hot air around without offering any relief, but he felt both excited and content. After he passed by the first farm, he saw the telltale metal windmill, a structure mounted on four poles with metal blades and a wind rudder extending out the back. It turned slowly in hesitant jerks and when he came closer, he could hear the rusted parts grinding against each other.

Besides the large, painted barn with a tin roof, there were several other outbuildings and sheds, a chicken coop, a small fenced-in orchard, and then, set back from all of them, a large whitewashed wooden house, shaded by large elms at either side. The symmetry of the arrangement spoke of care, and Watson wondered if Mr. Campbell might be a follower of advice from President Lincoln's new Bureau of Agriculture. The house itself could easily have been located on West Cherry Street for it had many of the same features as its town cousins: two stories, a large front sitting porch, and big, rectangular windows. He could see the bottoms of light-colored curtains in each billowing gently in the breeze. Walking up the path and then onto the wooden steps of the porch, he was about to knock, when the door opened suddenly as if he were expected. A girl, about 19 or 20, dressed in blue and white with a faded apron, stood looking at him, her eyes bright with an anticipation that gave him a twinge of guilt and embarrassment. This must be Delia. Did she scrutinize the face of every young stranger for a trace of her young, dead soldier lover? Was every new countenance that appeared in town a reminder and thus a disappointment?

"Hello, Miss," he said quickly. "I'm Watson. I've come to speak to Mr. and Mrs. Campbell. I have a message to deliver."

She remained silent for a moment, studying him, as if holding the still impossible hope that he might be her returned beau in disguise. Then she shook her head and focused her eyes on him.

"Are you that Dr. Watson? Why we have a very kind letter from you. I'm Delia."

"I'm terribly sorry, Miss, about that letter. But you see, yes, I was at the hospital when he died." He wasn't sure why he avoided pronouncing the boy's name. Did he feel guilty that he could only be the messenger and not her lover?

"It was our duty to write to the parents. The army had a formula to follow...I did it for so many of the wounded."

"It is with the most painful feeling that I sit down to impart to you the sad tidings..." She recited his words from memory and without expression. He was shocked to hear how empty they sounded coming from her lips.

"I got to know him at the hospital before the fever took him off. He told me about growing up here on the farm and about you and all of his dreams and plans. Right before he died, he gave me your picture...and a ring...and

I felt obliged to bring it to you and his parents. It's here in my pocket...if I could come in for just a moment. Then I'll be on my way again; won't trouble you more."

"Of course, I'm sorry to be rude. And it's not even my own door I'm standing here blocking." She stepped back, opening a space for him, and he entered the cool hallway.

"Mother Campbell," she shouted into the dark depths of the corridor. "It's a soldier who knew Elbert. Come quick." She led him into the parlor just as a middle-aged woman appeared. Her face was ruddy and lined from seasons of outdoor work, but Watson noticed her hands most: rough, energetic, powerful hands smoothing her calico housedress.

Seeing Watson, she called out. "Father Campbell! Come to the parlor right now. We got a guest."

Mr. Campbell, a grizzled and sun-burned man, entered and held out his hand. There was an awkward moment before his wife said, "Sit down, young man. Goodness, we aren't showing any hospitality; it's just the surprise. Can I get you something? And you said your name was?"

Her confusion embarrassed her, but Watson understood, and took a seat in a stiff wooden chair with a basket weave seat.

"Watson," he said, "David Watson."

"He knew Elbert in the last days at the hospital; he was the one wrote us that beautiful letter," said Delia, explaining. "It made me cry so..."

Mrs. Campbell still seemed uncomfortable and blurted out, "Oh yes, the letter. Go fetch it will you, dear."

The girl turned and ran quickly out of the room and as she left, but still within hearing, Mrs. Campbell said, "She's been such a comfort to us...almost like the daughter we would have...Well, she would have been, wouldn't she, Father. I mean, they intended to marry the moment he came home." Quite suddenly, she began to sob, quietly, "But not that way, never that way!" she blurted out. After wiping her eyes, she resumed: "Did you know him well, Mr...?" In her grief, she had already forgotten his name.

"Watson...yes, I knew him. I was the doctor's assistant at the hospital."

He said nothing more, but he could have added a great deal, for in their lucid moments before death, when they understood that infection or fever would carry them away, in those intimate seconds before the throes set on, he had heard so many of their stories. So many! In these moments, he never felt like a priest or confessor, listening to the unburdening of regrets and errors. It was a curious fact, instead, that the dying confided their hopes to him, their loves, their aspirations, and the futures they would never have. He had tried to learn as much as he could about each man, so that they would not die as strangers in the filth and agony and impersonality of the makeshift hospital. It cost him a terrible sorrow—each of their passings—but to him, such rituals had become the meaning of doctoring. That was to be a friend at death, and not to judge, nor to whisper false hopes of some resurrection that he knew was in vain, but to be like a member of the family and the treasurer of their memories. And for some reason he could not fathom, none more so than Elbert Campbell.

Delia re-entered the room gripping a folded, yellowed paper, a document that was weathered and aged, not by time, but the studied reading and rereading by its recipients. As she handed it to him, he looked at her carefully for the first time. In the confusion of the first moments, he had not observed her closely. Now he saw that she was tall and fair and large-boned and, he guessed, of German stock, like so many immigrants in this area, although her only accent was the rolling and melodious softening of the ends of words that he associated with this country wedged between North and South. She had wispy blond hair that she wore pinned back and braided. Her cheeks were round and touched with sun, and her green eyes brilliant and penetrating. The nondescript blouse and gingham jumper she wore must be designed only for convenience, to help with work around the farm. There was, in fact, nothing striking about any single feature; she wasn't even beautiful, but he thought she held herself with extraordinary grace.

"We've read it so many times," she explained, "that we know the words by heart. They're very beautiful; very like a poem."

"It is with great sadness," she began, closing her eyes and placing her hand clutching the open letter across her breast:

"It is with great sadness that I write to inform you of the decease of you son Elbert, who died a hero's death in the service of his nation. He was a patriot who gave his life to a cause hallowed by his sacrifice and a purpose consecrated by his blood. In his last days, he spoke with great love of his mother, his father, his future bride, and the small town where he was born: there to which he will return in spirit, once again, fallen in flesh, but quick in memory. Signed Lieutenant Longacre, Army of the North, (David Watson, amanuensis)."

Watson knew the words well since he had written

them about Elbert and slightly different versions for many of the others whose young lives had ended at the hospital. None of them quite true, he knew. The task fell to him because he had a fair hand and a way with words. As the surgeon in charge confided in him, "Persuading the living of a good death can be as important as handling a scalpel with skill. You'll learn soon that one's duty as a doctor is as much to the living as to the dying. Never forget that."

When Watson heard his own words read back to him, he thought they had never sounded this good when he wrote them...or as sad.

"Yes," he said, breaking the pause that followed, "the Lieutenant took special pride in knowing his men. I also knew Elbert in his last days, and he made me promise to come here, to Marion, after the war, and bring you his ring." Reaching into his shirt pocket, he pulled out the cheap metal band that Elbert had confided to him just before he passed, pressing it into his palm, and asking him, as one last favor, to deliver it to Delia. Many of the other patients in the hospital had tried to obligate him in some such fashion, and he had always been wary of deathbed assurances. He often wondered if these extracted promises were somehow a last, desperate grasp at immortality, and it worried him that he felt obliged to acquiesce on so many occasions when he had no intention or possibility of carrying out these last, anxious wishes. Why he willingly agreed and acted in this one case still puzzled him. Perhaps, he thought now, it had been her picture. But he also realized that he too had been searching; perhaps for such a small town as this. The Campbells sat, stoically, he thought, trying to suppress tears, but Delia's face was flushed with a kind of joy.

"You came all this way to bring me his ring? You and he must have had a mighty friendship."

"I don't rightly know what it was, Miss Delia," he broke in. "I just felt I had to do it. There was something about him. Perhaps it was because I wanted to bring an end to the war by myself; and this was my way."

"And we are so grateful to you," said Mrs. Campbell. "Will you stay a piece then? We'll be having supper soon. It won't be much, but we would be honored to have Elbert's friend and doctor."

Watson hesitated for a moment, although he had already decided to stay. In fact, when he looked again at their eager faces, pausing to examine Delia's sad eyes, he knew he would stay for more than just dinner if they would have him.

Later that night, back in his room at Miss Adams', he sat fully dressed on the narrow bed, propped up against the hard pillow he had placed against the wall. A square of moonlight splayed on the floor through the open window was the only illumination. But he did not require light to contemplate the possibilities that were coursing through his mind. He had always loved such moments of solitude, when he could consider the future, make plans, and imagine himself in new circumstances. Even though they never happened, there would still be the left-over traces of possibilities that he could take up again the next time he found himself alone facing new opportunities. His thoughts raced along the known to the unknown.

First, he would open a medical practice in Marion. It ought to be easy to find space for a small office. With the nearest doctor miles away, despite his youth, he would probably find enough patients, especially when the townsfolk learned he had worked for a Union hospital. During his stint in Missouri, he learned he would have to acquire further medical training. The head surgeon had explained that the new American Medical Association was pressing for state systems of approval and licensing. He could do anything required of him: courses, a diploma, even though he knew that his apprenticeship at the field hospital would be the best training he could ever get. He knew of no nearby colleges in Illinois except the Rush Medical College in Chicago. Several physicians he encountered in Missouri were known as "Rush Doctors" and they advised him that a year spent there was the best and easiest available education in the Midwest.

If he returned to this little town and his practice thrived, he would find a wife and build a house on such a street as this. A wife like Delia. Far too soon to think of that of course. But never, he corrected himself, never too early for a young man to dream.

Edna Turnbull

With no children of her own to distract her, and therefore confident that she had an unprejudiced eye for such matters, Edna Turnbull knew herself to be an expert at spotting the unruly boy who needed attention to manners or a dose of brown soap administered with a rough cloth. No wrinkled pinafore or scuffed shoe passed unnoticed by her critical glance. When she cleared her throat it was like a drill sargent calling attention. Of course, she never said a word to the parents about these errors of comportment—as the wife of the Methodist Minister, she had no need to speak—because her frown of disapproval was enough to bring a silent pledge of amendment to the most incompetent and harried of mothers. Sometimes, when she conversed about it, she admitted to resenting the town for placing the burden of enforcing good manners and proper behavior on her shoulders.

"It's not a task that I welcome," she told anyone who asked. "No. It was an obligation and a calling thrust upon me."

Whenever the subject came up in a circle of acquaintances at the Methodist Chapel, or among a few close friends during afternoon tea, she always sighed and remarked:

"I don't know what is to become of us proper folks here in Marion. There has been such a decline in behavior and a flood of such terrible and unsuitable people with their foreign ways. You know who I mean, of course."

She would exclaim this, looking for approval from whatever mute and pliant audience she had gathered about her.

"And those awful novels that young people read nowadays! Who will uphold standards if not we few," she might ask, waving her hand as a sign of generous inclusion.

"I have spoken several times already to Miss Butler at the library. Thank goodness she agrees with me that such salacious books have no place freely available to the young. One cannot be too vigilant."

She would say this, raising her heavy dark eyebrows in a gesture that might remind an amused observer of the shadowy archways of some sacred place. The rest of the architecture of her countenance was the color of aged sandstone: heavy lips, untouched by any artifice; teeth which she bared when the rare occasion demanded a smile or more often, which she revealed when she breathed in audibly as a sign of disapproval. The severity of this impression would have been complete but for her extraordinary figure. Whereas other women of her middle age had broadened, with bodies dragged down by the gravity of years, which the shapeless cotton house dresses they fancied only emphasized rather than disguised, Edna was as thin-waisted as a young girl, with large breasts that commanded attention, and a light and graceful carriage that baffled anyone who knew her sharp demeanor. She was, her husband often said in private, a puzzle of opposites.

But behind all her bluster, Edna had a secret that she held close to her memorable breasts, a thing which if it escaped into the public would by her own reckoning destroy years of meticulous efforts to establish an unsullied reputation and a position at the head of a small group of the best families in Marion. This life-long struggle had been a climb upward from mistakes made when she was a naïve and dreamy girl living on a small mud farm twenty miles east of Cairo between Sandy Slough and Barlow, Illinois. A useful marriage and absolute silence about what had happened to her thirty years earlier, and a precise and utterly false story of her origins, made her a stalwart of the town's elite and the feared gamekeeper of the foxhounds of rumors and gossip she could let loose in pursuit of anyone who challenged her position.

While her place was as secure as the leading minister's wife could claim title to, there were moments when she was alone, when the whole, sordid past swept over her in an uninvited surge of emotion, almost like the onset of a sudden fever. At such times, she would shiver violently as if the shaking of her body could throw off the repugnant memories: the guilt and shame that pried open her past. At those times she could not escape the returning visions of the dilapidated, unpainted farmhouse with the close-by pigsty and the muddy lane that led up the road toward Barlow. In spring and summer, the farm seemed to be an island on a viscous riverbed of heavy dark clay, next to a barn shaped like an inverted Noah's Ark sheltering the beasts her father kept for the slaughter. Even the odor of fresh hay, piled up in the barn, provided only a sweet overtone to the stench of animal smells and smoking manure piles that let off a bluish gas along with the fetid steam that escaped following a flooding rain. Her mother had struggled valiantly to create an orderly house, to keep the farm outside of the parlor full of her meager best furniture, lamps, and portraits of stiff-backed relatives. The family (which meant her father) was allowed into this room only for a brief sit-down before Sunday supper and after church. In Edna's memory, such moments of clumsy, forced conversation only reminded her that her father was a stranger, because with his child, he was remote and knew only to complain about the work that he would have to undertake once the wasteful day of rest had passed.

Edna thought she must have inherited her refusal to belong to this world, and her wish to escape to its margins from the wistful personality of her mother. Herself a farm girl who had never traveled to the great cities she often spoke about—St. Louis and Chicago—she had somehow taken a terrible wrong turn and ended in this marriage of hard work and stretched-out silences. Nonetheless, she had aspirations with which she infected Edna, when they spent evenings together at the kitchen table looking over well-thumbed old copies of *Godey's Lady's Book* that sat on a small bookshelf in the parlor next to the family Bible. On Sundays, when her father read aloud from the Holy Book in a slow and halting monotone, she and her mother (the best dishes washed and put away for another week) sat together on the uncomfortable sofa, looking at the tinted fashion plates, reading the stories that Mr. Godey chose: Poe (when she was old enough), Washington Irving, and Oliver Wendell Holmes. Although they had no piano or other musical instrument, her mother often took out the tattered sheet music sent along with the publication and tried to hum the melodies. Together they imagined a dance floor and an orchestra, and the rhythmic bodies, moving, swirling together, and sweeping around the room in unison, like the waltzing hands of a clock in three/four time. How her mother knew of such things or obtained these journals always puzzled Edna, but she understood that she used this Sunday respite to instill in her a vision constructed of her own brightest hopes, illusions, and deepest regrets. What they imagined together was an open door to the future through which only the younger one of them might still pass. Yet for many years the only other door of any consequence in Edna's world (beyond the white-washed church in Barlow), led into the crude, one-room school she attended, where the horizons of hope and accomplishment were as low as the small red-brick building that confined them.

The dreamy moments spent with her mother, against the background murmur of monotonous Bible verses, became, in retrospect, times of anguish and gloom. At first, Edna could not understand their purpose: why did her mother unfold these creased and yellowing pages of a magazine world and set them out before her, like the spoiled leftovers of a feast whose invitation to attend had arrived too late? Why, if her mother desired such worlds so intensely, did she find herself married to misery, and tethered to an unending workday in an overgrown shack with only one decent room?

Gradually, as the measure of discontent and desire grew inside her, Edna began to resent her mother's vivid fancies. It increased her distress to imagine worlds that existed beyond the cornfields and listless summers, and the drafty unheated school where a parade of teachers tried to instruct her sullen classmates. Until one fall a new young and fresh face appeared, a teacher scarcely older than she was. Up to then, she had paid no attention to the strict matrons who sought to instruct them. The lessons were so simple for her and her abilities so outshone the others, that school was mostly a time for daydreams while the others plodded along. This new teacher with a curious name—Aiden O'Connor—told them, on the first day of a hot September afternoon:

"Education is like a lantern in a dark night."

Edna was so struck by this idea that she promised herself she would heed his words, push back the shadows, and peer into the future with the light of learning.

Almost alone among her classmates, she responded to his urging, and she began to read, first borrowing the leather-bound novels and histories that sat on a small shelf in the corner of the classroom, and then, after exhausting this meager stock, she asked the teacher if he might have some books of his own that she could borrow.

He had looked puzzled for a moment; perhaps, she thought, he had never encountered a student who demanded more work. It was his first teaching position, and he had been grief-stricken to see the small schoolhouse with its shabby wooden desks and rows of students with faces like tarnished brass buttons, wearing clothing whose next existence would be for an unfortunate younger sibling or the ragbag for patching and mending.

Having graduated from Normal School near Bloomington just two years earlier, he had taken this first offer sight unseen, not realizing that the area around Cairo, known as Little Egypt, with its mysterious and classic names, was a rich and fertile farmland but as dry a desert of culture as the sand-blown expanse around the pyramids of Giza. Except for the occasional itinerant minister or Chautauqua gathering, Aiden looked up-river to St. Louis for the possibility of communication with the rest of the world. It would not be easy to make his way to that booming German metropolis, but its very existence made his ambition for a different sort of life and a better position a distinct, albeit distant, possibility. He therefore supposed his job in the dreary county school to be an apprenticeship, and a step in a direction that he calculated would bring him to a larger city and the excitement of teaching eager young minds. That, he assured himself, would make his years of preparation, and this miserable detour, worthwhile.

As far as any social life, Aiden found only the Methodist church to be a meeting place of any consequence, for it was the center of local life, even for those few farmers and their wives who spurned the confession itself. In fact, it mattered not at all if a person was Methodist or Baptist or some odd sect like Mennonite. The church was the only hub of the slow turning wheel of social life whose spokes included lemonade picnics, a choir and ladies' and men's clubs and a Sunday school.

At first, Aiden had attended out of curiosity and then returned from his persistent feeling of loneliness and isolation. He proved to be a popular figure and he noticed the lingering stares of several young women. On one or two occasions he was invited to Sunday supper at one of the better, well-tended farmsteads where, inevitably there was a daughter, slightly younger than he, who blushed and spoke hesitantly, if at all, throughout the meal. He tried his best to fill the empty and awkward silences that followed comments about the weather, the price of livestock and grain, and on occasion, the changes that were sweeping through the area since the war had ended. But he usually found that conversation fell off quickly, and only the clink of tin on cheap pottery dishes, or the satisfied animal-like sighs and grunts of the eaters filled these moments. Sometimes he thought that his looks inhibited the young women: his thick black hair, pale white skin and green eyes; they stared at him as if they had never seen an Irishman before. His mother had always called him, "My beautiful boi; my lovely lad." He had not let this attention turn his head, because he knew that all Irish mothers heaped sweet names on their sons, but sometimes, he thought, maybe, just maybe, it was true.

Toward the end of his first teaching year, in a new class of students, Aiden had noticed the intelligent-looking and enthusiastic student named Edna, who held back after classes ended, quizzing him about the novels he might lend her. She seemed full of dreamy ideas, and once she read them, she demanded to know more about the heroines of *Little Women* and *The Scarlet Letter*. He had debated whether he should lend her Hawthorne's dramatic tale of passion and adultery, and he was troubled and amused when she returned with an interpretation that he thought completely misread the point. She was quick, but had such an overwrought imagination that she scarcely understood the grim meaning of the burning red A pinned to Hester

Prynne's breast in the story.

It gave him an odd sensation to lead her to great literature only to have her naïve enthusiasm twist its significance and substitute a young girl's wild imaginings. Nevertheless, he thought that education and knowledge would come. He could help her realize the profound anguish and guilt that cast shadows on every character in this bleak Puritan history. At the same time, he could not help feeling that perhaps her innocent pleasure at the sexual freedom that led Hester to commit adultery was feigned. Perhaps she was teasing him. Maybe she understood all too well. Was she urging him on with a stare that implied both curiosity and calculation, tempting him to cross the invisible line that separated them into student and teacher as it had separated Hester Prynne from her minister?

There were times when Aiden became aware of unspoken words that passed between them that felt rather like a sudden wave of energy, a hot flash of emotion. Over the course of the year, he observed that she had suddenly lost her childish figure. He could see this happening in most of the girls of her age. From one angle, they looked older and more mature, and then, suddenly, from another, still like children. He knew this was a dangerous time, and he was cautious about what he said to older girls, careful to look through their momentary adulthood to the child that still lived beneath, to assume nothing.

With Edna, however, something was different. Some compulsion urged him on and tempted and emboldened him to respond to the obvious delight she took from the books and from his company. He convinced himself that this was an act of compassion, helping her to rise up from the squalor and tedium of her family's farm, to encourage her thoughts of escape into a better life. Wasn't that the purpose of teaching, he assured himself, to set souls afire, to stoke dissatisfaction? Sure of his own motivations, Aiden relaxed around his pupil and even thought up excuses for her to tarry after school.

For her part, Edna did not wish to rush home to help her mother with the chores that seemed to be an endless round of drudgery—a cycle of the same dreary tasks that repeated as regularly as the days of the week. She despised the dirt and smell of the farm: the dust that blew through the ill-fitting window and door frames that had to be swept up every day, and the clots of mud that stuck to her boots when she fed the chickens or fetched eggs. She hated the sickening, heavy, sweet stink of the pigs that made her eyes water when the wind blew the smell into the house. Her mother struggled valiantly against these abuses to the senses, scrubbing floors, washing sheets and curtains, and carrying on an endless campaign against her husband who seemed not to recognize the circumstances of their poverty.

Edna knew she was the solitary conscript in this war of her mother's against their sordid existence, and she adopted her mother's dissatisfactions as her own. On occasion, she watched her mother's relentless toil and wondered. What had brought these two ill-suited parents together? Had they once been different and full of hope? But the answer never came and her wonder only increased her disgust and growing determination to escape.

Her reading at night by the kerosene lamp, the bright days at school, and Mr. O'Connor: these became the only realities to her; for only in dreams and imagination could she redeem her hopes. Sometimes she even dared to think of her teacher as a companion, and she imagined waiting at the train station, carpetbag in hand and his large leather valise at his feet, waiting to climb aboard a life in some big city: Chicago, New York, even Paris.

Maybe, she thought, they would escape together, for she recognized in their discussions of novels, his own mood of dissatisfaction, the hint of desire to be somewhere else that was anywhere but the shabby rural schoolhouse set on the blanket of cornfields and cottonwood trees clinging to the creek beds that crisscrossed the fallow pastures and fields of dry stubble. Thus, the intimacy that grew between them was entirely based upon the thought of being someone and somewhere else. Theirs was the entangled imagining of something better in which each dreamed the dreams of the other.

Still, Edna recognized, even if her understanding of romance came solely from novels (she refused to believe that the brief, violent coupling of farm animals had anything to do with love), that there was an undercurrent of something real and tangible hidden precariously beneath their chat about the fate of literary heroines. Sometimes she listened to his voice so intently that she lost the meaning of the words, particularly when he read aloud. What was unsaid distracted her, and she almost felt dazed, with a warm sensation that rose through her body like a blush, a tingling in her arms that provoked a nervous shudder of pleasure. At such moments, she felt compelled to stretch out her arms or to stand even, to gain control of her senses again. When she studied his face, looking intently at him until he looked up from the book and returned her stare, she marveled at the contrast between his thick black hair and the pallor of his skin that never seemed to tan or blacken, even in the intense sun of Little Egypt. Everything about him signaled that he was from elsewhere and that was the mystery of him.

Being older, if inexperienced in such matters, Aiden realized how attractive his prize student was becoming. Her breasts were suddenly fuller, obvious even under the shapeless dresses she wore, and her narrow waist and thin legs reminded him of the fashionable girls he admired on his occasional trips to St. Louis. She always smelled faintly of freshly mown grass, a sweet fresh odor, completely unlike her sour-scented fellows. During their afterschool sessions, sharing a book, he found himself relishing the accidental touch of her thigh against his and the soft, pink forearm which he occasionally stroked, as if by chance.

This courtship by proximity and accident deepened almost imperceptibly. Neither Edna nor Aiden ever gave words to it. Their conversation always lodged on some elevated plain, and so the reality of their encounters intensified by unremarked stages: first a gentle, accidental kiss, his hand on her firm breast, the tips of her fingers wandering on his leg. Neither of them knew, or would admit to knowing, that a growing physical desire had replaced the dream of escape until, almost inevitably, they found themselves on the floor, she lying on his coat, dress pulled up around her waist, and he, hard and stiff inside her. When they finished, neither spoke until they had adjusted their clothing and she said goodbye as she edged toward the door of the school and back home to her grinding duties. It felt as if she had just finished reading a scene in a romantic novel and then had put the book up for another day.

Their encounters after school continued as if nothing had changed in their relationship. Of course, Edna understood what she was doing when she thought about it, but it was so bound up in her imagination that she refused to recognize any peril. She could only think that she finally understood Hester Prynne and her determination to be happy. Sometimes she wondered would she also someday proudly wear a scarlet A? Would there be a little Pearl?

All this while, her mother said nothing so long as Edna finished her chores by suppertime. Until one evening, when she arrived home particularly late, her mother seemed suddenly to notice her distracted, unhappy look when she trudged into the house.

"I know you do your chores," she began, confronting her at the door. "But what keeps you at school so late? Your father has been asking about you. He's worried that you might have fallen behind. 'Course I told him that weren't possible, and that you was a fine student, even if you sometimes stray off into the clouds."

"It's the reading, Mama. Mr. O'Connor is lending me his own books, and I sometimes stay after school to talk to him about them. I was sure you wouldn't mind. It's so exciting; there is such an interesting world out and beyond this farm. I want to know all about it."

"Well, if you do your work and keep your father content, then I s'pose it's all right. Try not to tarry too long, though. The days are shorter now, and I won't have you traipsin' around in the dark...Now you need to tend to them chickens...and let me look over some of those books your teacher is lending you."

Edna was relieved that she had brought home Louisa

May Alcott's *Little Men* and not *The Scarlet Letter*. When this thought came to her, she felt a twinge of guilt, for to be calculating was to admit to herself that the affair with Aiden had become physical and real. She turned her face away, in case her realization somehow showed. Her mother usually knew when she harbored a secret thought, and Edna was determined not to reveal anything. In fact, she put it entirely out of her mind: it was another girl she could almost see—not her—but a tragic heroine who occupied her body, walking on a lonely moor toward a secret encounter as she and her teacher rolled on the hard wood floor of the school. If she allowed the reality of it, she knew it would become unbearably actual, mean and tawdry instead of what she imagined it to be: a scene from the wonderful novel of her life.

Nonetheless, after that evening and her mother's curiosity, Edna became more cautious and reticent about staying after school. At first Aiden was puzzled, but when she explained that her chores demanded that she return early, he seemed satisfied. Not once did either of them mention the passion they had shared, displacing it entirely into their now brief conversations about books and characters. They only seemed able to communicate through imaginary beings, with fiction the only means to express an emotion.

Toward Thanksgiving, the new holiday that President Lincoln had proclaimed during the War, and that Edna's mother had read about in one of her magazines, the family celebrated with an extra-long Sunday meal, although after the hard work of baking and preparing, both Edna and her mother were more than relieved when it was over. The day had been gloomy and cold, and promised nothing but rain, mud and chill for the next four months, and a larder that always seemed to shrink too fast. Edna had another reason to be upset. For the last week or so, she had felt alternatively light-headed and then nauseous, her food rising suddenly and uncontrollably into her mouth, leaving the bitter taste of bile. She said nothing to anyone, thinking it would pass, but that day she caught her mother looking oddly at her, up and down her body as if sizing her for a new dress. These inspections made Edna deeply uncomfortable, and she stared back until her mother relented.

"Is there something wrong, Mama?" she finally asked after they took the last dishes to the tin washtub and began to scour the pot that had held the fatted hen.

"You tell me. You seem a bit peaked. Are you in trouble Edna? Have you been seeing someone?"

"Mama, what in the world do you mean?" Edna almost shouted out.

"Shush! Keep your voice down...your father! I thought you had better sense. I thought you staying at school was just innocent learnin'. Is it some boy...not that teacher I hope?"

When Edna realized what her mother was implying, she felt a wave of shame and bewilderment pass over her. Her nausea suddenly welled up, and she ran to the door and to the outhouse in the back yard. When she returned, pale and chilled, her apron almost frozen where she had wiped her hands, her mother stood waiting.

"So it's true, is it," she said, and then suddenly began to sob. "I blame myself for putting notions in your head. It's my fault, I can see that now. You've made the same terrible mistake I did. But I'll never have you marrying beneath you. We have to plan carefully. Of course you'll have to go away. I'll find a place for you somewhere in St. Louis. I can write my sister tomorrow. She'll know what for. And your father can't ever be told. Never!"

"Oh Mama, I didn't know what I was doing. He was so kind and gentle and there were the books...I thought..."

"So it was the teacher. Then I'll be off to see him tomorrow and set things right. There's no question of marryin'. You are far too young, and anyway, he will have to be leaving on account of the disgrace."

Both Aiden and Edna departed the darkened wintry fields at about the same time. But not in the way either of them had imagined. She never knew where he went, and, after several weeks of intense longing for him, wanting to be with him, she began to blame him, with her anger rising as her belly swelled and her breasts became enlarged and tender. True to her plan, her mother had written to the sister in St. Louis, someone whom Edna had only seen once, but who promised to help with "the situation" as they termed it. Edna packed a slim suitcase of clothes, none of which would quite fit her now, and climbed aboard the train bound for St. Louis. She had to cross the Mississippi by ferry and then travel to the center of the city where her aunt greeted her. Instead of taking her in, however, which she explained would be an embarrassment for them all, she had found a place where she could board through the St. Louis Women's Christian Association. In this manner, Edna was handed around as if she were something spoiled and distasteful, met with disdain and disapproval by anyone who recognized her condition.

The months that followed tried her patience, with little to occupy her other than charity sewing assigned to her by the Association, and, of course, the discomforts of a solitary pregnancy. Alone and shunned, she spent long hours thinking about her situation and the possibilities of the future. Upon occasion, she attempted to read, and on the rare occasions when allowed to wander out, she found a cheap bookseller where she purchased several books including the new novel by Harriet Beecher Stowe, *The Minister's Wooing.* But she found the plot silly and contrived. She feared—she knew—that her imagination had become dulled by the misfortune that befell her and the tawdry reality of the boarding house. In disgust, she threw the book down. She could no longer bear the sentimental prose or the intricate theme of the plot, the passivity of the heroine—all of these disgusted her. Although she did not realize it at the time, this was the beginning of her transformation.

As her belly grew, stretching and distending to accommodate the growth of the thing inside her, her anger at her mother and at Aiden intensified. She knew she would never return to the farm. Disgraced or forgiven, she could never bear the sight of them again. She determined never to be used again; she refused to be complicit in their judgement of her with no future and cast out to become an old breed sow. She had made one terrible mistake, but she vowed that the rest of her life—should she be able to construct something anew—would be a testament to the powers of denial: to liberate herself from her rude upbringing and girlish sentimentality. She determined she would start by turning away from the child lodged in her. When it was born, and safely given to the Children's

Home, she would be free to discard her childhood folly, like an old coat hanging on the hook of bad memories, never to be taken down again and of no use against the cold.

For her, the birth of her daughter, attended by a rough and unfriendly midwife, marked the abrupt and painful end to the first half of her life. When she heard the baby squeal in protest at the indignity and stress of labor, she turned her face to the wall without any sympathy or interest, and cried softly.

"Do you want to hold her, to look at her before I take her away?" asked Mrs. Wilson, the midwife, in too loud a voice, as if Edna stood across the room instead of lying in a heap of bloody sheets on the cramped bed jammed against the wall of her lodgings.

"No. Take her away. She's all in the past. But if you want you can call her Pearl, little Pearl." She then covered her eyes and shuddered.

Edna spent her lying-in back with her St. Louis aunt who welcomed her tentatively, at first, into the small, ill-furnished townhouse where she lived with her husband and two children. As soon as she was strong enough to help, she took up the washing and cooking for the family. No one ever spoke about her circumstances, and she discouraged even the mention of her mother and father. Like the rest of her past, she was determined to forget them. In the few spare moments earned, she began reading again, but she had forever cast aside novels. At the St. Louis Library, she discovered books by the other Beecher sister, Catherine, whose advice on morals and righteous living she read with enthusiasm. Of course, the religious aspects of the books meant nothing to Edna, but she found the advice in the *Treatises*, as Beecher called them, about womanly duties to be compelling. The author's strong opposition to female suffrage particularly intrigued her. She thought she understood why Beecher so adamantly opposed the vote. Edna recognized a clever strategy: pretend to relinquish a power to men that they already possessed in order to seize control of everything else. This would allow women to regulate their social lives and administer their morals. Not only could a woman exert self-control, but also authority in all else that mattered. This was a devilish bargain, she concluded, but Edna vowed to live by these precepts. The only puzzle remaining was how two sisters (Harriet and Catherine) could be the authors of such different descriptions of life. Harriet was a sentimentalist, a novelist of tears and weakness, of unrealistic coincidences and impossible lovers miraculously united. Catherine was a hard-as-nails essayist, a determined prophet of self-sufficiency. She wondered until she thought she understood. "Yes," she said, "I am those two sisters together in myself: once the fool whose head was turned by fiction and sentiment. But, now I intend to be a creature of self-creation if my will is strong enough."

From then on, the process of reconstruction occupied Edna's every waking moment. Even while performing the most menial tasks or minding the children, or on those rare occasions when she accompanied her aunt to an afternoon meeting of her religious circle, she was plotting her future. The family still carefully excluded her from most social visits, but nothing mattered to her except the plan. Even word of her mother's last fatal illness only momentarily interrupted her determined course. She took two days to deviate from her purpose to accompany her aunt back to the farm for the funeral. It amazed her to realize how diminutive and crude everything seemed: even more so than ever the farmhouse had shrunk from her recollection of it and the school house which they passed seemed nothing more than a tumbledown shack. It did not surprise her to learn that the schoolmaster had disappeared. As one of her mother's friends whispered behind her hand in confidence:

"He's probably in Chicago or even Boston."

She did not care.

Her father also seemed diminished, older and more wizened in just two years, with an unkempt lawn of dirty whisker stubble around his chin that meandered to the top of his pale cheeks. She felt a momentary sadness for him, but she could scarcely admit that she was related to him. She despised the shameful state of his mourning clothes: the stiff black suit, high-necked celluloid collar and the frayed white shirt that followed his wrists out of his coat sleeves. He wore a black tie, knotted and clumsily stuffed into the space between his second and third buttons. Was it cruel to think he looked like a bereaved scarecrow flapping its arms to frighten away the wings of sorrow? As for her mother, she felt a faint stab of grief, remembering the person who by accident set her on a path of escape, filling her pliable imagination with notions of travel and glamour, and pointing her unsuspecting toward the disastrous relationship with Aiden.

Well, she thought, that is all resolved now. I am entirely free of the past. She is dead and the person I was has gone.

Back in St. Louis, Edna labored diligently at her project

of self-improvement and found that her aunt and uncle gradually accepted her role as an elder daughter, housekeeper, and on occasion, friend. She made herself indispensable, and this, in turn, allowed her to move out from the shadow of scandal. She realized that she could never hope to find a handsome young man or pass through the giddy stages of courtship with its frivolous secret notes, embarrassed glimpses, and furtive longings. She would have to settle for something less, but it would be on her own terms. Even though she developed into a beautiful young woman, there was always something about her look—a frown of disapproval that was perhaps the first line of self-defense that would discourage a young man, looking for innocence. She decided to marry, if possible, someone older who had been disappointed in love, someone who would accept her as a bargain.

Remarkably, the person that she had prefigured in her mind turned out to be her uncle's younger brother, a Methodist minister some ten years her elder, who had already hardened into strange and solitary ways. Almost immediately, she realized that he would do. He was neither comely or plain; indeed when she tried to call up his image, she could think of no distinctive features, just a pleasant, if gruff, presence, and a man requiring guidance and a woman's firm hand. If he knew anything of her past or her family (and she suspected he did), he never uttered a word to her, although there were times when she sensed that he had accepted her in marriage to absolve her of her sins. Nonetheless, he allowed himself to be guided through careful steps into a partnership that suited them both. When he suggested that they move to Marion, she hesitated only long enough to discover on the map that it was a safe distance from the family farm and sufficient miles from her memories.

To her surprise, Reverend Turnbull turned out to be a popular preacher, whose placid and friendly demeanor encouraged parishioners to confide in him. He knew more about the citizens of this small bustling town than any of them might imagine, and certainly more even than he realized. His position and connections to St. Louis made it natural for everyone to think of him as a scholar, although his education had been narrow and limited, and he frowned upon excessive book learning. It was merely a sign of respect and perhaps more to do with the upstanding character of his wife that made his elevated position in town a natural assumption. In fact, however, his only interest was in local matters, and he filled his conversation at home in the parlor with Edna with references to townsfolk and their doings.

Guided by her careful, if seemingly trivial questions, he revealed far more than he should, and Edna stored this information in the annals of her orderly mind. She found that she almost never had to use this information, for she could convince anyone telling a story or whispering a piece of gossip that she already knew more details than the teller. She realized this to be a gift of power over others and she used it to establish herself as the matron of the town, the keeper of secrets, and the arbiter of morals, feared and respected, but never loved. The latter had never been important to her plan. To maintain herself secure in this position, she never once again opened a novel or a story of fiction herself and deplored their harmful effects on young minds. The hard truth of the present and the folly of others gave her enough to contemplate without delving into the imagination or conjuring up the past and its dangerous secrets.

Doc Watson

David Watson quickly lost all mention of his first name, and to the patients he acquired and the rest of the town he answered simply to "Doc" or "Watson." To begin his practice, he rented a small house near the central square where he could receive patients in the front room and maintain a residence in the back. At first, he found that his visitors usually suffered from only the most calamitous injuries: the fall from a spooked horse, some accident with a farm machine, a broken arm or leg—all wounds that his experience in the Union hospital had made him an expert on. Knowing the general privations and penury of the community, he charged only a meager fee, and sometimes nothing at all. Nonetheless, over several months he managed to earn sufficiently to save up for his expected trip to Chicago to enroll in the Rush Medical School.

As word spread that he could be trusted with confidences, a second sort of client, mostly timid at first—he thought because of his young age—began to appear.

Many of these came with marital complaints in the guise of physical maladies, and he quickly learned to separate their symptoms of despair from the ravages of disease and old age. When he analyzed it, he thought there might be something about his demeanor, perhaps in the way he listened quietly, that inspired women as well as men to discuss problems that stemmed from ignorance about sex, or prudery, or misapplied faith in folk wisdom.

Usually such patients were women who started to talk in confused circles round and around what was bothering them, until he interrupted and steered them away from their embarrassment right up to the subject he discerned beneath their hesitations. He quickly learned that many of the women he consulted gravely feared pregnancy and the agonies and dangers of another childbirth. Sometimes they begged him to learn how to prevent yet another child. He could hardly prescribe condoms because they were expensive and generally illegal to purchase, but he did counsel women about when they must abstain from sex before their monthlies. On occasion, a desperate woman came to him seeking an abortion. He never agreed to perform one, but in a few cases had to treat a woman who had taken some harsh emetic or injured herself in attempting a termination. He discovered one local midwife in West Frankfurt who performed abortions. He decided not to interfere until one of her patients died of infection. Hearing of this, he immediately rode out in his buggy to visit the small cottage where she performed her operations and persuaded her (with overt threats) to stop her activities. It was not that he opposed abortion on moral grounds; there was too much suffering around pregnancy to take to the high road of judgment, but it was dangerous, and the practice of amateurs simply compounded the risk.

Not, of course, that Watson was beyond interfering on occasion, in a birth that he knew would have cruel consequences and prolonged misery for the parents. He never felt a minute's guilt about this. Medicine and doctors were for the living, he always reminded himself; he had seen too much suffering already. Sometimes, when a baby was born deformed or severely crippled, he neglected to perform the heroics needed to save it. He knew this to be an ethical decision, not a medical one, but he would be intervening into a tragedy with consequences whichever way he acted. Failure to take special measures could save a family a lifetime of heartache. This was not something he ever discussed with anyone else. It was his decision alone, and to share it would raise the practice to the level of principle; he would then have to confront questions he did not wish to face. He understood it was right when he saw the grief-stricken relief of parents when he told them that their severely deformed baby had died. Sometimes he thought he had been steeled to such decisions by the terrible destruction he witnessed in the Union hospital: so much needless death, so many deformities inflicted on the living. He simply refused to add to them.

If female complaints of one sort or another occupied much of his practice, aside from setting broken bones and administering cathartics or presiding over fevers and infections, he could only muster kind words and sympathy for cancers and heart ailments. Perhaps his strangest cases were the bashful men who sat opposite in the chair in his office, across from his oak desk, twisting their caps silently, provoking him to draw them out. He could often guess the problem before he had backed them into a corner confessional. He knew he was their only confidant; they would never approach their mothers or wives and especially not a minister with their questions. Most of the time he knew, from their reticence, that the problem was sexual. The boys and men in Marion certainly understood the mechanics of sex, for it was visible everywhere around them in the world of dogs and horses and chickens and randy sheep. Unfortunately, he concluded, these violent and brief sex lessons, and the myths and crudities whispered in school or in drunken banter in the hotel saloon, only intensified their fears and confusions.

Not only did he have to treat the rare case of venereal disease that someone brought back to town from a visit to St. Louis or an infection spread by the traveling salesmen and circus performers who passed through the area, he often had to explain the mechanics of love-making and the benefits of hygiene. The hardest cases were a few young men who sat in the patient's chair and talked in circular nonsense until they burst into tears. He understood their problem and sympathized, but could offer no hope other than advise them to leave Marion and find a city where they might find other men of their sort. If he thought that was an impossible choice, he might advise them to bury their desires in work or marriage.

While he found satisfaction in his work, it was his joy to visit the Campbell farm. At first, he only went on an infrequent Sunday for a dinner of roasted chicken, beans and corn, biscuits and pie. It began to confuse him, however, when both Mr. and Mrs. Campbell began to address him as "son." He wondered if they were simply referring to his age or whether there might be some deeper meaning that he had become the substitute for Elbert. It might be, but it made him uncomfortable.

Delia was present on many of these occasions, silent, helpful, and attentive. He found himself more and more attracted to her. No longer did she wear the sadness and yearning of the daguerreotype photo he kept in his desk, or show the disappointment he recognized in the fleeting impression of their first meeting. As the year darkened into fall and then winter, with the weather colder and the sun slanting early in the west, they sat together after dinner on the front porch, saying little, but watching the night creep up and the pinpricks of stars emerge through the dusky pleats of the sky.

Toward spring, when the winter cold had finally broken and they could sit for a length of time, Watson dared to say out loud what he had practiced so many times in private.

"You know I'm planning on a spell in Chicago to earn my license. Thinking of going rather soon. And you know I plan to return to Marion. This is the place I've decided never to leave."

"We'll all be very unhappy to lose our only doctor, even for a short time. I don't know what we'll do."

"Are you speaking now for the town, Delia, or do you mean yourself?"

"Why of course for myself too. And for the Campbells. They've come to cherish you."

"Like a son?"

"Yes, that..."

"But Delia, I don't want to be a substitute. I'm not Elbert. Can't be if I tried. It would be wrong. Terrible wrong."

"Perhaps they do think that just a bit. You can't blame them. But I don't."

She reached over the arm of her chair and gripped his wrist.

"You're only yourself. Not for a minute..."

"You mean you'd consider me?"

"Of course I will."

"Then will you wait for me until I come back? It's only to be a few months."

"Do you see that moon rising over to the left, David, over the barn? Do you see how the light it's bringing coats everything with a gleam like silver, making mysterious shapes and shadows?"

"Yes, I can see that, but..."

"Well, I'll wait for you to come back, and wait to share this beautiful moonlight with you and we'll figure out all its meaning, and then the sunlit days we'll spend together."

"Then we'll marry? You mean to share that kind of moonlight with me?"

"Yes, that's what I mean."

Irving Gold

Something about the pronunciation of the word "jeweler" distressed Irving Gold. To begin with there was the local accent that fell hard on the first syllable. Of course, he understood this was merely the lazy way his neighbors had of talking where only the initial sounds of words were distinct, with the rest floating on diminished effort, as if the speaker were running out of breath. In his dark moments–and they came upon him suddenly and without reason sometimes–he thought they really meant to say it that way: "Jew; JEW-ler." Jew, the noun; Jew, the person; Jew, the stranger; the peddler with his pushcart of cheap bargains; Jew the money-changer in the Temple; Christ-killer; Jew the verb: "to jew; to jew someone." He had heard it often enough when local farmers, unaware of his presence, or just unmindful of what they said, discussing a hard bargain, a negotiation that verged on cheating: "to jew somebody down." Indeed, it was such an ordinary part of speech that on occasion a customer might warn him jokingly: "Now Mr. Gold: Don't jew me 'bout that price!" Then the two would laugh as if they shared some secret, a conspiracy of mutual understanding. To jew; to be a Jew.

In fact, Goldmann was the name to which his ancestors had originally answered. However, his parents shortened it when they arrived in New York harbor and were asked by the immigration officials for an identity. His father had often joked that this had been his moment of rebirth: that by lopping off the distinguishing German ending, it would better prepare him and his young bride for America where he had heard that everyone was in a rush. Better to have a name that everyone could pronounce and remember easily. To shed the marker of an immigrant was, for such an ambitious man, as easy as changing clothes. Irving himself felt otherwise. Yes, his father was an ambitious man and an opportunist. He had decided (wisely it turned out) during the violent uprisings of 1848 to leave the German-speaking area of Western Poland and head out to the United States. But he was still a Jew and there was no disguising that.

At first, the elder Gold had thought to travel as far as the West Coast, but his money and energy ran dangerously low by the time the couple reached St. Louis. He thought it fortunate to find a flourishing German-American city on the Mississippi River, where his language and accent would present no obstacle. Only his religion, which he quietly practiced at home, observing only the major holidays, could be a possible hindrance. After laboring for a few years at one of the local breweries, he had saved enough money to open a small jewelry shop. In its early days, the store also operated as a second-hand shop, but as soon as he could, he moved his family and his business to a better neighborhood. It was around then that his son Irving was born. As the only son, who arrived unexpectedly and late, he received lavish attention from his surprised and fortunate parents.

Gradually the Golds moved into better and better circumstances, and would have been entirely content but for mounting anti-Semitism touched off by distrust of the increasing flow of Jews from Poland and Russia that became a flood in the 1880s. Irving's father shared this disdain and tried, as far as possible, to distance himself from these crude newcomers. He had already halved his name and further proceeded to disguise the Jewish portion of his identity, joining the German-speaking St. Louis Bayern Verein, even though he was not from Bavaria, and had the wrong accent. He faithfully read the *Westlische Post* to keep abreast of events in his adopted city. He and his wife joined the local Singverein, which performed concerts at Christmas and mid-summer. There was never a question of belonging to one of the Jewish congregations or attending Schule on holidays. It was not, Irving's father always assured him, a heritage to be ashamed of, just bad for business. Nonetheless, Irving had been circumcised at birth and he carried this evidence as a private reminder of his origin.

As he grew older and into a better understanding of his circumstances, he became more intensely aware of the edge of contradiction along which his parents defined themselves. In public, they were merely Germans, or better, German-Americans. Irving's father gradually accumulated enough capital to open a fine jewelry and watch retail business near the downtown. Sometimes when customers asked about his lingering German accent, he mentioned Bavaria or Switzerland. The latter was, after all, a plausible explanation for his expertise in timepieces. This usually satisfied any vague curiosity. On occasion, because he often clerked at the store with his father, Irving overheard this dubious assertion and felt an inexplicable shame, although not knowing if it came from the untruth or, in fact, from the truth that he was a Jew living in a world where many would consider this an unpardonable blemish. He never mustered the courage to correct his father, because he knew that the stern response, when it came, would be harsh and critical of him. It was as if his father and mother, too, expected him to understand the need for disguise, as if some secret incident had happened to the family in Poland, which still cast a shadow over the possibility of candor. Thus, Irving grew up mindful of the distance between his home life and its private rituals of tradition and the German-American identity his parents pretended in public. Much later in life, he thought he had come to a better understanding of them. It was simply their way of becoming American: to be a German-American first, lost in a huge population of immigrants, and then, after they learned English, to leave him a heritage without a hyphen.

At the same time, he could not help but recognize that he looked darker, even exotic next to the other boys who attended the German language school where his parents first enrolled him. With his black curly hair, pale, almost fragile looking face, he knew that he resembled his mother's family. There were occasions even, when he thought his friends might recognize his origins. When he saw his reflection in the mirror, he thought he looked Jewish. There was simply no way around it.

When Irving was nineteen and began to show an interest in girls, his parents, oddly enough, never seemed to approve of any of the young Germans he mentioned. There was always something wrong in their eyes: rumors of a dissolute father, their plain looks, some blemish on their potential that they discovered. It was not long before he realized that they were trying to steer him to marry into another Jewish family that his father knew through business. When he recognized their attempt to direct his rather aimless amorous meanderings, he was puzzled and angry. Why, he asked himself, if they were so reluctant to celebrate being Jewish, would they object to his marriage to a gentile girl? Wasn't that the goal of their vague dissimulation, their division between orthodoxy at home and their public persona of the good German-American immigrant? He neither understood nor sympathized, and once he even confronted them about their caution: "This is America," he had said, "not Poland; not the old country. What could happen here?"

"It's a matter of good business," his father replied. "No need to advertise; no need to create prejudice."

"But everyone knows we're Jewish," he had exclaimed once. "And I don't see or feel the difference."

"Well, you can't be sure," his mother said. "You mustn't always be so trusting. Things can always change. Believe you me!"

By this time, after helping his father on weekends and then, when high school had finished, as his permanent assistant, Irving had learned the jewelry and watch trade well. He even showed a proficient skill at repairing a broken timepiece and became an expert at replacing the crystals that frequently broke on expensive watches. Most of the customers were, of course, women, who purchased strands of silver filigree and cut glass broaches or semi-precious stones that his father had set in gold or silver bands. On occasion, he was asked to identify a stone—usually a shard of crystal glass pretending to be a diamond, or a common lapis-lazuli or bit of amber. He became very adept at determining these identities and estimating their worth, although he never quite mastered his father's gentle way of informing a patron that her heirloom from the old country was only an ordinary piece of colored glass. Nonetheless, he began to enjoy his days in the store and realized that he was good at his work and popular with customers. He came to love the feel of jewelry, the warm, almost liquid surfaces of heavy gold and silver settings and the sharp cuts of glass and the spikey points of the occasional diamond. All of these pieces seemed to him to possess an inner energy, something that radiated out and caressed the soft pads of his fingertips. Looking through his jeweler's monocle, he loved to study the wavy lines and spots of turquoise and pick out the tiny flaws that broke the surface.

He also began to recognize that with many customers there was something more than a simple transaction: an undercurrent of unspoken words that bothered him. It was not hostility—he knew enough to recognize unpleasantness—but a gesture of hurry, as if the client was about to speak, but then thought the better of it. Usually this occurred during the discussion of the price, when on occasion, a customer made a ridiculously lower offer to pay for services or for a new item. Irving thought of it as a kind of test, of him and of them, but it never amused him as much as it did his father. Once when he remarked about such an incident after a man had repeatedly tried to bargain for something he never intended to buy, Gold senior just said simply, "They just assume all jewelers are Jews. And sometimes they think we're selling from a pushcart. Just ignore it, Irving. It comes with the business." Irving didn't press the issue but thought he understood its meaning, and it gave him a certain wariness with every new customer which he tried to disguise with an ingratiating smile.

If Irving was the pride of his parents and the delight of his father as an heir to the business he had built up in St. Louis and the position of respect he occupied in the German-American community, there was one issue between them that defeated this happy continuity, this smooth passage from one generation to the next. Irving was courting a Lutheran girl, of German background, both of whose parents had passed away. Hoping that this would please his parents, instead, it only inspired sullen warnings from his father and a growing coldness in his mother's eye. This was a situation Irving could not tolerate. If his parents were only Jewish inside, privately, at home, and lived their public lives in the religious chaos of sects and beliefs that characterized turn-of-the-century St. Louis, what, he reasoned, did it matter? Why couldn't he marry outside the faith, if indeed his parents' odd form of adherence could really be called a faith at all?

Stubbornly, Irving continued to see the dark-haired, German girl, Greta, who almost looked Jewish, with her thick dark and wavy hair and stout figure. There was an irony, thought Irving: "I'm cautioned not to marry a girl who looks Jewish but isn't, and urged on to court someone more passably German who is." He despaired of ever understanding his parents and their alien hypocrisies, but he was as stubborn in his choice as they in their prejudice. He would never understand the "accommodation" as his father once called it.

The argument between them ran deep and corrosive, and Irving realized eventually that if he actually married Greta, he would have to leave St. Louis. His father had not actually said as much, but he understood the friction between them would never diminish, and the arrival of children would merely add a dimension to the unpleasantness between them. Because jewelry was the only business he knew or understood, he could not imagine setting up in competition with his father. No matter how vast the city or diverse the places where he might locate, he knew he could not remain.

When his parents realized that his choice was irrevocable, they consented to attend his small, non-sectarian wedding, although he came to understand that for them, the ceremony was more the interment of their hopes and expectations. He knew he would see them infrequently, wherever he and Greta decided to locate and he understood that any such meetings would be clumsy and cold. However, the family bond, stretched and worn, still existed, despite the hurt that his parents' disapproval had inflicted.

After the wedding, which took place in the dull, little Protestant chapel, witnessed by his parents and Greta's brother, and eventually at odds with the approval of all of them, Irving and Greta set off on a brief honeymoon to Chicago, the most memorable part of which was a whole day spent at Marshall Field's new department store. They both marveled at the cool, ornate, and brightly lighted interior and the sparkling counters and rows and racks of clothing, shoes, and household furnishings. Greta was enchanted by the subdued elegance of the tearoom, which Irving also found charming. For her, the ladies' retiring chamber was a marvel of convenience and extravagance. For his part, Irving could not erase from his mind the brilliant impression of the jewelry display, the casual, draped elegance of gold and silver necklaces and the brilliant stones, the real stones, set handsomely in rings and broaches. It was a memory he would always carry with him.

After the bliss and excitement of Chicago, the couple returned to St. Louis. There they found a small apartment, rented by the month, near the downtown. It was temporary because Irving was planning to move as soon as he could find a suitable storefront in a new town to set up business. It was not an easy search. At first, he looked in local newspapers in the announcements section on the off chance that a jewelry business might be for sale. He consulted city directories in Missouri, where they existed, for the names and locations of stores—so he could avoid setting up in an area already covered by one jeweler. After several weeks, he decided to travel east into Illinois, which was more settled and established, to see if he could find just the right location. At first, he set his eye on West Frankfort, thinking it might harbor a large Germany population (because of the name). When he visited, he was amused at his error—the spelling was wrong—and while a few German families resided in the town, there was already a watch and jewelry business right on the main square.

Traveling straight south about 15 miles he came to

Marion. It was still a smallish settlement and seemed to him like every other Midwest city he had visited, striving to establish itself as an upcoming economic center amid the corn fields and orchards. Nonetheless, he thought there was something inviting about the place. Perhaps it was the large elm trees, the street names, the white frame houses, all of which he had seen elsewhere. Something else caught his attention; the town's thriving business section lacked a jewelry business. When he inquired at the local bank about renting a storefront on Illinois Square, right at the center of town, he found a very suitable property. Without consulting Greta, he signed a contract with the owner. It was now merely a question of moving his bride, his life, and his future to Marion.

Living in Marion away from the sadness and disappointment of his parents was more than matched by the happiness he found with his new wife. Greta surprised him by her rambunctious pleasure-seeking in bed. Indeed, he was somewhat taken aback at first, until he realized that his reticence only dampened the delight that both experienced in the other's body. He brought only a boy's rudimentary knowledge of sex to their coupling, based on vague and impossibly exaggerated stories he had heard, and a measure of off-color jokes that his friends had bandied about, which contained a good deal of misinformation and bravado. On one occasion, his father had tried to talk to him about sex, but he stumbled over the words as he tried to describe in a clinical and abstract way the act, for which Irving only knew slang terms that he knew would be offensive to mention. Inevitably, his father took his silence for understanding rather than its opposite, which was much closer to reality. Thus, Irving allowed himself to be guided by Greta, not even pretending that he was an experienced or accomplished lover. In all, it was a revelation to him.

In matters of the new jewelry business, however, Irving was master. Gradually he built up a stock of items: wedding rings, silver plate dishes and flatware, glass and pottery dishes and vases and cheap watches. He learned quickly that the customers who came into his store wanted luxury at a bargain price. He also recognized the town hierarchy: those few families at the top of this small heap of humanity: Doc Watson, the Reverend Turnbull's, the banker, lawyers, and school principals. These potential patrons had the money, if only limited taste, to buy the objects that would advertise their status. Below them were the poorer farmers who came in to buy a timepiece or a thin gold wedding band that might be the only valuables they would ever possess. In hard times, when the crops failed, and during the Great Depression of 1893, he lent money on the value of a family heirloom, or even an item he had previously sold.

In the aftermath of that distressed time, specifically in 1894 when the Depression struck Illinois the hardest, Irving Gold began to feel something he had never experienced. Lending money and acting the pawnbroker to troubled customers, suddenly gave him a new and dubious reputation. He became someone viewed with considerable suspicion and embarrassment. He understood the reasons: he knew the shame of families whose livelihood had been scraped to the bone by the hard times; he knew how much they suffered, and what they owed. He also recognized their nervous suspicion that the value he gave to objects when they placed them on the glass counter of his shop was far lower than their true worth. If he lent money on an object he had sold, he was always careful to match the purchase price in his appraisal. But he still saw the anger and disappointment in the eyes of clients who expected more, and surely, in their own eyes, deserved more.

During those moments of transaction, Irving also felt something almost palpable in the space across the counter, a sentiment that he only later gave the name anti-Semitism. He knew, of course, that he looked Jewish—if indeed there was such a look—although he wondered how the good citizens of Marion had come to their stereotype. There were, as far as he knew, no other Jewish families in the town, if indeed his mixed marriage could be called by that name. He wondered: was it in looking at him that they had formulated a picture of the only Jew they knew and then applied it generally? Was he a stereotype with his short, curly hair, pale skin and the dark beard that shaded his face by early afternoon? The clipped, Germanic city accent he had picked up during his St. Louis childhood or his slightly bent and rounded shoulders, and his quick and eager fingers that he struggled to control? Did all of these traits add up to something more than a picture of himself? Did that person, positioned in his store, behind the counter of cheap treasures, make him a model even if he had renounced any practice of Jewish customs and married out of the faith? Did he deserve this unfair prejudice?

On one particularly hot, still summer day in 1894, with cicadas buzzing in the air made brittle from the drought that had wilted the corn and burned the tops of squash and potato plants, he could sense the nervousness of everyone he encountered. It was as if the anxious wait for rain that refused to come, the vain look for the roiling clouds that might promise a cooling storm, had shortened the temper of the whole impatient town. There had only been one customer up to the late afternoon, the Reverend Mrs. Turnbull, the middle-aged woman who often stopped to inspect the merchandise but had never—he was sure he remembered—purchased anything. He had begun to think that her visits were merely reminders of her disapproval, a renewal of personal dislike she had somehow come to harbor for him.

This afternoon, in the sullen heat and the closeness of the store, he saw that she was perspiring freely, with little droplets forming on her brow, threatening to run in rivulets into her eyes. Self-consciously, she wiped her face with a white lace-edged handkerchief. If this embarrassed her, she disguised it with a frown, and then began a series of questions about a ring she had asked to examine.

Turning it over repeatedly in her small hands, as if searching for flaws, she spoke without looking up:

"I'd fancy this ring," she said in a voice that almost crackled with static electricity, "but, of course I know your price would be far too high."

Irving shifted from one foot to the other behind the counter as he reached for a wedge of blue velvet mounted on cardboard and placed it before her.

"Why don't you look at it on this," he said, gesturing to the board, "and afterwards, if you want, you can try it. You can see that the gold is very dark and rich and the stone is a small diamond. I don't have many others like it. There's not much call for sophisticated taste in Marion."

She looked at him, taking in his words, which she had heard many times before, and then did what he suggested, placing the ring on the velvet and squinting to catch the sparkle of its facets. Smoothing her white bodice and then bending over again slightly, she continued:

"But I think I see flaws in it. See here, this tiny dark line. That must surely lower its value; not of course that I would ever care to bargain with you over something that was imperfect."

"No, Mrs. Turnbull," he responded quickly. "There are no flaws. That I can assure you. And I've examined it carefully with the glass."

"Well, I suppose you know best about such matters. It is your trade. But I would want reassurance that it wasn't just a piece of cut crystal done up in a plated mount."

Irving looked again at her and decided, suddenly, that her attempt to disparage the ring was an opening gambit, in preparation for a session of what could be serious bargaining, by suggesting reasons why this ring might not be genuine. In fact, it was one of the most expensive items in the store: not a false bauble or a fake. It was a measure of her attitude to him that she spoke in such denigrating terms even before asking its price.

"No," he reiterated, "it's a very fine gem and the gold is heavy, 18 carat, and the mounting has a beautiful filigree construction. Why don't you try it? Of course, I can size it to fit if you should decide..." He said this with as much sincerity as he could muster because he was certain this game would have no result.

"And how much are you asking for it?" she resumed, suddenly looking him squarely, almost defiantly in the face.

"Oh," he said, "it's two hundred dollars. Why not try it," he urged, remembering the many times they had reached such a point in their fruitless transactions.

"You people," she said suddenly in disgust, "you have such a devious way of selling things, tempting me like that! Do you actually think if I try it on my finger I will suddenly weaken and pay your ridiculous price? Is that how you do it?"

Irving's smile remained, but he had to force it to linger. *You people...you Jews*, he added to himself silently.

"I think it would be a very handsome complement to you, Mrs. Turnbull," he said. "Do try it."

She did. Abruptly, she grasped the ring with her right hand and slid it over the knuckle of the fourth finger of her left hand. Then she held her hand away, stiff and with her fingers tilted upward in a gesture of inspection.

"I still think I see flaws," she continued. "Perhaps it's not really worth $200. Something considerably less I would estimate."

Irving was outraged and struggled to suppress the unkind remark that sat at the tip of his tongue. What was the purpose of this hostile banter, he wondered? Why insult him this way? He knew from experience she would never buy anything, and the way she bargained now, exposing her scornful assumptions about him, was deeply wounding. Yet, as he fought to suppress his anger, to put "a good face on it," an outrageous idea came to him, as if the heat, and the dry, impossible afternoon, the madness of the situation had made him giddy: he would accept her challenge and push her to the limit, just to see what she was capable of saying.

"Well then, perhaps, you are right," he began, observing the sudden surprise that appeared in her eyes. "There may be a tiny flaw here or there. But it's still a beautiful ring. What would you be willing to pay for it?"

She looked shocked and puzzled at his unexpected question. Stretching out her left hand again to gain a moment of composure, and with her other, simultaneously daubing her brow and cheeks, even damper now with anxiety, she replied:

"Oh, I don't know," she began deliberately, "I don't really need it, and there are the flaws and that cheap gold plate that you mentioned. I suppose about $20 if that, and I think it's a generous price, really...for something I don't need," she repeated.

"All right," Irving said, almost beside himself with a thrill of excited anger.

"Oh, I really couldn't," she replied quickly. "I didn't really mean..."

"But it's yours for $20," he repeated, suddenly lightheaded with the folly that his fury was urging him to commit.

"All right," she said squinting, her eyes greedy with the sudden possibility of possession. "I suppose I could pay $15 for it."

For a moment, he thought she was trying to sabotage the purchase, but then he realized that having come this far, having become in her eyes the haggling Jew with tawdry goods, he would not allow her this escape.

"Sold," he said, too loud, determined he would not let her change her mind. "It's yours. I'll put it in a box and even if you don't have the money with you, you can pay me later."

She glanced at him, puzzled but now as resolute and excited as he was, and reached into her sack that lay on its side on the counter. She drew out a five-dollar gold coin and placed it on the velvet board as if money too was a jewel and they, two merchants exchanging goods. Then she removed the ring and passed it back to him. He took it quickly, fearing that she might once again lower her offer. He pulled out a small cardboard box and placed the ring, diamond up, into the slot in its black cloth base so that the jewel glistened against the dark setting.

Shall I wrap it?" he asked.

"Oh no," she replied, "I really must be off. I have other shopping to do. I didn't mean to...I wonder about what Mr. Turnbull will say. He doesn't approve of finery you know." She turned, clutching the box and snatching up her purse. She walked out into the hot dusty afternoon sunlight without a backward glance.

When Irving reached home after closing up the shop that evening, he greeted his wife with an uncustomary warm embrace. Taking off his outer, dark jacket, he fussed with his cuffs in embarrassed silence. For a moment, he felt as if he were engaged in a solitary celebration, a ritual, rolling up his shirtsleeves in preparation for an ecstatic dance. He could not be sure of what Greta thought as she looked at him, appraising his odd behavior.

"You have a spring in your step tonight, Irving. Did something good happen today? Something at the store?"

He paused for a minute to collect his thoughts although he knew in advance that he would tell her nothing. On the walk home, he had debated with himself, but quickly decided that there was no explaining what he had done, no rational reason to justify his rash decision, or his elation at triumphing over Mrs. Turnbull's arrogant prejudice—if this self-inflicted wound was, indeed, a triumph. There was no way to explain that he had suddenly made her into the embodiment of her own bigotry: a bargaining, grasping caricature of what she despised. Greta would never understand the gratification that made him flush again with nervous excitement as he remembered the transaction; on the contrary, she would worry that he had lost his mind.

"Nothing much out of the ordinary occurred," he said. "A day like any other in Marion." He reached out suddenly with his right hand and grasped her shoulder, touching the soft fabric of her blouse, and turning her slightly.

"Do you ever regret coming here?" he asked, "Not going to some larger place?"

"Oh no," she cried. "Not at all. We've made a pleasant life here...It's such a fine little town." She let her voice trail off as if she had another thought. Irving clearly expected her to qualify her expression of happiness, but she just looked at him curiously.

"I'm mighty hungry," he said, breaking up the silence that had settled between them. "Could we eat soon?"

"Of course," she answered, turning toward the kitchen. "It won't be but a minute or two. I'll fetch you when it's ready."

He watched her as she walked down the hallway to the half-open door. In the shadows, she reminded him suddenly of the girl he had courted twenty years earlier. For a moment, he thought of the heavy, matronly German women in St. Louis, gossiping on the street corners or in clusters around the stoop of a townhouse. Not Greta, who still moved with the liveliness of a young woman; there was yet hope in her step. Now he feared he had done something terrible to destroy it. He walked into the living room, settled into his favorite armchair and wondered how his rash action that afternoon would end.

The next morning, he entered the shop with a feeling of excitement and expectation. He realized it was almost the sensation of fear at what the day might bring. As he turned the key and opened the door, he wondered if the store would look the same. Would it show signs of his sudden irrational and destructive act? He half expected to see its reflection in a disordered interior as if the merchandise had been pawed over by thieves. But nothing was out of place. Indeed, nothing happened at all and, he thought, perhaps the remembered events of yesterday were just his imagination. He had no customers that morning and so he spent his time polishing the glass of the display cases before he placed the watches and jewelry in them that he took from the heavy safe in his office. With this accomplished, he decided to wash the front windows. As he worked, he noticed the same two or three women pass by the shop. They looked in briefly, but their eyes never met his, and he thought nothing more of it until later. After a small lunch of sandwiches that Greta had made, he sat in his office reading yesterday's *St. Louis Post-Dispatch* which arrived by train and was delivered by the mailman. His family had always been loyal readers of the *Westliche Post* and when Joseph Pulitzer transformed it into an English language paper he had followed along. As he was turning the last pages, looking briefly and nervously, but unable to concentrate on any of the stories, he heard the bell tinkle as someone entered the store. It was Mrs. Simpson, the dry goods shopkeeper's wife, and, he realized, one of the women who had paced in front of the store earlier that morning. He wondered if those crisscrossings were efforts to gather up the courage to enter.

"Good afternoon, Mr. Gold," she said, as he emerged from the office and stood behind the counter. Her voice was hesitant and loud with embarrassment.

"Yes, Mrs. Simpson. May I be of assistance?" he answered.

She continued with more confidence: "If I might look at rings. Something nice, but not too expensive. Or perhaps a necklace?" Her eyes brightened. He wondered if they were lighted by the glint of greed?

"Certainly," he said, pulling out from the display case, a cardboard box with several rings inserted in the cutouts–missing only one: the diamond he had sold to Mrs. Turnbull yesterday.

"Yes," she said, "quite lovely. But I imagine that they are all very expensive." Her voice trailed off as if anticipating disappointment.

"No, not at all," Gold responded. "It depends upon the stone and the setting. I also have some lovely costume pieces if you prefer. It's very hard to tell the difference."

"Oh no," she said with a cluck of disapproval. "I wouldn't want something fake."

"Well then," he answered, "You should concentrate on the top row here. There are two small diamonds, sapphires, one ruby and an amethyst. The row below is lesser stones: lapis lazuli, garnet, crystal. For the latter, the gold is only 14 carats."

"Yes, then," she said fingering one of the expensive rings. "And how much is the sapphire? I've always loved that stone; and the name is so exotic don't you think, like the mysteries of the East."

"Oh I do agree. And that is a lovely setting too. I ordered it from Chicago."

"You tempt me, Mr. Gold," she responded. "But I suppose I could never afford it what with the terrible state of business. Mr. Simpson..."

"It's $150 and worth every bit of that."

"Oh dear, just as I feared! I could never pay that. Mr. Simpson would never forgive me...think me vain and self-centered." Nonetheless, she slipped the ring on her finger and looked intently at it.

He had fully expected the conversation to turn to this moment. Then, almost in spite of himself, he said softly, "How much could you pay?"

Her eyes widened as if a truth had suddenly been confirmed–the promise of gossip and rumor made manifest.

"Oh, I couldn't bargain with you," she said hastily, and then blurted out: "thirty dollars."

"I would be pleased to accept that," he said, as if he too had found a sudden truth in their transaction.

"Well then," she said with finality. "That's fine," and reaching into her purse, she withdrew two gold pieces and laid them on the glass counter. "I'll pass by later with the rest...and fetch the ring." She turned and hastened out the door, hurried on by the fear that her good fortune might prove illusory.

Again that evening Irving felt strangely elated and anxious at the same time. During the afternoon, several more women, the wives of the town's gentry, had stopped in the store to bargain for his most expensive pieces. He also sold two watches. He recognized that this brisk business was evidence of the spreading rumor of his folly, his uncontrollable madness, as if a stone had dropped into a pond and the first waves of the select were responding to the energy, and then sending out hints of opportunity to those less fortunate at its further circumference. But he could not stop himself. The next day proved to be similar except that now, as his stock of finery was rapidly depleted, the clientele had changed and the store became crowded with the curious and embarrassed wives of railway workers, the postman's wife, school teachers, and an occasional young grocery boy or farm hand. They were excited, but several expressed anger and even some sharp words, because as late comers, they believed they had been cheated out of opportunities to carry away their share of the pillage.

Each transaction went the same way: Irving mentioned an initial fair price; the customer would respond with a ludicrous offer, and then he agreed to accept a pittance of the value. With each bargain, he felt the same alarming sense of confirmation, as if he had discovered something deeply evil in the souls of his fellow townsfolk. They knew they were swindling him, but they could not resist the temptation he placed before them. With each sale, he became more excited and less able to control his emotions, barely suppressing the feeling of a dizzy elation. In these moments, he thought he understood the frenzied agitation that seized someone before the act of suicide and the huge emotional energy it took to destroy oneself. Or maybe it was like the endless, stretched-out seconds waiting for the bugle to announce the beginning of a battle, where the mind was utterly clear in intent, and the body listless and unresponsive, waiting for an encounter with death and destruction? He wondered if he was going mad, and yet he could not stop or even pause in the relentless liquidation of his livelihood and destruction of his very identity.

On Friday evening, when he returned home to the small house on West Elm, he had a sense of foreboding. As he walked wearily up the wooden steps of the front porch, the door opened and Greta stood, arms limp at her sides and her cheeks streaked with tears, the striations of her grief. She knew, he realized, and her silent greeting only confirmed the hurt that she was suffering.

"What have you done, Irving? Why? I don't understand!" she sobbed after a minute. "Why? Everything? Is it all gone?"

"So you know," he said softly, touching her elbow and guiding her back into the house. "So you know," he said again, feeling for the first time in several days the burden of his anxiety lift. "So you know," he repeated, unable to think of anything else to say.

"How could I not know? The whole town is talking. What has come over you, Irving? Think of the consequences for us. I scarcely know you anymore. How could you do such a thing?"

Irving paused, and then gripped both of her shoulders and looked into her eyes, as if searching for his reflection, to find himself in her vision.

"I don't know what made me do it. It was a sudden impulse. I couldn't stop."

"But you've ruined us! What made you do it? Who are you? I don't know who you are anymore!" she cried bitterly.

Irving waited almost thirty seconds as his mind raced, choosing and rejecting explanations, before he could admit what had pushed him to act.

"All I can say, Greta, and maybe you will never understand this, is that I'm just not that grasping Jew. I had enough! Something inside me made me want to rip the skin off the prejudice that's living in this town. To prove that they were worse than anything they ever thought about me. Show them who I was. And now all I've done is to destroy us.

High Pockets

"So this is it and no further; where it ends," John Clarke said to himself, as he descended the iron steps of the rail car and looked around at the discouraging brick station. Two small suitcases, one filled with books and the other his clothes: these and the memories that punished him when he allowed them attention were his only possessions. There was no one to meet him, no friend or acquaintance, just the promise of the job and the oblivion of miles—the distance between who he had been back in Baltimore and the possibility of escape. Here, he thought, I will be just John Clarke and not some vicious caricature.

If asked, he could tell the world a thing or two about the pain of nicknames. As long as he remembered, some sort of hurtful epithet followed him as surely as the long shadows cast at sunset. There were times when the palpability of this unwanted attention made him stop suddenly to turn around and glimpse whoever or whatever was in pursuit, to catch their eye in the act of passing judgment on him. He was rarely successful, but nonetheless knew that he was peculiar to the tastes of others and this strangeness provoked their need to label him and exaggerate some quality to stand in for the whole of his character. Ever since he was a boy, growing up in a neighborhood of row houses near the docks of Baltimore, he had suffered one offensive name after another: "Ladder Boy," "Miss Fussy," "Ichabod Crane" (after the class had read Washington Irving's short story in 6th grade), and the worst: "Mama's Favorite." Somewhere he had heard the phrase, "to earn a nickname," but he assured himself he had done nothing to deserve such spite. As a precaution, he tried to make himself stand out less at school, slouching down the edge of hallways, never walking confidently in the middle, and making as little noise as possible when he entered a classroom. Nor was there solace at home, for he feared that even his parents were unlikely to think of him simply as John.

There were many times when he considered this situation in the small mirror on the wall of his bedroom, looking for whatever it was that incited others to such malevolent humor. Often when he walked by and glanced into it, he hoped to see another person, a better, handsomer and rougher version of himself, someone he could admire. Instead, it always threw back an image that embarrassed him and made him turn away in shame. In high school, he was taller than most boys his age and so he slumped over, rounding his shoulders and thrusting his head forward to diminish his stature. This odd posture only emphasized his jerky gait and slight build. His face was pleasant, although by then, his skin was inflamed and violent with acne. His hazel eyes often glazed over as he imagined himself elsewhere, like the hero of the fiction he discovered later in life—Tarzan or John Carter from one of E. R. Burroughs' other novels. Most noticeable was his twitching left eye, which others sometimes mistook for a wink, and which he struggled to calm when in the company of his classmates and parents. Only in moments of solitary and absent-minded adventure, when he imagined himself elsewhere and otherwise, could he forget what others thought of him; only then could he truly relax.

John's family had occupied the same small row house on Fells Point for two generations, and everyone expected that he, his brother, and all his male cousins would follow their fathers onto the nearby docks as a stevedore or some other longshoreman. The family was proud that it had maintained its place as one of the few Irish groups in a work world that was increasingly Polish. The Clarkes preserved a close network of family relationships that ensured stable work and sometimes even promotion. However, John's odd demeanor, his slight, unsuited build, and his bookish dreaming worried his parents, who sought to encourage him, at opportune moments, with stories of hard work triumphant, and the rise of some in his extended family to become the superintendent of a warehouse or head of a gang of 'wharfies.' In his own house, just inside the marble steps and the wide wooden door, were hangers where his father and older brother placed their dockworker's hooks and watch caps every evening after work in a display of masculine pride. Glancing at this array, John knew that such a future was impossible for him, although he sometimes regretted that he had neither the stamina nor the will to follow in their footsteps.

He excelled at school (another source of potential ridicule), and learned to read at a very young age. Often, he hid these skills in a retiring shyness and wished himself only to be that which was impossible: a sturdy, hard-working and hard-drinking man like his father. Only his mother intervened now and again when his father chided him for sitting in his room studying. On occasion, she rewarded him by presenting him with a dime for the odd jobs around the house which she knew he would spend on his "adventure novels" as he called them.

When he was ten or eleven, his favorites were *Ivanhoe* and the *Knights of the Round Table.* He loved to follow their adventures and sometimes woke at night from an urgent dream in which he pictured himself as Sir Galahad's squire or page, attending Court, listening to the strange Anglo-Saxon accents and then the tender words of courtly love. Most of all, he liked the pictures of these dashing heroes with their saintly faces printed in the color books he borrowed from the Baltimore Public Library. He wondered if someday he could buy an illustrated collection of the tales of the Crusades and King Richard the Lion-Hearted for his own room. The knights were equally handsome, he decided, in their beaten steel-plate armor or courtly silks and velvets.

Yet this infatuation with medieval adventures did not survive the appeal of the more exotic, and his favorite characters soon became Robinson Crusoe and his friend Friday. Even when he was much older, as an adult, adventure stories still intrigued him, and he subscribed to pulp magazines for many years. When it appeared in 1912, Edgar Rice Burroughs's *Tarzan* became his favorite tale. Even more, he loved the author's John Carter series. Of course, he knew these stories were preposterous, even silly, and he realized that Burroughs set them in the jungle or on Mars only because he could fashion a world to his own liking and people it with animals and human-like creatures entirely of his own invention. Nonetheless, he often stared at the drawings of John Carter with his rippling muscles, charmed by his hero's uncanny physical and mental prowess. And then there were the animals conceived out of the author's febrile mind—the dangerous poisonous lizards, the brilliant plumed birds, and the strange mammal equivalents of Earth's dogs, cats, horses, and draft animals. He loved to contemplate the miraculous power of evolution, the mysterious force that Burroughs summoned up to explain his odd Martian landscapes. Of course, he never admitted his odd taste to anyone or his continued, secret infatuation with adventure stories intended for young boys.

When he turned 17, now forced to contemplate the future, he began to consider continuing his studies at the University. Years past, his father and older brother had ceased to persuade him to follow them to the docks, and he began to feel like a boarder in his own family home. His heart sank when he came home from school and saw his mother scrubbing the marble steps in front of the house. He only half listened to the brusque talk of his father and brother as they recounted the day's lifting and stowing of heavy crates and cargo. He no longer felt a part of their world and wanted more than anything to escape. Not that he was unsentimental about his neighborhood on occasion; he knew he loved his parents, but felt shy and clumsy around them. He often wondered how he could express his feeling for them when they themselves seemed so fearful of even the hint of affection.

Gradually, he had begun to suggest his ambitions to them, encouraged by his high school biology teacher to think of a career in science. Most of all he wanted to be associated with two great Baltimore institutions. Both the Johns Hopkins University on Howard Street and the Baltimore Zoo on the north side of the city opened simultaneously, and he considered it fate that had established what he hoped would be two focal points of his life. More and more, he set his sights in their direction, away from the port and the docks where he knew he could not remain.

He also hoped he could escape from the relentless teasing he received in high school, remarks about his odd posture, and, of course, the nicknames that some of the boys attached to him. For this reason, he had few friends and trusted no one. Anyone in his class who might have approached him feared sharing in his ostracism. There was only one small Polish boy, blond and very feminine looking who made advances that were friendly, and who hailed him in the hallways and smiled with a look that lingered, as if the two of them shared some secret bond. But John was terrified of this attention from Ambrozy and his overtures, and he fixed a sullen look on his face and managed only curt responses to signal his rejection and disapproval to any other boys who might be watching. To rid himself of the odd feeling of shame and guilt inspired by this unwanted adulation would be another reward of his new life, where no one knew him.

By the time he graduated, only a few boys remained in his class. Most had dropped out to take jobs on the docks with their fathers. He often saw them in the street, but they rarely acknowledged him now, or if they did, they shouted at him with a remembered nickname. What amazed him in these encounters was how much the others had changed and hardened. Their faces were rougher and livid from their strenuous outdoor work and hard drinking, and their shoulders seemed broader. They now walked with a swagger that came from their new status, although he imagined he could also see a look of incipient fatigue, the tired and drawn aspect of a discouraging and hapless adulthood. He shuddered sometimes to think this might have been his fate. Had he followed his father, would he too have the large, cracked hands of a dockworker and their lusterless eyes?

Getting to Johns Hopkins was a long trolley ride through the center of Baltimore, but the real journey was to pass through its limestone portals as a scholarship boy. His parents could afford nothing for tuition and he knew, besides, that his father disapproved of "book learning" and could not imagine his son, a Clarke, living the soft life of a scholar. Nonetheless, his biology teacher had pushed him to apply and mentioned that he had some influence as a distant relation to President Gilman. So it was arranged for John to begin his classes in the fall. He could not afford to move anywhere near the elegant neighborhood where the University stood, and continued to sleep at home, spending as much time as he could in the biology laboratory and at the library.

During the summer, waiting for classes to begin, he often wandered through the Baltimore Zoo, looking at the animals and chatting with the keepers who seemed to enjoy filling his ears with the exciting stories of mishaps with the big cats, the moody, savage behavior of caged animals, and the uncanny human-like qualities of monkeys and apes. Looking back on these days, he recognized what Burroughs himself had observed that laid the foundation for his wild imagination of the cruel beasts of Mars. John also realized that his enthusiasms for his favorite author were frozen in permanent adolescence. His love of fantasy belonged to another part of his nature. In the real world, there were explanations for animal behavior, and he wanted to be a scientist and someone whom the perplexed zoo attendants might call upon to explain how to preserve the animals in their keep.

When the semester at Hopkins began in the fall, John timidly entered the lecture hall of his first class and immediately recognized a familiar stir of attention, an undercurrent of derision that he judged to be focused on his appearance. He had dressed in his only Sunday suit, a combination that, if he hitched his pants to his true waist, revealed his thin ankles, his black stockings and scuffed shoes. The jacket likewise was too short, although more than ample in the shoulders, as if still draped on a wooden hanger. The combination emphasized his narrow, pinched chest. His long arms stood out from his sleeves like handles of a butter churn: in all, he was the very caricature of a scholarship boy. He managed an apologetic smile and took a seat at the back of the room. Whatever the attitude of his classmates, he pledged at that moment to ignore them. No matter the cost, he would not allow the mockery and ridicule of the port to follow him here. The university situation offered different possibilities. The boys of Fells Point had teased him for being too good, and for showing them the narrow confines of their futures by his example. Here it would be different. These were the sons of doctors and merchants. While they might scorn him because he came from the bottom rung, and represented a world that their academic degrees and family fortunes would save them from even imagining, he knew this was a portal to a different future. If he succeeded here, if he learned their words and gestures, they would have to accept him. Above all, he hoped they would never invent the terrible nicknames that had made him blanch and cringe.

As the year passed, John continued to journey almost daily from the cramped town house by the docks to the leafy expanse of the Hopkins campus. Besides his lectures, he spent hours in the biology laboratory, studying the animal and plant specimens and skeletal remains of animals and humans. He always managed several afternoons a week at the zoo where he had now taken on a part-time position as watchman, janitor, and assistant keeper. He scarcely ever thought about his family or spoke more than perfunctory greetings when he was at home, and planned to leave as soon as he could afford other accommodations. Life was gradually opening wider for him, and he began to stand straighter and address his fellow students with greater confidence. He suddenly realized this was the first time in his life that he had felt joy.

That feeling of elation only increased when he made his first real friend, another scholarship boy who had come to Baltimore from Philadelphia to study biology. At first, John was tentative and shy around him, hesitant to assume too much. Unlike most of the other students who wore their family pedigrees like exclusive club insignias, David Smith always gave him a friendly smile and spoke often about assignments. He was shorter than John was and seemed genuinely interested in him. His skin was dark, almost swarthy, with deep black eyes and stiff unruly hair. His most striking feature was his delicate hands that seemed to parody the intense masculinity of his square stature. In other words, he looked quite the opposite of John and that was, perhaps one source of his attraction.

Almost without knowing when it actually happened, the two became fast friends. Not only did they share lectures and lab work, but regularly lunched together. John gradually told David about his family and growing up on the docks, and his intense desire to escape that rough world. One day, he even felt confident enough to admit jokingly his love of reading adventure stories.

"I have a question for you, David," he began, "but first I have a strange confession to make."

David gave him an odd look that quickly turned into a smile of encouragement.

"I decided on biology for the strangest of reasons. Not because there was much nature to study on Fells Point besides rats and dogs and horses, and of course fish. No trees even on our street although my mother coaxed a few flowers out of the back garden from time to time. No birds but sparrows and pigeons and gulls. In fact, I think it was the absence of nature that attracted me to explore what was missing. I knew an altogether different world existed somewhere. And then...please don't laugh at me...I began to read *Robinson Crusoe* and I credit his odd story with my love of biology. Of course, that's preposterous and Defoe's fantasies are impossible and juvenile, but somehow he made the force of nature, the vitality of life in strange places, seem real to me."

"That's the oddest inspiration I've ever encountered,"

laughed David. "But I think I can see what you mean."

"You won't tell any of the others, will you? They would only tease me and invent some sort of terrible nickname like 'Ship-wreck Boy.'"

"No, I won't say a word if you let me call you 'Ship-wreck Boy.'"

John's face dropped and then, when he realized that David's proposal came from affection, he laughed.

"Sure. I'll even answer you; but no jungle calls! And now you have to tell me why you became interested in biology. You probably have as odd a story as mine. Is there much nature in Philadelphia?"

"Well," David began, "we do have a share of parks and a fine zoo. But I spent considerable time at the YMCA where we had a wonderful reading room. My favorite books were studies of anatomy and a collection of beautiful Audubon prints. I imagine I just fell in love with knowing about insects and birds, and I convinced my mother and father, who really could not afford it, to buy me nature books and nature stories. Sometimes they protested that it would do me no good and advised me to interest myself in something that would earn a good living. I always answered that I could teach school. There's always a position in the natural sciences in the best and even more so in the worst high schools. So here I am."

John thought for a minute. "I'm not so sure I want to teach," he said, imagining for an uneasy moment the nicknames unruly students might confer on him. "I have always wanted to work in a zoo or as a park naturalist. That's why I took my part-time job. Maybe I could find a position in research once I earn a degree. I would love to direct a laboratory. Or be a naturalist on a ship, like

Darwin."

"You are a dreamer. But then, we need our dreams, I think. After all: what others have done, we can surely do."

After this lunch of brief confessions, David and John became even closer friends, and following the long listless summer vacation of their first year when they were apart, enthusiastically greeted each other on the first day of classes in September. The joy of being back in the laboratory among the specimens and bones and anatomical drawings was like a return home. Nevertheless, after they greeted each other, David seemed to retreat into himself.

"Is something the matter?" inquired John. "You seem distracted."

"Nothing really terrible. It's just that the boarding house where I rented last year is scheduled to be torn down for a block of new row houses, and I shall have to move. I don't quite know where."

"I have an idea," said John as suddenly as the thought came to him. "Why don't we find lodgings together? I'm certain it would be cheaper to live as two. Perhaps we could rent part of a house if we put our money together. I would love to leave Fells Point. I feel like a boarder with my parents and a foreigner in that neighborhood."

John was more excited at the thought than he let on. He had always been skilled at hiding his emotions, although he sometimes feared that others could detect the brightening of his eyes. At the same time, he wondered why he should hide his delight at living together. This was his best and only friend, and they already spent most of their days together in class or long afternoons in the laboratory memorizing the Latin names for specimens and dissecting animals. It would be wonderful, he thought, to move out of his dingy room with his parents, and he knew that they would also be greatly relieved. Of course, they tried to understand him, but could scarcely comprehend how their own son had become so different, like a changeling. How, from the same mold, had he grown into a gangly, shy stranger? He might miss them, he thought, but he could return for birthdays and special masses at St. Michael's. Yet, these visits, he knew, would only serve to measure the distance he traveled from his birthplace and toward the future he had chosen for a life of science.

David and John spent the next several weekends and any time they could borrow from their studies, looking for a room to rent. By pooling their money, they thought they could afford at least two rooms: a bedroom and study and sitting room with, perhaps, some sort of cooking arrangement. Since meals were only a few pennies in bars, they could eat out frequently. Their search widened around the university partly because the neighborhood where it was situated consisted mostly of elegant houses. Some of the students managed to find a nearby room, but their limited finances pushed them east into Old Town along Monument Street. That area consisted mostly of small houses and a few tenements, but neither boy worried much about the neighborhood so long as they could find a satisfactory place.

Their search finally ended one Saturday morning when they stopped at a house on East Monument where a handwritten note propped between the front window and the lace curtain behind it read: "Rooms to Let." An elderly woman, heavy set and tired-looking answered, opening the door cautiously.

"Yes, young men?" she asked.

"We've come about the rooms...in the window." said David. "We're students at the University," he added to reassure her of their reliability. She opened the door wider and stepped back, revealing a gloomy beige hallway that led almost immediately to a carpeted staircase, and then beyond, down on the left, to a door that must have opened into the kitchen. The only light came through the archway on the left from the living room.

"The rent for the room is $4.00 a week with breakfast and dinner included. No late meals and no use of the kitchen. You can come and go as you please, although I don't harken to late hours. And no guests, absolutely no guests. Do you want to see it?"

John looked at David and then answered for both of them: "Yes, please."

"Then follow me," she commanded and turned to hobble up the steps, hitching up her dress as she lifted one heavy leg after the other. David had a peculiar and amused look on his face, and went first, John following.

"The room is in the front over the living room facing the street. Down the hall...that white door is the bathroom; the commode is next to it," she said as she reached the landing. She opened the door into the long, sunny bedroom. The walls were covered by a pink and white paper that had begun to separate and hang loose in a few spots. White lace curtains fluttered in the breeze from the open window. There was a piece of oriental-style carpet in the center of the room, a half-open closet door, a dresser with five drawers on the right, and a large bed against the left wall. Over it hung a small portrait of Jesus with long, amber hair and a blue and white robe.

John looked at David, knowing that this was the best place they had yet encountered. So many of the other rooms had been cramped or in noisy rooming houses.

"Could we get a desk and chair?" he said. "There's ample room for it."

"Yes," she exclaimed, "of course. And I can find you two beds instead of this if you prefer. My son can bring them over in a week or two. You'll have to share for now if you decide to take it. I'll leave you a moment to discuss the matter. Come back downstairs to the sitting room. I'm Mrs. Spenser; you'll be obliged to pay me in advance each Friday," she added, and turned to walk out of the room. They could hear her heavy steps as she descended.

David walked around the room as if pacing off its measurements, and then sat down on the quilt that covered the bed.

"I think it's the best we've seen and the best we will find for the money," he exclaimed. "And it's on the trolley line that goes up to the university."

"And not far from the zoo in the other direction," added John enthusiastically. "Yes, why don't we tell her, yes? Perhaps we can move in tomorrow. I haven't much to bring: just my clothes and books. And the eating arrangement, that sounds perfect."

"All right then," concluded David. "We can probably locate an old table and a couple of chairs for a desk. And there is ample room for two beds," he added. "But I don't mind sharing for a while."

"Yes, it's fine," said John. "I slept in the same bed with my older brother until I was ten."

They walked out of the room, closed the door carefully, and went back downstairs to find Mrs. Spenser sitting expectantly on a small sofa.

"We'll take it," said David. "And if we could move in tomorrow that would be wonderful. We haven't much to bring. Here's a week's rent," he added, pulling four dollars out of his pocket.

"I thought as much," she said. "But I'll also need a deposit of a week's rent too. We'll set it to come due on Friday mornings as I said."

John looked at David, and then reached into his pocket and handed four more bills to Mrs. Spenser.

"Here's the keys," she continued, producing a large iron key that obviously opened the front lock. "The smaller one is to your room. And one other thing while it's on my mind. I don't fix breakfast on Sundays. I'll be at church early. I can show you where it is; just a few blocks over. It's a Baptist Chapel, not that I care what religion you keep...so many odd faiths in Baltimore these days. Not that it matters much so long as you observe. 'Godly in the eyes of God' I always says."

David and John left and turned back to the house as they reached the sidewalk.

"It will be fine, I think," said John. "Mrs. Spenser seems nice enough. I didn't have the courage to tell her I'm a Catholic—one of those strange religions I think she must mean."

"Yes, and I don't believe I will ask her about church. I'd just as soon avoid getting tangled up in religion right now. I don't think I could bear another sermon preached against evolution," David added.

"Nor could I," interrupted John with half a laugh. "It can be so narrow...religion...it pinches off thinking. I'm hoping Mrs. Spenser won't try to convert us."

The two boys moved in the following day, arranging their few things in the closet and dresser. John spent the next afternoon in a nearby used furniture store and bargained for an old painted table and two stiff wooden chairs that cost next to nothing. In fact, he thought, the storeowner was more than relieved to find a buyer for the old chipped stock that he could never put out in obvious view of customers. Nonetheless, he bickered for half an hour over the price and then sought an excessive delivery charge. Since John had been raised in a frugal household, and he had watched his mother wear down storeowners, he knew the value of things and an honest price, and finally convinced the owner. With a place to study and the eventual delivery of two beds, the boys settled into a routine of morning classes, John's afternoons at the zoo, and meals with Mrs. Spenser. David found part-time employment as a towel boy and general handyman at the Pierce and Schroeder YMCA that had recently opened at the intersection of those two streets in downtown Baltimore.

Evenings, after supper with Mrs. Spenser, they both studied by the light of a single lamp that stood on the table and just barely pushed the dark back against the walls. Its glare made reading difficult and David and John quickly tired and were usually in bed by 9:30 or so. At first, both boys were shy about the sleeping arrangement. Although he never said a word about it, John frequently woke in the middle of the night, listening to David's deep, slow breathing, and feeling his warm body against his. Sometimes he even imagined that David put an arm around his chest and held him in an unconscious embrace. It was disturbing to wake in this fashion and not to know exactly what had interrupted his sleep or why his dreams were so vivid. He knew he should move to the edge of the bed, and sometimes he did, but the sagging mattress always pulled them together at the center.

After almost a month, Mrs. Spenser announced that her son would deliver the two beds the next day. John looked at David as she spoke, but his face showed no reaction. After all, thought John, it would be a much more suitable arrangement.

"Thank you," he said to Mrs. Spenser, finishing the last biscuit and gravy that had been a chicken pie (it was Thursday and this was the regular offering in a never varying menu).

The next day when their beds arrived, Mrs. Spenser's son carried the wooden frames up the stairs and placed them side by side, where the other bed had stood. Later that night, when it was time to turn in, the two boys sat facing each other.

"This mattress feels lumpy and hard," said David, sitting down abruptly on one of them. "I might well miss the old one."

"I guess I will too," exclaimed John, turning off the light.

If John expected a calm night, he was wrong. He woke several times to hear David's rhythmic breathing. He mentioned nothing about his troubled sleep until about a week later when David looked at him carefully, as if he were studying a patient with a puzzling condition.

"Is something wrong?" he asked.

"Well, no, not really. I'm just not sleeping well. It will pass."

"I think I know what you mean," replied David, almost

too rapidly. "I've been having nightmares. I hope I haven't wakened you."

"Perhaps you have," said John cautiously. "But it isn't serious. Just the new bed," he ventured.

David didn't react, but then suddenly brightened and laughed, "It could be the long-term effects of Mrs. Spenser's cooking. I think she could make a rock edible if she stewed it long enough."

The subject never came up again, and as the weeks passed, their lives settled down into a routine broken only by John's stories about odd problems at the zoo. The worst were the obstreperous visitors who threw objects and food into the cages trying to arouse some imagined ferocity of the cats and antics of the apes. What those impatient tourists did not understand, of course, was that the giant carnivores and simians spent most of their time sleeping in the sun, with only an occasional twitch of a tail or an outstretched arm as evidence of life. David was also filled with tales about his job, and loved to talk of the youngsters who came off the streets for an afternoon of games and lectures at the YMCA. He often made jokes about the other workers at the facility, their cautionary tales about forming friendships with the boys, and the heavy dose of Christianity that they dispensed along with instructions in sports and games. Hearing this, John wondered how such a free spirit as David could bear the cloistered moralism of the Y staff.

Then, one afternoon about six months after they had settled in, on a day when the wind had swept away the last of the leaves from the few lonely trees in their neighborhood, stripping away all but red brick and marble steps and paving stones, John came home to find David sitting in the parlor with a ruddy-faced policeman. He paused, not knowing if he should leave them alone, but the officer spoke firmly.

"Are you the boy what shares a room with this young man?"

"Yes, sir, we rent a room together from Mrs. Spenser. But I'm sure David has told you that."

"Indeed, then, I'll oblige you to remain and listen. There is a situation I got to discuss with you. A friendly warning to pass on. You see, there is complaints at the YMCA. Your friend here was caught several times with the younger boys. I don't s'ppose to judge you two, but the Y is a power in the city. Of course, he's been let go. They summoned me to walk him home and give him a warning. It's a danger to the young lads there and, of course, it had to end. That's all I have to say now. I'll take my leave, and want nothing more than never to see either of you again."

He stood up heavily, looking grimly at David and John, and then walked out into the hall and out the door. David did not seem to be able to look John in the eye: he seemed preoccupied as if studying the faded pattern in the carpet.

"Is it true?" blurted out John.

"Yes," confessed David, looking up for a brief moment.

John paused and then stood up and put his hand on David's shoulder.

"It doesn't matter to me. I'm still your friend. I'm sorry though. What will you do?"

David remained silent as if consulting some inner voice of council.

"I don't know," he blurted out finally. "But we will have to leave. Mrs. Spenser knows—the policeman told her—and she'll put us out the door for sure. I'm sorry to involve you. It's nothing of your fault. But I just plan to go away. I've made a mess of my life. I really loved being here with you. But I can't destroy you too."

At that moment, Mrs. Spenser walked into the room. When she spoke, it was as if she suddenly picked her words from the middle of an inner monologue.

"Of course you boys will be leaving. Tomorrow at the very latest. Can't have the shame of it in my house. You can have supper and I'll return your paid-up rent for the week. It's what comes of not being a good Christian if I might say so. Do you want my advice...No, well, you know what's best. I don't need to tell you."

John looked at David and felt a shudder of humiliation and yearning pass through his body. He knew that they would have to separate. John couldn't face going back to the docks or even continuing at the University. They would surely find out, and he could never bear the revelation, the gossip, and the secret amusement of his fellow students or the bewilderment of his parents. He had done nothing except find this one true friend, but he also knew that he would have to leave Baltimore. He just wanted to hide somewhere from the strange feelings he had, from the embarrassment, from anything that would remind him of this time, when, in the eyes of others, his attachment to David had turned into something dirty and profane. It terrified him to go alone, but he knew that running away was the only solution. Maybe David might live on the edges of the normal world, in some place that would accept him, but he couldn't. He would have to say goodbye forever...and hide...from himself.

The following morning, with his bag packed, he stood in the front hall with David. Mrs. Spenser had retreated to the kitchen, but not before putting a new sign in the window: "Room to Let." It was her only gesture of goodbye.

"Where will you go?" asked David.

"Chicago, I think, and then from there, maybe to some small town that will hire me as a science teacher. There's always a place in some run-down village for biology."

"That's a wasted life!" David exclaimed. "You don't have to. Come with me. We'll manage together. Come to New York City. Work there. We'll find another place."

"I couldn't," said John. "I'm not brave enough."

John never explained to anyone how or why he ended up in Marion teaching biology in a world that clung fast to the golden words of William Jennings Bryan and his crusade against evolution. He had seen a notice in a Chicago newspaper advertising the position. On a gamble, he took the train to the little town. It was a compromise, but his life, when he thought seriously about it, was only a string of compromises and carefully anticipated consequences. He had escaped his past in Baltimore, but in doing so, by steering into this backwater of a town, he knew he also escaped having any future. What friends he would make were of necessity to prevent town gossip and to ward off the terrible bouts of loneliness he sometimes felt. There were times when he thought this had been a wrong and hasty decision, and that he should go to New York, find David, and pick up a new life in the anonymous possibilities of the city. But he knew he couldn't. He was too much of a coward. Maybe he could face the world, but he knew he could not face himself. He could not imagine himself in such a life, and he knew that without a mental picture of living this way, of actually seeing it in his imagination, he could never muster the energy to pursue it.

Such were his thoughts during the best of times. In his darkest moments, he felt that the disguise he wore for the benefit of others and himself was nothing but self-deception, and that hints of his true substance showed through for all to see. True enough, after awhile, rumors began to circulate in town that he wasn't "the marrying kind." On occasion, just to staunch the gossip, he stepped out to a church social with one of the unmarried teachers. Unfortunately, this stratagem did little to defer the gossip. Worst of all, he knew that the new boys in his classes, each year, picked up old nicknames for him, passed on by the older students. Sometimes he heard them whisper some insult just loud enough for him to hear: "Dr. Loner," "Bug Lover," "Mr. Sissy," and the worst: "High Pockets." At such moments, he couldn't help feeling that his life had doubled back upon itself, to replay the unhappiness of his childhood on the docks of Baltimore and the abrupt end to his temporary bliss with David. Even Marion, he knew in those few moments of honesty he allowed himself, was really nowhere to escape. No such place existed so long as he was in it.

Ralph

Ralph was born on February 29, 1896, and it was always an accounting problem to decide the proper day of his birthday. Much later, he told everyone—it was about his favorite joke—that he was the result of poor planning, a rainy June weekend, or maybe just bad luck: take your choice. He sometimes said, with a malicious grin, that his tightwad father thought to save a few pennies on birthday presents, and so purposely aimed for a leap year. Many of his friends, when they began to understand the oddity of his not being born in the regular cycle of things and not appearing on the calendar except once every four years, found this a good explanation for his quirky habits and sense of humor, and his solitary ways. He was a boy born between times.

However odd the circumstances of his birth, there was no mistaking that he belonged among the Ceciles. Like his two older sisters and younger brother, he presented his mother's German and English blood: reddish hair—hers had already turned several shades darker with flecks of grey at the temples—and pale blue eyes. Like them, he had a small head and face so that his features seemed exaggerated and crowded together. Particularly when he was young, and before he grew into them, his ears looked like cupped hands, and his mother, exasperated by the surprising look of her son, tried taping them back to encourage growth in a more normal direction. Like all of her attempts to improve his looks, this was to no avail. When the other boys of his age became old enough to understand that the most injurious insult was to mock a physical attribute, they dubbed him "Elephant Ears" or "Donkey Ears" or just "Old Flappy." At first, this hurt him deeply and he inflicted several nosebleeds and bruises in retaliation, but eventually he learned that attention was attention, however earned, and he grew to tolerate his nicknames just as he finally began to grow into his prodigious ears.

As with everyone with his heritage, although exaggerated in boys, his pale skin developed a patchwork of freckles in all shapes and sizes that intensified in the hot sun and faded back in the winter. This visual reaction to the long, humid summers of southern Illinois was perhaps a signal that this population of immigrants had passed too far south for its own good. They settled a region that for a hundred years had been almost a border state of its own at the bottom of Illinois, neither North nor South, with a population that fanned out along the Ohio River and spread across into Kentucky. Why newcomers stopped there, aside from sheer exhaustion, was a mystery, because the rolling hills and dense woods, with their harsh seasons were inhospitable both to the staple crops further down South and unfriendly to the corn and wheat of the

Great Plains. Inevitably, the population remained thin and grew slowly by natural increase, until the railroads began to hatch-mark the section tying it to markets in Chicago and St. Louis, and again setting off another influx when the coalmines began to open. Thereafter, society settled into three layers, with the boisterous southern European immigrants at the bottom along with a sparse population of freedmen and ex-slaves. Next were farmers, their wives and broods of fat, dirty children in the middle, and finally the town gentry, to which Ralph belonged by virtue of his father's small law office, on top. Being one of the town's two legal experts with a genuine degree, and a diploma that hung in a mahagony frame behind his desk, Mr. Cecil knew most of Marion's history and understood the tangled skein of legal and family relations and obligations that made it a community. "A good lawyer," he always said, "never talks about his clients: not to anyone." This was good advice since most of the town came to him to decide minor disputes over land and property. He was like advocate and court in one, but never the source of any gossip, unlike old Reverend Turnbull whom everyone suspected of telling stories to his wife. He recognized that wills, bequests and other legal documents recorded most of the meaningful history of small town lives, and his studied silence in all such matters just increased his value as a confidant. That was far more than the Reverend, who sometimes preached sermons aimed directly at a single sinner in his congregation.

Mr. Cecil's silent demeanor and public scruples also meant that the whole family enjoyed an extra foot of social space. Mrs. Cecil always considered this a sign of respect, but her husband knew that it had to do with the fear that he might reveal the town's secrets. If Ralph noticed any of this, he never discussed it, and, in any case, he had enough peculiarities his own making than to worry about grown-up talk from adults that he saw on church mornings or visiting days at home.

Of course, Ralph did not think of himself as a problem or anything unusual, but from the age of four or five, he began collecting the bodies of animals and birds. These latter were especially plentiful in the spring and fall during migrations when clouds of songbirds seemed to pass over the vacant fields around town, sometimes to descend onto the barren fields to feed on the uncollected remains of the harvest. Sometimes Ralph found a sluggish or injured bird and, carefully folding its fluttering wings against its fragile, hot body, he took it and placed it in a large birdcage that he had found in a shed behind the house to nurse back to health. Even in winter, despite his entreaties, his parents would not allow him to bring these foundlings to his room. It was just as well because they often died, despite the care and food he gave them.

When he was eight, his father, who was a confirmed and avid duck hunter, presented him with his first gun, a slim, light air rifle that shot small lead pellets. This was a practice weapon because the potential damage it could inflict on anything living was slight. Nonetheless, his father placed hand-drawn paper targets of animals on the big elm tree behind the house and insisted that Ralph show him the results of his efforts. Dutifully, Ralph stepped off thirty paces and loaded the rifle from the red tin box of lead shot, pumped the handle three times, and aimed at the target. After a number of days, he became adept at hitting the bull's-eye, or bird's eye, and his father proudly exclaimed that it would not be long before Ralph could join the men in a fall duck hunt or quail shoot.

Except that Ralph had no intention ever to shoot any living thing. His obstinacy in this matter puzzled him because he knew that killing was expected of all men, and that when "bird season" approached in the fall, most of the elder townsfolk and older boys began to rehearse stories of famous past hunts, talking proudly of bagging incredible numbers of birds and the occasional rabbit or fox. All this strutting made them stand just a bit straighter when they walked around town and in the hallways at school. Hunting signaled the end of growing up (what "men folks did"), but Ralph determined he would never join them in this ritual coming-of-age. Part of his distaste came from his duty at an early age to clean the ducks his father brought home after a day's shoot at a nearby farm that had a large lake. To attract the birds as they migrated south, the farmer would let the grass grow tall and leave a patch of unharvested corn and wheat.

On those cool fall Sundays, after the previous day's shoot, and while his mother was preparing their one big meal of the day, Ralph and his brother climbed down into the dank basement to dress the birds. It was messy, smelly work. Before his brother sliced open the carcasses to rip out the guts, his job was to remove the feathers by dunking the dead bird into a pot of scalding water and then stripping off the singed feathers in damp handfuls. Repeating this process several times, he could finally rid the bird of its down, until only a few sharp and stubborn pinfeathers remained. Once he pried these out, the naked bird, reduced and scrawny with only a ring of remaining feathers around the neck and head, its skin puckered and rough from repeated immersion in hot water, was ready for his brother's knife. Then his older brother would remove the head and innards and the duck would be ready to cook. Even though Ralph performed this duty without complaint, the whole process made him sad. There was beauty in these limp, dead animals with their glazed-over eyes, the translucent blue-green of their feathers, and the buoyancy of their fragile bodies that, only a few hours previously, had made them able to soar in the air or float on the pond.

Ralph had always thought that his dog Tippy shared his view of hunting. She was a female pointer of about four years, and now the family pet. His father kept other dogs too, boarded with the local farmer, but they were never allowed into the house or even in the yard, and never petted for fear that affection would turn them to pleasing rather than obeying. This might have been Tippy's fate too, except that she was gun shy, and every time she heard the crack of a rifle, she disappeared, tail between her legs, into the bushes. Some dogs were just like that, his father explained, and so she became a house pet. Too bad, he had added, because she had every instinct of the hunt but the kill, and had proved better than all the others in her brood at finding quail and pointing them out, her nose straight and tail stiff as an arrow so you could draw a straight line from tip to tip to the quarry. But that mattered little because she would run off after the first shot.

Ralph and Tippy were inseparable on long summer days and then after school; they both loved to run in the woods and nearby fields, flushing birds and animals. They learned the best places to roam: the shallow creek that wound around through the hills on the north side of town and the woods, with its countless familiar rabbits and squirrels. Although Tippy quickly became bored with chasing the chattering squirrels around tree trunks, she never tired of pointing rabbits that froze in the mistaken belief in their invisibility. On occasion, they encountered a woodchuck that scurried angrily into his hole, or caught the glimpse of a red fox. More than anything, Ralph wanted to bring some of these animals back to the house and keep them caged in the small barn that now served as a stable for their horse and buggy. His mother did not object to the odd turtle or salamander, but she worried that wild animals might carry sickness with a bite that could be fatal. His father apparently could not see much beyond death in them. "Whatever were animals for," he often exclaimed, "except to shoot?" To him, everything in the wild had its allotted season except, of course for varmints like groundhogs that could be hunted year round. Nonetheless, Ralph built a large cage out of wood ends, wire and screen, just in case they relented.

As he grew older, Ralph had a difficult time understanding the attitude of his parents and the other boys in his classes who talked endlessly of the next season's duck hunt. He concluded that it was a sport where prowess brought prestige. But in this regard, he was the odd boy out, the sideliner who rarely if ever ventured into the woods in October, and always found an excuse to refuse his father's insistent demand that he join the adults and dogs on a quail hunt. He vowed he would never get up at dawn to sit in a freezing duck blind and wait for the beautiful birds to descend to their death. Once, he tried to joke about it, saying that it was something like trench warfare against defenseless animals. But his father's glare and older brother's smirk showed how little they understood him. Thereafter, he understood the necessity of silence in such matters.

Consequently, Ralph developed something of the reputation of a loner, a freckle-faced boy who seemed to excel at nothing in particular and who had learned to keep his enthusiasms private. By the time he had graduated into high school, even his dog could no longer muster the energy to run in the woods with him. Only Mr. Clarke, the biology instructor, warmed to him. This was perplexing to Ralph. Mr. Clarke, whose watery eyes magnified by his thick round glasses and stooped shoulders made him the butt of jokes that picked apart the traits of his odd appearance, provoked nicknames that brought a murmur of laughter to his classes. With unkempt brown hair and a small effeminate voice, his greatest peculiarity was his embroidered suspenders, which held his pants too high above his waist. This odd garb earned him the name "High Pockets...Old High Pockets" which Ralph understood to be words for "fussy," "prudish" or even "sissy." Nevertheless, Ralph genuinely liked Mr. Clarke and happily stayed after school helping to clean the makeshift biology lab and to talk about animals. Mr. Clarke, he discovered, had once been a zookeeper in Baltimore before he moved to southern Illinois, and he knew the common and Latin names and habits, not just of animals in the United States, but also of the collection of African elephants and giraffes, and zebras and lions that were the pride of that Eastern city. Ralph sometimes wanted to query Mr. Clarke about why he had abandoned his wonderful career, but never did ask, sensing that he might uncover some private embarrassment. If his father knew anything of the circumstances of this earlier history, he never said anything about it except to tender the advice never to be too friendly with teachers. He would always follow this with a chuckle and the comment that southern Illinois seemed to attract the oddest characters, as if its very ordinariness and obscurity led the unsuccessful, the worn-out pioneers, the lovelorn and penniless widows and other types and specimens of failure to seek it out. He sometimes added that it was a place "coming from everywhere and going to nowhere." This comment made Ralph wonder if these words expressed a personal regret or were just the result of knowing too much about the lives of his neighbors in a place where gossip spread like a fire in the prairie in a dry August.

Despite its small size, Marion was substantial enough to draw Chautauqua lectures and the occasional one-ring traveling circus during the summer months. The whole town turned out for these events, climbing onto makeshift bleachers at the campgrounds to listen to Irish Bell Ringers, political speeches, talk labeled "hygiene" that Ralph did not particularly understand, but which embarrassed his mother. They heard recitals of poetry—even Shakespeare—and travel adventures recounted about Egypt and the Orient and other exotic and maybe imaginary places (there was no knowing if the speaker had ever visited these countries). But Ralph counted the days until the circus arrived. When his science teacher secured permission to take him behind the tent to the area with the cages of performing animals, he rejoiced. Mr. Clarke even knew some of the trainers by their real names, and Ralph was surprised by the discovery that Koubow the Lion-Tamer was really an Irishman from New York named

O'Reilly in his swarthy greasepaint. Underneath his costume, the circus clown (the "Grand Guignol") was actually the lady trapeze artist, a German woman with slim strong arms and a thick harsh accent.

Ralph loved these disguises and the magic of the ring, the smell of the animals, the sawdust floor, and the sour blare of the small brass band sometimes augmented by enthusiastic amateur local players. The lure of the circus was its ability to transport ordinary life into the remarkable. And every employee, he soon found out, had many roles to play, doubling as roustabouts, musicians, "arteests" of one sort or another, clowns, animal trainers, and ticket takers: it seemed to be a whole world of masquerades and possibilities.

Sometimes when Mr. Clarke failed to attend a performance, Ralph wondered if the animals might have reminded him of happier times in Baltimore. Or maybe he was just bored to keep company with his young student. Then Ralph went on his own to assist in feeding the animals, sweeping out the sawdust floor of the ring, helping to tighten the ropes of the big top, or just listening to the performers spin their long stories about travel around the circuit of small-town America. He loved their descriptions of where to find the best audiences and cheapest food, and where to avoid the worst weather—like "Tornado Alley" in Kansas. Ralph delighted in the musty odor of the animals: the four white horses that two clowns rode standing, a foot on either back; reins tightly gripped holding them together as they raced around the ring. He listened raptly for the occasional snarl of the big cats—the two mangy lions that reluctantly struggled up on stools at the crack of the trainer's whip, when they seemed only to want to slink noiselessly behind him. Because he observed these acts so many times, Ralph knew that even these stealthy moves were part of the charade, designed to provoke squeals of fear in the audience and shouts of warning to the trainer who seemed oblivious to the danger creeping up on him.

Happy as he was, something always worried Ralph during these visits. At first, this concern appeared only a small blemish on the experience, but it seemed to darken and spread over his delight every time he went backstage. When they were not performing, all the animals were penned up in tiny hot metal cages only half shaded by two large beech trees. The more fortunate horses were tethered nearby in the shadows. There was scarcely room to turn around in these steel contrivances that were built to be loaded off and onto a railroad flatbed. The heat seemed to enervate even the lions who lay stretched on their sides with their mouths hanging open and long pink tongues dripping saliva over the edges of their massive jaws. And the monkeys, when he passed by, stirred briefly to grasp the hot bars and look out, their pleading eyes fixed on him as if hoping he could release them from their misery. The trainer warned him not to put his hand inside the cages, for despite the languid, friendly movements of the animals, they could turn, in an instant, on any act of sympathy. Ralph never quite believed this and thought it must be standard advice given to outsiders who might be keen to bother or tease them. Surely not him, he thought.

The circus came every July right after Independence Day, during the hottest weather of the year, just about the time when the corn ears had developed tousled crowns of yellow silk, when the wind stopped blowing, and the air was always still and heavy and damp. Even the birds seemed less frenetic, their young broods now fully feathered and fending for themselves. Only the cicadas buzzing in undulating waves of loud and soft defied the indolence of the summer heat. At night, even the fireflies seemed to be blinking their last "come hither" lanterns. That was when the circus appeared, regular as the Summer Solstice, arriving at the small brick railroad station, with boldly painted boxcars announcing the "Greatest Show on Earth." Ralph and the other boys would rush to the siding to help load the wagons bound for the Chautauqua campground at the edge of town, hoisting huge crates crammed with costumes, ropes, trapezes, and sections of tents for the performance. As always, there were the animal cages to handle with extra care. Two boxcars served as residences for the performers, although the ringmaster and his wife (the sometimes ticket taker and bookkeeper) always boarded at widow Barclay's near Main Street. For a week, the town stirred out of its summer-time torpor, as wagonloads of farmers and their families drove in from the countryside to sit in the makeshift bleachers inside the hot, dusty tent, to watch the performances as if they had never seen the like.

Ralph always wanted to be present, so much so that his parents sometimes feared that the slick, worldly folk, whose stage names sounded Italian and German and Hungarian, might tempt him away. Circus people had that reputation, like the gypsies that Ralph knew from the book of folk tales his mother liked to read to him when he was younger. He could certainly see the resemblance: circus folk with their strange names and uncanny skills with animals and acrobatics, their love of sleight-of-hand tricks with cards and ropes, puzzled and intrigued him, as if these people, like the gypsies and characters out of Grimm, came from lands with fantastic names. He liked to imagine this even though he knew, as his father had told him, that everything in the circus was just for show. Most performers were small town folk like himself. But that fact only set him to wondering and dreaming.

In the summer of 1912, after the circus packed up and left the fairgrounds empty of all traces of music and commotion, Ralph made a decision—something entirely private that he would keep to himself, ponder and plan and turn over in his mind for the whole next year. He made a private vow to tell no one or even hint at his decision, and he knew he could keep to this promise for he had learned to be a secretive person. Anyway, who would understand if he did tell them? Next year he planned to make himself indispensable to the circus, so familiar a face that they would never notice him, just another roustabout. He would jump onto the freight train as it pulled out of town and hide until the hands were called out again in the next small town. What could they say? He was a good worker and he knew the animals; he would remain invisible until the work conjured him up.

Ralph also realized that his plan required a disguise, a false front that he must put between himself and his parents. He certainly did not hate or even dislike them, but to take this step of running away, he knew that he had to create a safe distance from them (it was for himself), so that he could be brave enough to leave and so they would accept his departure as natural and inevitable. He had always been known as a solitary boy who wandered through his lessons at high school, who spoke politely when addressed, who was friendly and warm but never entirely present because his thoughts always seemed somewhere else. It had always served him well to be unnoticed.

When the circus cars pulled onto the siding in July the next summer, Ralph could scarcely contain his excitement. He was the first of the local boys to lend a hand unloading the animal cages, the heavy burlap sacks of rope, as difficult to grab and hold as a bag of snakes, and the neatly folded sections of canvas tent. He was tireless in carrying the large square metal cases of costumes, the bleacher planks for the audience, all destined for wagons that would trek back and forth along the brick main street to the fairgrounds where the encampment gradually took shape with each load. Old friends and performers were present along with a new group of roustabouts. They all worked together, like a geared machine, each element of labor fitting into the next. Circus men and women were like interchangeable parts, he thought, for every one of them worked at several jobs and tasks. They spoke in short bursts of a strange slang that Ralph loved to hear and imitate.

It took a full day of exhausting work, but the first show was ready for that evening. Inside the closed tent the heat and smell of the damp canvas and fresh sawdust was overwhelming, and the air scarcely circulated until the performance began and some of the side flaps could be opened. That first night, Ralph's job was to police one of these openings, to prevent anyone from sneaking in without a ticket. Try as they might, his friends from school could not persuade him to let them slip through. This was his circus and his first loyalty.

After several late mornings—Ralph explained to his mother that the circus people only occupied the middle and ends of the day—he felt theirs was becoming his own rhythm of life. He woke up at ten when the sun heated up his small bedroom unbearably, and dressed quickly and eagerly, not knowing or even daring to guess what his assignment that day might be. Each time he asked the animal trainer if he could help with the horses and maybe even feed the old sluggish lions. More than anything, he wanted to be inside the ring with the animals, cracking his whip as Simba and Mantoo (the lions) protested with feeble snarls about having to hop up on the red, three-legged stools. Ralph understood that the snap of the whip and the vocal protests were both for show, because both lion and trainer were actors in a routine so old and practiced that it resembled sleepwalking. He wondered if he could teach the lions a new trick, something that looked dangerous enough to frighten the audience into screams and applause.

The hot July morning before the last matinee and before the circus hastened to pack up and load, Ralph was particularly nervous and excited because he was ready to act on his secret decision. No one, he thought, would even notice his presence on the train until they were well underway. He had left a long note on his bed, addressed to his mother and father, a kind of apology for not telling them outright. He feared they might dissuade him and he was determined. Of course, he promised to write them postcards from all the towns they visited. Above all, he begged them not to send the sheriff after him. That morning, when his mother left the kitchen, he departed, allowing the screen door to close gently behind him, carrying a small bag of underwear and socks and one change of clothes. He was on his way to his new life...joining the greatest show on earth.

After the last blare of the tinny band rippled through the still air and the final stragglers among the audience had made their way out into the hot, sunny afternoon, the entire circus family peeled off their costumes and worked quickly to disassemble the tent. Pulling down the poles, winding up the ropes, they loaded the moveable entertainment back into crates and canvas bags for the waiting boxcars. Ralph loved this work because it signaled the beginning of his great adventure. When the last animal cage had been secured, he jumped aboard one of the wagons to ride to the station.

He had said nothing to the ringmaster or his wife about signing onto the circus for a stint; still he suspected that his presence, if discovered, would present no surprise once the train began to move slowly out into the countryside, headed for Springfield and a week's occupation of the county fairgrounds there. The circus reminded him of a demonstration in Mr. Clarke's science class: it was like a slow-moving magnet passing through a pile of charged-up boys like himself, attracting and holding some who would find a permanent place and casting off those who became bored or tired or troublesome. That's what it was like, he thought.

He was bone-weary when they reached the rail siding near Springfield. Smells of creosote and coal smoke hung in the air. Having dozed uncomfortably on a canvas bag in one of the boxcars, Ralph tried to rub the ache out of his stiff legs and arms and wipe away the glaze of a fitful sleep. He found he was not alone. Some of the other roustabouts had discovered makeshift bedding in corners in the rough, jolting car, and its load of carefully piled boxes. Just as he stood, one of the circus acrobats slid open the door with a rough thud. A long shaft of morning sunlight burst into the darkened room, illuminating its contents and revealing a fountain of shimmering straw particles that floated in the air. Ralph coughed involuntarily when he saw the thick air that he had been breathing all night. With the other boys, he jumped down onto the broken ground and gravel that spilled out beyond the railroad ties, and walked off to report for work. While he waited for his assignment, he accepted a piece of stale bread and a cup of strong black coffee from the cook.

By now, of course, Ralph knew the routine of setting up, and he helped pile the crates onto wagons as the ringmaster barked out instructions. Under the early hot sun, he and the others sweated through their work, piling boxes on and then removing them from the wagons. At the fairgrounds, the tent rose up on poles, pulled by the ropes that he and the others tightened and then staked into the ground. All the while, he wondered about the animals: the two lions, the horses, the monkeys that wore silk trousers and cardboard hats when they performed. Were they as hot and exhausted as he was?

As soon as the canvas cover had been secured and the trapeze and rope ladders were bound tightly to hooks at the top of the tent poles, he walked slowly around to the back where the cages of the menagerie had been unloaded onto a bed of wood shavings. Each cage or enclosure had its own metal feed trough and water bucket, but, unlike the Chautauqua grounds in Marion, there was no shade here at all, and the merciless sun already coaxed the animals to lie flat to absorb whatever cool remained on the bottom of their cages.

This distressed Ralph, and he went off to question the animal trainer who seemed unconcerned, assuring him that the sun in Africa was far hotter than central Illinois. That seemed a cruel and thoughtless answer, and Ralph remained particularly worried about the monkeys who seemed lethargic, breathing hard with their mouths open as if the oxygen had been burned out of the air.

The circus was completely unpacked and set up by noon, and the exhausted performers and roustabouts milled around the tent, chatting, stretching, snacking on sandwiches and lemonade, although Ralph saw several of them take long swigs from the hip flasks that they passed around. The boredom, he sensed, was as intense as the sun beating down, and they both combined to make him drowsy. What kept him from nodding off was the constant reminder of the animals basted by the hot overhead sunlight. Would they survive until the evening performance, he wondered? He even asked one of the experienced hands about their safety. The other just chuckled and reassured him that winter in Florida was far hotter and unrelenting and the animals seemed not to mind at all. He wondered, suddenly, if this wasn't something like his father's attitude: animals were animals. He had expected much better of the circus.

By 2:00 Ralph was worried to a panic and he came to a sudden decision. He might be an impulsive boy, but he thought his instincts were right. He went to the small sleeping tent that he intended to share with several of the other circus hands and gathered up his bag and took it back to the monkey cage. He quietly opened it up and snapped a leash that he had found around the neck of the exhausted monkey, picked him up and pulled him out of the cage. It was only a short distance to the railroad station by foot. Stopping once as he made his way, he fashioned a sack from a buttoned-up shirt into which he placed the drowsy animal. He had just enough money for a trip back home on the 3:00 express. If the circus could not take care of its animals, he decided, he would do it for them. He could use the cage in the shed—it had hardly been occupied—and he could keep the animal as a pet. The monkey could have the liberty of the whole building, and eventually, he might come into the house. He knew his parents would object at first, but what could they say when he appeared at the door with his charge? They would probably be so happy to see him that one extra monkey would not matter much. Anyway, he had rescued it from the torture of neglect.

When the conductor took his ticket, he looked with suspicion at the wriggling bundle on the seat next to Ralph. "It's my pet," explained Ralph, "just taking him back home. You can see that he's no trouble."

"Mind that he ain't, young man, or I'll charge you double."

Ralph arrived in Marion around 8:00 in the evening and walked quickly from the station to the back yard of his house and into the shed, still carrying the monkey in his shirt parcel. Opening the door, he stepped inside. There was still just enough light to work quickly to untie the knotted sleeves and undo the buttons. The monkey who had been still and quiet, suddenly jumped up and raced around the small room, chattering wildly and then disappeared up into the rafters, knocking off a shower of dust. Ralph feared that his parents might hear the commotion, and so he backed out of the building, closed the door, and then headed for the kitchen where he knew his mother would be cleaning up after dinner.

He scuffed his steps loudly as he approached, so his mother would be prepared when he opened the door.

"Hello, Mama," he said, nonchalantly, as he pushed open the screened door. "I'm back from the circus. I decided I didn't want to run away after all." He had improvised this explanation during the train ride, and he hoped it would serve until he could explain about the monkey in the barn.

"Yes, Son, we know that you're back. Your father is in the living room right now, talking to Sheriff Bennington. He's told us all about it."

"All about what, Mama?" Ralph said in a surprised voice that he tried to disguise by repeating himself. "About what?"

"That there monkey you kidnapped," she said abruptly. "The circus sent a wire to the Sheriff down here in Marion, and he's come to pick it up. He's brought a cage and all. The circus said they just wanted him back...no explanations or questions asked, so you'd better fetch him from wherever you've got him hid."

Ralph was amazed that the circus had figured out what happened and worried about catching the monkey swinging around the rafters in the barn. Nonetheless, he retraced his steps and slipped quietly into the shed. He could scarcely see, but he could sense the quiet. In the dim light, he saw the monkey sitting placidly inside the cage that Ralph had left open. It was as if he knew he belonged inside the wire enclosure; maybe he even wanted to be there. Ralph wondered if he missed the confinement.

Ralph walked over quickly, reached inside, and the monkey jumped out and onto his shoulder. Together, the two of them emerged from the shed, then around the house to the front door. Ralph opened it timidly and went into the living room where his father sat with Sheriff Bennington, a man with ruddy cheeks, bleary eyes and a sloppy blue uniform that seemed ready to burst around his extended middle. The room smelled uncharacteristically of drink.

"There you are, Son, and that monkey too," said his father. "No harm done then. Sheriff Bennington and I were just speculating as to when you would show up. Of course, you'll have to give up your friend there. He's wanted back at the circus and from the looks of him, he'd be mighty happy to go back. They're sending someone down in the morning to pick him up. But for now, you can just put him in the cage outside in Sheriff Bennington's wagon. He'll send a wire back to let them know that all is well."

Without a word, Ralph meekly followed the sheriff out the door and down the front steps to the wagon which held a large wooden crate with open slats. The monkey eagerly jumped off his shoulder and hopped in as soon as the sheriff slid off the lid.

"I reckon you thought you understood animals," he said. "But I'm supposing they're a lot more complicated than you expected, just like people are. This one here is probably circus born and bred and wouldn't know a jungle from a cornfield. He'd never make you a pet, and he'd probably die from missing the audience and the applause and his trainer. You go back in now and talk to your mom and dad. Maybe they can figure out what to do with you. I ain't got an idea."

"Thank you, Sheriff," he blurted out, as he turned toward the front steps. "But I think I know what to do, what I want to be. Maybe, just maybe, I can convince Mr. Clarke up at the high school to put in a good word for me at the Baltimore Zoo where he used to work. They'll always be wanting someone to help with the animals, someone who sees them more than an entertainment or dinner. Maybe that way I can begin to figure them out. Sure easier than trying to figure out who I am."

Young Ed Watson

One day, when young Ed Watson was only eight years old, Delia's father remarked, "That boy has got himself the voice to be a preacher man!" By this time, scarcely anyone in town who knew him doubted that the young man would receive the call. Even the Methodist Reverend Turnbull's wife censored her general disapproval of all young boys when he greeted her with a polite and mellifluous "Hello." The voice itself was unnaturally deep and mellow, like the gurgle of a stream at flood time, although Ed himself was shy and small for his age, with sandy brown hair and bleached out blue eyes. There was little else, at this age, to commend him to the Lord's work, although he attended the local Baptist Church with his mother and prayed fervently, when he really wanted something around Christmas time or his birthday. His father, Doc Watson, whose practice ranged from female complaints to lame horses, thought that Sundays were intended as days of leisure, and this meant a visit to friends, some work in his garden, but never church. He had let it be known around town that Sunday was not an appropriate day to fall ill or suffer an accident, or discover a sick animal or even think about salvation. Rest was rest.

Young Ed was considerably shorter than his older brother, Cal, a disadvantage in a family where hand-me-down trousers and shirts had to be mended and re-sewn to fit his smaller frame. Despite his mother's agile needle and thread, his wardrobe bore evidence of a patchwork of tears and stains, as if they retained the memory of the rough play of their former owner. If Ed resented inhabiting these clothes he never bothered to complain to anyone, and his mother neglected to worry about her youngest son who was not troublesome and who willingly accepted his smaller share. He even seemed content to be the second son in his father's eye.

There were times, however, when Ed wondered if his whole being was borrowed from someone else's castoff life, and it made him worry about his future. Would he be the object of everyone else's plans, a blueprint with the white lines of his personality etched in by some parent or stranger?

When he turned seventeen and had only a year left of schooling, his parents finally showed an interest in his future. It was as if he had been sitting at the table silently and then suddenly they heard him ask for the salt with his surprising, low voice. He sensed that their attention, however, was troubled more by questions than genuine concern. More than once, he had heard his mother say in a hushed voice behind her hand: "What's to become of Ed, Mr. Watson? He doesn't seem to take to anything special and we just can't have him waiting around for something to happen."

"If I knew," replied the doctor, "I'd certainly say it to you plain out. Do you suppose he might be a preacher like his grandfather always says? Blessed with a voice like that he might go far."

"But do you think him to be convicted," objected his mother.

"As much as the next fellow. Doesn't matter much what you believe on the inside, I suppose, as to what the outside looks like. And he's certainly got the sound of it."

That evening after dinner, when his mother came into the sitting room still wringing her hands on the front of her apron, Ed and his older brother were reading while his father paced around, picking up his pipe and tobacco and preparing for his smoke.

"Your father, Ed," she began hesitantly, sitting down on the edge of a stiff-backed chair, "has something to say to you."

"Yes, sir," said Ed, looking up from his book and glancing anxiously at his brother for a reassuring nod. Instead, the latter just pushed his nose deeper into his own book and paid no obvious attention even if at the end of several minutes he had failed to turn a single page.

"Your mother and I," began the doctor, "believe it's high time you began to think of the rest of your life. You know that your schooling ends soon and you've never once spoken of the work you'd like to do. Can't have you falling off the log into the water to swim with the common folk around here. And not much opportunity in Marion unless you want to tend a store. I could see about fixing you up as an assistant at the General Emporium, but that isn't much of a future. There's the law, of course, and you might want to run up to Springfield and try your hand at that. And being a doctor. It's harder nowadays. You can't apprentice like I did. You'll need a license and an education at one of those new-fangled universities. Can't say you'd be cut out for that anyway. And then, of course, there's the ministry. Have you thought much about that, Son?" he said, finally coming to the point.

Ed shook his head, "Not too much yet, sir, but I know I should."

His mother, who had listened to the doctor's unpromising list of professions, said gently, as if the thought had just occurred to her, "Why not think about the ministry, Ed? You'd be a wonderful preacher, and I know you've got the talent. I can speak to Reverend Turnbull. He's been very excited, of late, about a new school up in Chicago, the Moody Bible College, or some such name as that. We could find out more and see if it's the right thing for you. Of course, that would be in the city and I'm not sure you're quite ready for that yet. But if it's a genuine Bible College..." Her voice trailed off, but Ed could sense that she had already convinced herself.

He looked at his preoccupied brother, who was listening inconspicuously, and then at his parents, wondering if he had the power to stand up against their apparent resolution.

It didn't matter much what he did, he told himself, if his parents thought it was right.

"So, I'll be a preacher then maybe," he said, allowing his voice to deepen as if to underscore his consent.

That was how his parents persuaded young Ed to travel to Chicago for study at Reverend Moody's new school. After several letters and the exchange of a small fee, his parents arranged for him to travel by train to the city's Union Station in April. The school secretary wrote a long letter describing what clothing and sundries he would require, but most of his words were vague warnings about the city and its temptations. "Forewarned is foresworn," he said, and in words intended just for Ed, cautioned him about the perils of Chicago, its temptations and "cesspools" of intrigue.

Ed was fascinated and frightened by these words, not quite knowing what they meant, but he believed he could trust the teachers to keep him on a straight path, just as his parents had always guided him through situations he scarcely understood. If he was not concerned, his mother one late evening confided her own worries to the doctor: "I'm not sure about that boy, Mr. Watson," she began. "He's never shown much pluck. He just seems to mind the last voice that calls out to him. I've never had any sense of who he really is. A polite boy, so eager to please, and well spoken, but without gumption."

"I think it will do him good to study the Gospels," replied Doc Watson. "It'll give him the strength he needs. I'm sure he will find himself in its pages. Just as you've always said, Mrs. Watson, 'There's at least one righteous story in there that meets any situation a person can imagine.' And even if he doesn't take to it, what's the harm in a bit of education? I'm not worried at all. We need to let the boy go, put him out in the world. It's high time."

Two weeks later, in late April, 1910, Ed found himself on the express train for Chicago, as fresh and unformed as the new century and ready, insofar as his limited experience allowed him, to encounter the city.

When the engine rolled into the Central Station and he

emerged onto the platform, Ed was exhausted and bewildered. Clouds of hot steam shot out from under the train, showering the hurrying passengers with coal smuts and dust. Ed gripped his slim valise tightly, having been warned against thieves and pickpockets who preyed upon the unmindful. He looked no one in the eye, as Mr. Moody's lieutenant had cautioned in a letter, for a single, prolonged glance might be interpreted as a signal to an evil-intentioned lookout for a lost or bewildered traveler. Ed could not imagine what such threats meant, but he dutifully kept his vision fixed on the doorway that exited into the great hall, not even turning when he thought a man whispered to him and brushed against his arm.

Once outside, Ed paused and looked with amazement at the city around him, and then up and back to the huge red brick building he had just exited. On the plaza in front, horse carts and carriages and spindly looking automobiles swarmed around the entrance. The pungent smell of animal dung mingled with smoke filled his nostrils. Across the busy street, he saw a sign for the electric streetcar stop, and carefully stepped through the teeming traffic toward it. The stop had a confusion of signs and indications, so he had to ask which of them might convey him to the downtown YMCA where he was to report. He quietly approached a woman dressed in a greyish suit wearing a large hat. (His mother had advised him that women with large hats might be trusted.) Despite his attempts to muffle his booming voice, however, its unexpected volume attracted the amused glances of several of the waiting passengers.

He knew Farwell Hall, his destination, was downtown and very close to the Moody Institute where he was to study. He would have simple, safe lodgings and meals, and, as Reverend Torrey had assured his mother, the wholesome companionship of other boys and the diligent oversight of a dedicated adult staff. His mother had read encouraging testimonials about the YMCA in both the *Herald of the Prairies* and the *Northern Christian Advocate*. For a boy who did not much know his own mind, she had said, this was a perfect arrangement.

When it finally rumbled up to the stop, the streetcar was already crowded, and Ed had to push his way into the front. He had already counted out the coins, which he clutched so tightly in his fist that they left welts and the grimy smell of copper when he handed them to the conductor. "Downtown YMCA," he mumbled, and the man responded, "I'll let you know when we arrive, lad."

The trip from Grant Park into the city seemed to Ed like approaching a mountain range of high buildings: first the foothills, three or four stories high, and then, in the distance, the mysterious, jagged outline of the skyscrapers that he had seen in stereographs of Chicago. By the time they entered the downtown, the intensity of traffic and the shadows, cast by the buildings, shrouded the city in confusion. Crowds of pedestrians crossed in front of the streetcar, moving in every direction. When he finally stepped off, he was swept along as if he had no will of his own, a tiny eddy spinning in this choppy wave of bustling humanity. Somehow, however, he found himself standing in front of the Central YMCA at LaSalle Street. He walked up the stone steps and into the lobby and set his bag down in front of the reception desk. An elderly man with a pock-marked face peered at him over the newspaper he was reading and asked, "What's it for, young man?"

"I've come to attend Mr. Moody's Bible College," Ed proclaimed, "and I have a letter from Reverend James Gray to report to the YMCA when I reach Chicago. So here I am."

"Well, you'll be wanting the YMCA Hotel, I'm sure," said the man, folding his newspaper in half and looking more intently at Ed. "It's where we send all the young men these days. You'll find it's a long walk, south on LaSalle St, and then east of here. Not perilous this time of day. Just go out the door, continue east to Wabash, and then go about eight blocks south. You can't miss it. A brand new, red brick building, tall as a skyscraper. They'll give you a room. Won't be much, but you pays for what you gets, don't ya?" The old man almost cackled at what he thought was a joke, his eyes bulging out of a cadaverous face. "And report back to The Moody School tomorrow morning. Boys often mistake and come here first. Now off you go. Don't talk to no one in the street. You have a hayseed look about you."

Ed was embarrassed and could only stammer a "thank you," and then turned to head out of the building back into the roaring city. He easily followed the instructions—all of them—ignoring inquisitive looks and avoiding the broken sidewalks and perilous street crossings where the traffic moved in and out in a continuous stream of vehicles, animals, and humanity. As he traveled away from the downtown, the traffic moved even faster, with sputtering motor cars weaving around wagons, and streetcars clattering and complaining over their metal rails. By the time he reached the hotel, his shirt collar was wet and he thought it must be black with grime. The hotel was immense and imposing and he thought to himself, if this was somehow God's work, he wanted to be part of it. He walked into the front limestone entrance that covered two stories before the rows of vertical windows that rose up behind it. He didn't attempt to count the stories that mounted up high to the roof that hung over a series of arches. He had never seen such a building, let alone entered one, and he did so now with a knot of excitement gripping his stomach.

To the back of the lobby, a friendly looking woman stood behind a polished counter. Behind her were rows and stacks of open mailboxes, as many, Ed guessed, as there were rooms in this immense building.

"What can I do for you, young man," she beamed and then answered for him: "I suppose you've come about a room."

"Yes," replied Ed, "I'm going to attend Reverend Moody's School. I'm training for the ministry. And I was told to come here."

"And well you might do with that wonderful voice. This is the right place for you, then," she said, pulling out a large ledger book from under the counter and placing it atop. "It's $1.50 a week with breakfast. You'll need to register. You must always leave the key to your room with me. And the hours are definitive. Never come in after 9:00 in the evening. Breakfast from six to eight. Sign here. And absolutely no guests...ever!" She turned the book around and Ed carefully wrote his name and the words, "Marion, Illinois" on the line beneath the address entry.

As she watched him, she said under her breath: "Another southern Illinois boy! My goodness, what's happening down there to draw so many of you young ones to Chicago?"

Then she smiled, so Ed replied confidently, "I'm going back after a semester to be a preacher. They all say I should," he added.

"Well, son, you need to do what is best for you. That will be room 805. Take the elevator around the corner to your right. You'll find everything you need. Bathroom and toilets at each end of the hall. Here's the key. Remember to turn it back to me when you leave in the morning. You'll be wanting to pay me in advance, so I'll expect to see you tomorrow, early."

Ed took the key from her outstretched hand, picked up his bag and walked to the elevator. He had never ridden in one before (the tallest building in Marion was only three stories) and so he hesitated for a moment before the closed door. Finally, he pressed the button marked "up" and he heard the sound of metal engaging and felt a slight breeze. Over the door, a half clock face suddenly moved and the needle began to sweep from 10 toward one. When the car reached his floor, the door cranked opened, revealing a small, wizened man wearing a peculiar dark green suit with military stripes sitting on a stool like a leprechaun in livery. He pulled open the metal safety gate, which collapsed into the side of the elevator.

"Step in, young man," he barked, "and name the floor."

"I'm in 805, sir," Ed managed to say.

"I see that you're a new boy. So here's a piece of advice, right off. Learn it now, and you and I will get on perfect. You're not to be racing up and down, calling me at all hours, riding the elevator as if it's a just broke-in horse, like some country boys try to do to me. I'll leave you standing there, sure as anything if you try it. And I'll know if you do. Step in. I'm McGuiness."

Ed edged to the back of the elevator holding his bag tightly, and McGuiness pulled the metal safety door shut and turned the handle that closed the outside door. Then he engaged the hydraulic lift with a jerk. A similar half-moon clock over the inside door began to bump up as they rose to the eighth floor. When it reached that level, McGuiness stopped the elevator, collapsed the safety gate and opened the door.

"Thanks very much," said Ed, stepping out.

"To your right, boy."

Ed turned down the gloomy green hallway and walked past a number of similar entrances, equally spaced along the corridor until he reached 805. The door was ajar, and the room dimly lit by a window that faced an inner court. Ed found a light switch that lit up the tiny room with a stark glare that revealed every unforgiving corner of the small space. There was a simple metal-frame bed with a flat pillow and a sheet tightly tucked around a thin mattress. A rough-looking green wool blanket sat folded at the foot. The only other furniture in the room was a small wooden desk and chair, and a tall clothes closet with two drawers at the bottom. A small brass radiator, standing on four carved legs was tucked into a corner and attached to a long pipe leading up into the ceiling. A framed picture of the Reverend Moody, fierce in his white beard, hung on the wall over the desk.

Ed dropped his bag on the bed, making the springs snarl, pulled out the chair and sat down. This was to be his home for the next six months: a room with no object other than to incite the contemplation of self-control. He wondered what would become of him. He was alone for the first time in his life, but he knew, at the same time, that this was a place with no possible privacy. All his mail, if he ever got any, would rest in the open for everyone to see, and the key was available to any of the staff to enter his room while he was away.

He stood again, resolute to banish any suspicions, and opened his suitcase. On top was a paper bag with the remaining sandwiches his mother had packed for him, and underneath that, two neatly folded shirts, trousers, socks and underwear, and a sweater she had knitted from dark, maroon wool. If it got cold before summer term ended, he had instructions to buy a warm coat, and had a few dollars to do so, although he hoped it would not be necessary. He did not like the idea of spending his parents' money on this strange adventure that he was so unsure about.

He arranged his meager wardrobe in the closet and sat down to eat his sandwich. Looking around the barren room, he sensed something missing, and its absence puzzled him. Then he realized there was no mirror, and no way to see himself except perhaps in the oblique reflection of the window. Perhaps there was one in the communal bathroom, but this, he thought, would seem a strange and vacant room even when he was inside it, bearing no trace of his existence, no way for him to step outside of himself, to fashion the being that others would see. He would remain, he thought, the creation of everyone else while he waited for the call.

The next morning, Ed rose early and rode the elevator down to the basement floor to the breakfast room. It was a vast, low-vaulted cavern filled with tables and chairs, buzzing with the chatter of boys like himself. Some were dressed for outdoor work, some in neat suits or white shirts, and he stood, for a moment, imagining the hundreds of jobs and tasks that must have engaged them: a veritable boys' army of assistants and helpers. He found an empty spot at a table with five other boys and sat down. Suddenly, there was a hush, and from his right, he heard a bright, clear voice blessing the food and the day and thanking Reverend Moody's vision and support for the hotel. Just as suddenly, the undertow of conversation flowed back, and the doors to the kitchen swung open. A file of young waiters carrying huge trays balanced on their shoulders emerged and began to distribute the heavy china plates.

After breakfast, Ed (careful to leave his key) walked out the front door into the busy street, the dust and confusion of traffic already thick with commuters heading downtown. He wedged his way onto a crowded streetcar that sped recklessly toward the center of the city and his destination on the North Side: The Moody Bible Institute. When he finally arrived, he hopped out of the car and walked to the large red brick building. Everywhere inside there were signs of Reverend Moody, from his name in large lettering on the building, to the bearded portraits and photographs in the main entrance. He was amazed at the presence of the founder and wondered, for a moment, if it was not sacrilegious to put oneself before God in this fashion. Perhaps, he reasoned, this is what religion meant in the city, to be the follower of a great modern preacher, a great builder and organizer.

After asking directions to his classroom, he walked down the cool hallway to a large double door with opaque glass windows and an open transom through which he could hear the murmur of voices. Hesitantly, he turned the brass handle and walked in. Several tall windows illuminated the room. There were raised rows of desks in a semi-circle around a sunken stage on which sat a podium, an American flag, and a black upright piano and stool. It was nothing like a church, Ed thought, as he looked at the boys seated at their desks, chatting. He slid onto a bench near the door and waited expectantly until a handsome older man with a shock of silver hair and a red waxy face strode onto the stage, followed by a woman dressed simply in a ruffled blouse and long navy blue skirt and vest, carrying a large songbook. She sat down at the piano and adjusted her position, straightened her back, and then spread the book open. The man stood at the podium, gripping its sides with both hands and said in a booming voice: "The Ninety and Nine."

The piano played a few chords of introduction, and then the boys began to sing enthusiastically. Ed did not know the words, so he poked the boy next to him who pointed to a shelf under the desk that held a hymnal. "Page 240," he whispered.

Ed found the hymn and began to sing, hesitantly at first and then joined with enthusiasm in the joy he sensed around him, louder and louder:

"Rejoice: I have found my sheep!
Rejoice for the Lord brings back his own!"

For a moment, Ed lost himself in the optimism of the words about wayward sheep, imagining, perhaps, that this was what it meant to receive the call...that the words addressed him directly. When the echo of the music ceased, the man at the podium nodded to the piano player and then looked straight up at Ed.

"What a grand voice, son, a preacher's voice if I ever heard one. And who are you?"

Ed stood up, blushing and confused, and stammered, "Nobody, sir..." The boys around him roared with sarcastic laughter. "I mean, I'm Ed Watson from Marion, Illinois, sir."

"Well, son, don't you mind the scorn of your classmates. It's mere envy on their part. With a voice like that, and what we can teach you here at Moody, we'll bring you into the fold and then send you home a Minister of God."

"Thank you, sir," Ed managed to say. He slipped back into his seat, conscious of the stares of the other boys in the auditorium, curious faces like upturned pink petals set against the somber wood of the hall. He had never felt so alone or without purpose, and he wondered if this was the meaning of the hymn. Written just for boys like him? It was surely true, he reckoned, that one could be most lonesome in a crowd of strangers. And hadn't he heard somewhere that the sensation of emptiness occurred just before the infusion of God's Grace? He wanted to speed its arrival and experience the flush of belief and confidence...if it would just come.

The rest of the day was uneventful, filled with Bible study, special prayers, a meager, silent lunch, and an afternoon of hymn singing and inspirational lectures. Then it ended, and he found himself wedged into a streetcar, caroming through the city, back to the boys' hotel. When he approached the front, he remembered the unfriendly warning of the elevator man, and decided to eat in a small corner restaurant before retiring to his room.

Stepping inside the steamy, warm interior, cap in hand, Ed felt immediate pleasure, sensing the conflicting odors of hot grease, some boiling soup or stew, and cigar smoke. A tin counter ran most of the length of the room, with leather-topped stools in front. Three or four tables were set off in the corners. Only one of these was unoccupied, but not wanting to take up the space set for two or three, Ed edged onto a stool. Behind the counter through a large space that opened into the kitchen, he could see a woman busy at a black cast-iron cook stove. Another woman, about 40 or so, he guessed, large-boned, and friendly looking, with her hair tied up and wearing a white, but smeared apron, stood at the edge of the counter, ready to take orders or deliver plates. The menu was chalked on a large blackboard to the right end of the counter, and Ed could see that his choice was soup, an Irish stew, steak and potatoes, and pie. The prices surprised him, and he knew he would need to be very careful to make his allowance last. Despite his hunger, he decided on soup and bread, and a piece of pie. The waitress wrote his order on a small pad, and then, with a knowing smile, she said, "I can guess you're new to Mr. Moody's Hotel, ain't you, young man?"

"Yes," Ed responded, wondering if he was such an obvious greenhorn with no more attachment to the city than an empty room.

"Well, it ain't enough to eat nothing but soup at night. You'll end up skin and bones if you do. If you promise to give me your trade, I'll let you have a nice meal every night for half the price. Lots of the boys come here, but you look particularly peaked. Must have arrived just?"

"Yes, ma'am," Ed said enthusiastically. "That would be a genuine kindness. I'll come every day after I return from school; I promise."

"Then you're with the college too."

"Yes, I just started."

"Going to be a preacher? Lovely deep voice you have for it. Just hope you last. Most of the boys start out well enough, but the city tempts them away. You'll want to keep straight and narrow. It's the laziness catches them up into having fun instead of studying, I think."

"Yes, ma'am," he replied with more confidence than before, "I fully intend to. I've promised my parents and it's expected of me."

The next few weeks followed the same pattern: early mornings, a streetcar ride to the Institute; a day of classes; a hot meal at Mrs. O'Reilly's restaurant (he now knew her name), and then nights spent studying in the dim glare of his narrow room. As the weather warmed, he became restless and almost desperate with the routine that seemed not so much to quicken his soul, but to deaden his enthusiasm. Above all, he wanted friends, and so he sought out some of the other boys at the hotel. Two or three had been friendly at first, until they found out he was one of "Moody's Lads," and they suddenly went silent when he approached them or acted cautiously around him as if hiding away their sins. Undiscouraged, he persisted and tried to copy the city lingo he overheard, and gradually, they forgave him...or forgot...his professed ambition. Two boys especially caught his fancy for reasons he could not quite articulate. He thought he glimpsed tenderness in each of them beneath the big-city swagger they affected. Nick, the boot black, was a small boy with ruddy cheeks and an untidy mop of dark hair that spilled over his forehead and made him appear much younger than his years. Nick assured him that accentuating youth was the best way to attract customers: it was good business to seem innocent, slightly lost, and vulnerable. His friend Roger was a newsboy who got up very early each morning to fetch his lot of papers from the publishing house on the south side near the hotel. He would then station himself on a corner downtown, threatening any competitors away from his territory, and using his large size and dark, angry look to intimidate customers. It was an act, he confided, that half the time persuaded a passing businessman or secretary to pay a penny just to avoid the annoyance.

In the hotel or especially at O'Reilly's café, where they often met, however, the two boys were jolly and full of mischief, and for some reason they saw Ed as a possible accomplice in the larks that they planned as well as someone who might share in their game of stunts and deceptions. Perhaps they realized, as he did, that he was still awaiting some sort of certainty, and this played to their sense of possibility, and to his need to overcome insecurity and loneliness.

What the two conspirators most enjoyed on their Sundays off or on a rare summer holiday, was to ride the streetcars for free, evading the conductor as long as possible, clinging to the sides, disappearing among the passengers, and then jumping off, to repeat the game when the next car arrived. In this way, they went from one end of the line to the next, exploring the city but always risking the danger of a cuff on the head by a streetcar employee or a bruised knee from hopping off at full speed. It was the challenge that exhilarated them, and they worked and worked on Ed, tempting him with exaggerated stories of their adventures, of moments when capture seemed inevitable and escape thus the more thrilling, as they leapt and tumbled off the racing cars. Finally one Sunday, he agreed to accompany them, deciding that he could miss services just once at Moody. To his amazement, he found that this game of evasion was great fun, and henceforth, on several following Sundays, the three spent a jolly time wandering at the end of the line, along the beaches of the north side, traipsing down streets with elegant stone houses of a size that Ed could scarcely imagine to contain only one family. Sometimes, of course, the boys had to pay, especially as they returned, when customers were sparse. He found the pleasure, being half-stolen, never became tiresome.

Ed found himself looking forward more and more to these Sunday outings and the evening meals with Nick and Roger where they recounted the memories of these adventures to each other, each time with a new exaggeration or twist, and then imagined new escapades and escapes. His friends never quizzed him about classes at Moody, and he never volunteered even a tidbit of his day's schedule. Indeed, he found he could separate the studies that he performed dutifully from the pleasure he discovered with his new companions.

He was still the obliging boy...everyone at home had said so, and he always did the expected, but somehow, he felt, particularly on those weeknights after dinner when he studied the Bible or tried to memorize Mr. Sanky's hymns, that he was acting as the shadow of himself played for the anticipations of others. The more he performed these duties the less he knew of himself. That this did not worry him was perhaps the most surprising portion of his lot, even if he sometimes questioned his suitability for the ministry. Did one have to believe, truly and deeply, to convince others? Or was it like the world of commerce that Roger and Nick explained. They were always exploring new tricks of salesmanship, for neither of them cared a whit about the news or shiny, leather shoes, only about making the sale itself. Was that also the meaning of salvation: was it a transaction, recognizing the success of the sale, the gleam of credulity in another's eye? Would that be enough to bring him joy? Would this kind of success fill the void he felt?

Ed refused to linger on such thoughts, shaking them off and always, for at least a few minutes thereafter, renewed his concentration on his studies. To his surprise, he found that the double life he led, the able and yielding student at Moody and the joyful companion of his hotel friends, required no intersection. They were separate roads along which his spirit and body traveled, and he made no effort to connect them.

By summer's end, he was preparing for a long vacation back in Marion with his family. He had received an odd letter from Reverend Turnbull at the Methodist Church, inviting him to participate in services when he returned. "To give it a trial run," the old minister had explained. He suspected this to be his mother's plan, for he felt just as strongly that his father was dubious about churches and religion. Nonetheless, he wrote a short response, saying he would do as asked.

When he arrived at the station on Saturday, his mother greeted him with tears while his father stood off to the side as he always did when emotions showed, pretending a preoccupation with the paper schedule posted on a small column near the station master's glazed-in office window. Ed knew his father's reticence meant nothing, for he imagined that the death and grief and false hopes of his profession had killed, not kindness or concern, but any outward manifestation of his sentiments. Ed was astounded, not at his parents, but to realize the simple nature of things in Marion. His quiet town, which he had scarcely noticed before he left it, was just a tiny, partial intrusion on nature, whereas in Chicago, he had become used to the geometric shapes of concrete and brick, and the vast heights of buildings that defined the treeless landscape.

They walked together down Main Street to Elm and then up the worn and unpainted steps of the old house. Ed was practically bursting with descriptions of Chicago, its grand skyscrapers and avenues. It was nothing like St. Louis, he kept adding, although he had never actually been to that city. He was living in a hotel 10 stories high, riding streetcars, and eating in restaurants! For some reason he did not mention Moody at all until his mother asked.

"And tomorrow?" she said, "Bright and early after breakfast, Reverend Turnbull wants you to say the prayer at the first service. You should pick something beautiful from Mr. Moody's school. Just to show off what learning can be had in the city." Without thinking, Ed knew the words that he would read out to the congregation. Like all of Moody's prayers, at least to his limited acquaintance, this was a call to gather in, just like the hymn of the "Ninety and Nine." He would be prepared.

The next morning, after a half-eaten breakfast, he felt anything but ready and hung about the kitchen table until his mother, looking hurried and anxious shooed him upstairs to dress. When he returned, wearing a white shirt, dark blue tie and black trousers, his shoes shiny with a special polishing Nick had given them before he departed, his mother grasped his shoulders with both hands. "Well look at the young man of God!" she exclaimed. "Now you be off and don't look for me at the church. I'll be seated far in the back where you can't see me. It would be an act of pride to sit up front."

Ed nodded and walked out of the kitchen, onto the back porch, allowing the screen door to slam loosely behind him, and headed for the Methodist Chapel only three blocks away. The day was starting cool with a dry breeze that hinted of an early fall, but he was flushed and sweating with anticipation. He knew he was the vessel of so many hopes that he must not stumble now or show any hesitation or doubt. He walked on, kicking at the early seared leaves that had fallen on the brick sidewalk, feigning a carefree, almost childish gait. This was only a self-conscious diversion from his real feelings of excitement...and dread. The tension kept him from breathing deeply so that when he reached the chapel he found he was out of breath, as if he had run the whole way.

Walking up the steps and into the cool stillness of the narthex, he moved toward the altar, and then past the preacher's podium, to the door in the back that led to Reverend Turnbull's office. He knocked gently once, and then more firmly when there was no answer. He had forgotten the Reverend's hearing problem and remembered now to speak up. The door opened and the small, elderly man emerged, with just a fringe of white hair above his ears and around the back of his neck. He was fumbling clumsily with a black robe, trying to find an elusive armhole. It suddenly struck Ed that he was meant to replace Reverend Turnbull, to fill the position of leader of this congregation, when he retired under the strict stewardship of his wife to his rocking chair, his dog, and the small pleasures of watching the world recede slowly.

"Come in, Ed, and welcome. Just help me find this tangled up arm, and then we can set down a piece before the service. You are to give the prayer, you know. Just after the opening hymn. I've chosen one of Mr. Sankey's favorite compositions. Of course, you'll recognize it. Mrs. Johnson has been practicing it."

Ed sat down and the two chatted briefly although he paid attention mostly to the commotion from outside the office as the congregation began to shuffle in. What they discussed, other than his studies and some vague, safe impressions of Chicago that he imparted, slipped in and out of his consciousness because he was concentrating so hard on the upcoming service. He could not fathom why he felt such anxiety. He had read the prayer several times, indeed, committed it to memory although in his vest pocket he had copied the words in large, distinct letters so he could refer to it if needed.

After what seemed like ages, the time had come. Mrs. Johnson suddenly began the chords of the hymn, and Reverend Turnbull stood and led Ed out into the apse in front of the altar and then to the podium. Ed could see that the room was full. No doubt, his mother had talked up his coming, and the curious were present to witness his initiation. He joined in the singing, and it relaxed him to pronounce the familiar words. Just as suddenly as it began, the piano stopped, and the congregation settled back into their seats, all eyes fixed on him. He walked over to the podium, pulled out his sheet, smoothing its wrinkles to gain time, and then looked out over the audience. He saw many familiar faces, and found his mother's, at the far left corner of the back, and smiled.

"Now O Lord Jesus," he began, "give us a love for souls, give us a burning passion for souls..." He spoke slowly, trying to control the volume of his voice, which started low and deep, booming out in the small room. "May that be the desire of our hearts," he continued, "to lead some soul out of darkness to the light, out of bondage to liberty, to lead some poor wanderer out of the darkness of this world to the blessed gospel..." He paused because he suddenly sensed a stir of the congregation. He thought he heard the murmur of whispers and perhaps even a snigger. "...Out of the darkness of this world to the blessed gospel," he read on, "until their names are written in the Lamb's book of life..." Once more, an audible commotion interrupted his concentration; this time he was certain he heard a laugh. "Written in the Lamb's book of life...may we see wonders...may the work commence right here this morning and flow over the city..." He stopped again, this time because he could suddenly hear himself. His voice had reached a screechy, high pitch, brittle and cold as an icicle, and the congregation was now laughing openly at his embarrassment. He looked angrily at the words of the prayer in front of him and then wadded up the sheet and shoved it in his pocket. Turning, he walked clumsily back toward the Reverend's office door, fearing that his legs would buckle under him. He opened it, and escaped into the room, although the flimsy closure could not shut out the hilarity that had swept over the gathering.

That night at dinner, there was no conversation, only the sounds of chewing and the occasional request to pass a dish, and then, finally, the noise of his mother, standing to collect the plates to wash up in the kitchen. Unlike other nights, she did not leave the men at the table but returned almost immediately, sat down, and coughed as if to signal his father. Doc Watson began: "I heard your prayer this morning, Ed. Don't often go to church, but made an exception today. It wasn't so bad. Maybe with a little practice, you'll come to it; get over the fear."

"Yes," affirmed his mother. "After all, it was only this once."

Ed looked at his parents and then to his brother who always returned home for Sunday afternoon supper.

"I don't think," he began.

"Now don't be negative, Son," interrupted his mother. "It would be such a pity that our investment of hopes..."

"No," Ed said firmly. "I'll never make a preacher. I don't understand why everyone thought it was best for me, without asking me: you all just assumed. I'm not a ball of clay that you can just shape any way you want, you know."

Doc Watson was surprised at the vehemence of this response, but Ed thought he saw a hint of merriment.

"Now Ed, you know what your mother intended, what we all intended. What will you do if not take the collar?"

"I've decided already," continued Ed, ignoring his father. "I'll go back to Chicago. Start over again...I mean, I'll start a life there."

"But what will you do, young man?" broke in Mrs. Watson. "You're not suited for anything but the ministry. Have you just wasted all that time with Mr. Moody's school? Didn't they treat you well?"

"I don't know what will become of me," he said, choking back tears. "But whatever it is, I will decide. If it means being a boot black, well, then, I'll shine shoes for businessmen. If it means selling newspapers, I'll sell them on the street corner. But it will be me doing the shining and selling, not someone you imagine I am."

"But to start off so low!" exclaimed Mrs. Watson.

"Yes, and maybe even lower than that," said Ed. "But I need to go back to the beginning of myself to find whatever it is I have for a talent. When I choose to become something, it will be my choice, not yours or Grandfather's. You have to let me go...and let go of me. Don't worry, Mama, I'll find myself. Just wait."

True to his word, the next morning, Ed had packed his slim suitcase again and after a brief farewell to his family, walked with extra-long strides to the train station, confident for the first time in his life that he was truly on his own, that a life of his own making was about to begin.

The Gift

Thomas Patterson seemed a normal boy until around the age of nine or ten when his special gift showed itself. Those closest to him recognized a palpable strangeness to the way he talked, and after a while, even he began to recognize that he had a special gift. Up until that time, he was largely indistinguishable from his two brothers, who varied only in height and weight and the shade of their brown eyes. He played the usual games of catch and chase and learned to throw a ball accurately when his chores around the house were finished. Under the careful tutelage of his mother, he could pick potato bugs out of the back garden and wash the leaves of squash plants when they were invaded by the chalk-white mites that threatened to devour the crop before its due. When he was much older, he loved to work alongside his father in the evenings after a Sunday dinner, polishing the new black automobile and learning the funny French-sounding names of the parts that made it run. Most of all, he delighted in hearing stories: the history of his family; their long traipse from the East along the Ohio River and across Illinois; rumors of the mysterious Indian tribes that once occupied the land; the bitter Civil War battles that pitted one side of his heritage against the other; and the bits and pieces of gossip that his mother let slip about their Marion neighbors. He found that by constructing an outline in his mind, a pattern and a frame, he could place each memory in its proper place and recall it exactly as needed.

Patterson senior had great ambitions for his sons. He thought to send them to the new normal school in Carbondale where they might learn to be teachers. Or maybe to Springfield to study law. It would be a remarkable rise, like his own, from farm boy, to store clerk, and now to the manager of a business that bought and sold John Deering agricultural tools and machines. Among his brood of raucous sons, Thomas seemed the most promising at first, that is, until his strange gift became apparent.

With his prodigious memory, so exact in recall of detail that it closed off his imagination, or rather crowded out new thoughts with the precise and vivid pictures of what had already transpired, Thomas (Tommy) lacked his father's determination and pluck. Quite simply, he had no interest in the future, for forgetting is one measure of planning, and he neither wished to, nor could forget anything. At first, this ability made him the family keeper of dates: birthdays, holidays, train schedules, the day of the last and first frosts, and the names of his parents' friends and all their progeny. His mother noted this skill first and came to depend upon it. She could ask him the location of any misplaced item like a knitting needle or a kitchen utensil, or her reading spectacles. She thought nothing of it until one day, just to amuse himself, he said, "Your glasses are on the mantel in the parlor, unless you mean the last time you misplaced them before Christmas dinner last year when they were in the kitchen under a dish towel, and before that..." He stopped when he saw a very odd look spread across her face, as if she had suddenly discovered a stranger talking to her instead of her tow-headed son.

In the beginning, Tommy was unsure of what to make of this uncanny ability to remember, and there were times when he hid his gift in silence or feigned confusion. At other moments, however, he was immensely proud of his ability, correcting the details of a story told by one of his parents or relatives. Between the ages of 10 and 18, he remained cautious, in part because he took his father's joking admonition to be a serious warning: "Children are meant to be seen and not heard," he often proclaimed. Neither Tommy nor his brothers could quite tell when and if he meant it. Consequently, around the house, he listened to conversations. When visiting aunts and uncles in the towns around Marion, he amused himself to learn by heart all of the family stories in their various versions, without ever correcting the storyteller.

At school, he also tried to be an ordinary boy, although his ability to recall earned him a curious reputation. He could read passages of Emerson's long, dull speeches and then recite them flawlessly even if he did not understand the words. In science class, he had no problem remembering the complicated family trees of plants and animals. His teacher, Mr. Clarke, once remarked that he was a modern Linnaeus—a name he had to look up. Once seen, mathematics principles were as familiar and comfortable as the old oak furniture of his parents' living room. On the other hand, he encountered considerable difficulty writing essays and putting together new ideas. His English teacher often accused him of plagiarism—a word that he came to dread because of its truth. Obliged to invent original sentences, he found it impossible not to remember the better words and passages he had read elsewhere. Eventually, of course, he arrived at a solution, which was to jumble what he remembered into the semblance of something passably original. However, he was never good at it, and for all his efforts, he earned poor grades in the liberal arts. His parents put this down to a lack of concentration on his part, and rather naturally, their hopes and ambition began to shift toward his two younger brothers: Carl, still in primary school and Luke, only a year behind him.

As for boys his age, Tommy was rather a presence among chums than a leader. He grew taller than his father and, indeed, of greater stature than most lads of his age. He loved baseball and played sandlot games with his friends. Because of his height and skill with a bat, he once entertained the thought of trying out for a professional team. However, his poor eyesight and lazy fielding made this ambition impossible. He did possess a skill pertaining to the sport that was the envy of all his friends. He knew the rosters of every team in the World Series from 1903 on, and he could recite the batting averages and pitching statistics of every player with amazing accuracy. He became an expert on the complicated history of his favorite team, the St. Louis Brown Stockings, their first great World Series encounter with the Chicago White Stockings, and their eventual evolution into the Cardinals.

None of his friends could do more than begin a baseball story or express admiration for a player than Tommy trumped him with a rush of figures and percentages whose exactitude embarrassed them both. Once when he was 17, he persuaded his father to allow a trip to St. Louis with friends to see the Cardinals play. The outing proved to be a disaster, as Tommy recounted the statistics about every player and endlessly corrected every observation of his companions. After a hot afternoon at the ballpark, exhausted by the blazing sun and bored by the buzzing drone of batting averages and tidbits about every player, the other boys vowed never again to attend a game...at least with Tommy.

Around girls, Tommy was naturally shy and timid, compounded by his imposing physical presence. He particularly favored Ada Simpson, the daughter of the postmaster of Marion. She was a tall, lissome girl, with bouncing blond curls and an amusing turned-up nose, and very popular with the young men in town. To his wonder, she seemed to prefer Tommy, and when he called on her to sit in the parlor on Sunday afternoons, he did his best to please her and her parents. Seated in the room that was shrouded against the heat by heavy drawn curtains, it amused him to observe that her parents, one following the other, and at intervals no longer than ten minutes, contrived to find an excuse to enter into the room: to fetch a book, to fuss with a window, to ask Ada some insignificant question. Tommy understood the purpose of these ruses and often engaged them with a query of his own, thinking to ingratiate himself with the whole family. Gradually, before he quite realized it, he found that Mr. and Mrs. Simpson lingered to ask him questions about his mother and father, and about the town's history. If he became aware at these moments of Ada's increasing impatience, he paid slight attention because of his delight in recounting the past in precise detail to such an enthusiastic audience. Eventually, however, even they began to tire of his stories, and he came to realize that Ada's parents were merely testing him against their own memories of events. When his love of particulars overmatched anything they could reasonably recall, their questions became more difficult and abrupt. When Mr. Simpson couldn't stump him, or when he simply answered that he wasn't aware of some event, a sly look of pleasure flirted with a knowing smile on the man's face, and a meaningful "Uh huh," to his wife, as if a point had been proved.

Tommy might not have minded these memory tests until he realized they had curdled into mockery. Soon even Ada joined in, stirring in her own questions and souring their evenings together to the point where he wanted to call less and less frequently. Ada did not appear to mind his growing distance and one afternoon, he caught sight of her walking on Main St. with Clarence Baker, whose milk route took him past the Simpson house every morning. Tommy feared that he would only have memories of their times together in the parlor with nothing further from Ada, although he vowed to try one more time.

When he seriously contemplated it, he realized that his remarkable and uncontrollable memory cast a shadow in front and whichever way he turned it obscured the road forward. He understood he could not control his recollections, or keep his mind from flashing brilliant, clear pictures of the past in front of his eyes. He knew he would never cease to love this world once removed in all its intimate details. He vowed to disguise this obsessive ability the next time he visited Ada. Thus on a clear December morning (the 10th he later remembered), he paced around his room practicing what to say, pausing only to write down the phrases signaling forgetfulness—phrases that he almost never used: "I really don't remember that." "I'm sorry but the details escape me" (he liked that one). "It's been too long a time for me to recollect." "Was that last year, or the year before?" But the more ingenious his excuses, the more he felt disingenuous and feared that the Simpsons would detect the deception and send him and his excuses down the cold stone steps of their house and back into the street.

Finally, he decided not to alter his approach to Ada. If she wanted some young man who could only dream about the future, well then he thought: "Let her have him!" He said this out load, as he tore the practice pages from his notebook, crumpled them, and placed them carefully in the trash bin that stood beside his desk. Glaring into the lamp on the desk, with its new Edison incandescent bulb, he stared until the light blurred into fuzzy twin orbs...and he realized that he was crying. There was no turning back now. Ada would have to take him as he was or not at all. He knew, of course, that she would reject him, but he needed the finality of a decisive no. He could no more change his habits of mind than the color of his eyes; nor could he forget who he was. In fact, he couldn't forget anything at all. This realization became a powerful and frightening insight: he thought he had discovered what defined romance—and that was the ability to deny the past, who you were and where you came from, for the sake of merging with another person and living entirely in expectation and hope. If that was so, he knew he was doomed, for everything said to him simply conjured up an image that reminded him of something long forgotten by everyone else. He could do nothing about it. If anything, the older he got, the more crowded the recesses of his mind became and the more intensely his gift defined him.

Maybe his mother had been right when she once said to him on his 13th birthday, just after he had described all his previous celebrations and tallied the gifts he had received: perhaps it was an accident of his birth, she said with exasperation, because he took his first breath right during the first hours of the first day of the sign of Gemini when the first twin was still looking backwards. He admired his mother for making a joke of her vexation, but he could tell from the nervous way she cleared her throat, that she was annoyed and even fed up with her remarkable son. Just as many times before and after, when he was recounting a long story, she would nod quickly in agreement, or punctuate her silences with a barely vocalized, "yes," "yes," and "yeses" that came quicker and quicker as if she were urging him to the conclusion like a reluctant race horse meandering toward the finish line.

His father expressed an entirely different sort of impatience. He would furrow his brow, massage the front of his head where the hair had receded, and roll his eyes in disbelief. He never meant to be unkind—Tommy was sure of that—but his father often interrupted his stories, trying to terminate them when they had scarcely begun, announcing the denouement that Tommy would only reach after several minutes of exasperating explanations and multiple digressions. He knew when he talked he would be testing the limits of their toleration, but he was powerless to desist. Later, of course, he learned to put a terrible word to his condition: he had become an impossible bore. But he was beyond caring: the past remained ever more vividly colored and richer in detail than anything in the mundane world around him, at least, that is, until the present had faded into his total recall and took on the freshness of a memory.

After his inevitable failure with Ada, Tommy made two decisions. First, he agreed to go to the new Normal School at Carbondale and train to be a teacher of history or maybe biology. With his capacity to remember facts, he thought he might easily master the names of all the species and their characteristics. Or he might specialize in teaching the history of the great wars of Europe. His second decision, which he vowed to share with no one, was to remember the expressions of others as he was talking, in order to gauge their reaction when he began to ramble. When he could compile a comprehensive list, then perhaps he could better judge when to stop a story. After a week, he had jotted down a preliminary list, just to try out his powers of observation, although it made him very sad to do so.

1. Mother: clearing of throat, coughing.
2. Father: finishes story before it ends.
3. Ada: increasing nervousness; glancing around the room.
4. Brothers: teasing and laughter
5. Uncle Brockton: interruption and a gruff "Get on with it boy!"
6. Aunt Madge: a strange distant look as her focus dissolved and then an interruption with a completely irrelevant question: "Would you like a

glass of lemonade?"

He admitted to himself that to complete such a list would fill up three or four pages, and so he gave it up.

One evening, shortly after he graduated from Marion High School in June of the next summer, finding himself somewhere in the obscure middle of his class standing, Tommy sat with his parents and two brothers around the dining room table. He knew precisely what was in store for him because he had been forewarned of the conversation. His mother cleared her throat in her usual nervous way and patted her greying hair with hands that were red and cracked from the hot dishwater. His father, looking his gruffest and most philosophical, began a speech that Tommy would later remember, of course, by heart.

"Well, young man," he began, "you'll need to be thinking now of making something of yourself. Have you given any thought to continuing on to school somewhere? Carbondale, for example. You might be a teacher. Although with your marks, it might be a struggle. Of course, lawyering is out."

"I've tried to think, yes, sir," Tommy answered quickly. This was the truth. He had tried, searching for the horizon of his future, trying to imagine himself in a new place, even married and with children. This strategy failed; he found he could not concentrate for very long. The future bored him, and the thought of what might be and was yet to come seemed like a story whose conclusion he could not discern because the tangle of possibilities frightened him. He imagined this was no more reasonable than the excuse of the failed writer who blamed his unfinished story on the broken nub of his pencil.

"And what have you decided?" demanded his father, breaking into this silent dialogue.

"Well, nothing so much yet," he answered. "I think I'll be a bit like my friend Ralph. He's still in town and he hasn't decided yet either. You remember him; he ran off to the circus in the summer of 1908, June 30th, I believe, during the six day heat wave. Following their three days on the Chautauqua Grounds. And then he came back with the monkey and the sheriff arrived and took it away, and then Ralph..."

"Tommy!" exclaimed his father. "Please! Not another one of your stories! Try to think about your future. You'll never get anywhere if you just repeat all the old tales."

"I'm sorry, Father, but Ralph was so sad when he realized that the monkey loved living in a cage and really didn't want to be free. He just moped around with a long face and then..."

"But I've heard he's thinking to go off to Chicago to study at the University," broke in his mother.

"Well, I didn't know about that, Mother," exclaimed Tommy happily. "That's such a nice ending to the story, and it makes my point doesn't it? Everything will work out in the end."

"The next time you tell it and then the next and then a thousand times more," laughed his youngest brother, with a triumphant smirk on his face.

"I can't help having a good memory," said Tommy apologetically, his eyes slightly unfocused as if he was dreaming of being somewhere else.

Shortly after that discussion, Tommy did decide, or rather, was led with the firm guidance of his parents to apply to Southern Illinois Normal. He matriculated in the fall of 1910 and made the short journey east to Carbondale, driven in his uncle's shiny new Sears Motor buggy. During the trip, Tommy tried to recount one of his favorite stories about another family trip, but his teeth were set to chattering by the rough road stones and deep, muddy gullies that made him bounce on the hard seats until he lost the train of his thought. Several times, he tried to start over, but he began to suspect when he did, that his uncle sped up the car and purposely ran into ruts that made them sway perilously until he had to hold on for fear of plunging off the side. When they finally reached the town—familiar because Tommy's family was spread throughout the whole area and made regular visits to "kissing cousins"—they stopped on the street in front of the huge central building, "Old Main," an inappropriately named new red brick building with beautiful, large windows and arched cornices over the openings and entrance. Tommy learned later that it was a good example of "Illinois Gothic," with an admirable steep arch over the clock tower and a high-pitched tile roof.

The new student climbed out of the automobile and shouted a "thank you" over the rumble and sputter of the motor when his uncle engaged the drive and pulled away, leaving a puff of blue smoke and the whining noise of accelerating gears.

Standing in front of the rambling, red brick building, Tommy considered what he might encounter in the next two years of preparation to be a schoolteacher. Not surprisingly, he could not conjure himself standing before a class; he could only remember all the long, drowsy, and unhappy schooldays he had spent memorizing the singsong poetry and moral homilies in the *McGuffey*

Reader. Or sometimes dreaming about his favorite tales of medieval knights and ladies in King Arthur's Court from the big illustrated book of poetry by Tennyson that his mother had bought him (he had memorized most of it). Mathematics had been simple and unrewarding for him, and he thought of geometry as the study of lines and angles that never had anything to do with anything he could remember. Only history opened his eyes, but even there, he became alternately bored and frustrated because his own stories and memories infected all the old narratives. Often, he found himself confusing the two, not really knowing whether the narrative of his family's trek across Ohio and the down the river to Illinois was any different or less important than knights in armor plying the Rhine.

To his professors at Carbondale, Tommy proved an enigma and soon merely a bother. Reading and talking about education frustrated him immensely, and he found himself daydreaming in class, wandering through childhood memories like through a museum filled with vivid paintings. Night times were even worse, in his room at Mrs. Willis's boarding house when he stared at a white sheet of paper that should bear the words of his essays, but remained blank save for his name and the date. The other boy, Matthew Smith, who lodged with him, was the ambitious son of a farmer from Murphysboro. Tommy found him almost impossible to approach because he was always brusque and in a rush to read an assignment or finish some exercise. In fact, he often rudely interrupted Tommy when they began to chat, and raced through his meals as if excess chewing and swallowing were a tax on his time. Tommy did find a friend in Mrs. Willis who smiled and encouraged him to talk, and gave him gentle, reassuring nods until he realized the gravity of her deafness. That only made him speak louder to compensate, and the din drove Matthew to wolf down his dinner even faster and flee to his homework.

After nine months of this routine of classes, hasty meals, and long, lonely nights, the headmaster of the College, Dr. C. W. Price, called Tommy to his office for a conference. He had never entered the head bureau before, and so he arrived early, announcing himself to the clerk who sat officiously in his ill-fitting black suit and grimy celluloid collar at a desk just at the side of the entrance door. Tommy stationed himself on a low-backed wooden chair, as instructed, and tried to imagine what the purpose of this conference might be. Finally the clerk looked at his watch and then motioned to Tommy: "You may go in now; just knock quietly before you enter—please not too loud."

Tommy stood up abruptly and felt the blood rush from his brain in a dizzy evacuation. He walked clumsily to the heavy oak door, with its opaque glass window, and rapped gently with his middle knuckle. He heard the grating sound of a chair moving, and a voice commanded him to enter. When he walked through the door into the office, he almost missed seeing the tiny, white-haired man peering over the desk. Intricate, wooden shutters with thin parallel slats covered the windows, and the walls, lined with heavy shelves and leather-bound books, absorbed most of the illumination that came from the dim light of the desk lamp and made him almost invisible.

"Sit down, young man," said the Head, leaning over his desk and gesturing to stiff-backed chair. As he perched on it, Tommy decided this discomfort must be by design;

perhaps Dr. Price imagined that it added stature to his own diminutive presence.

"I'll get straight to the point, Mr...." he shuffled through his papers until he found a list.

"Patterson," they both said in unison.

"Yes, Patterson," confirmed the professor.

"I won't ask you to explain yourself," he continued, "but your marks are well below the norm, and we only took you on because you are a local boy. I think you will agree that you are ill-suited for academic work. To a man, your teachers have noted how your mind wanders and, well...how you tend to confuse the present with the past. You have to realize that class recitation isn't the occasion for family stories, especially not the long, drawn-out...well anyway...we have decided it would be best if you went back to Marion to find some sort of work there that suits you better."

Tommy understood, but at the same time, he couldn't help thinking about home...home...home sweet home and he began to recite the lyrics of that song to himself. Suddenly he remembered the curious tale about how Abraham Lincoln had loved the melody and requested its performance in 1862 at the White House, but had forbidden Union troops to sing it for fear of raising sentiments of desperation and desertion.

"Young man, are you listening to me?" demanded Dr. Price.

"Of course, sir. It's just that I was reminded of the song...you know...'Home Sweet Home' and all that I know about it; its bittersweet Civil War history."

"You see; that's what I mean. You wander off by yourself into your own world, and that just won't do. I see no necessity to discuss the matter further. I'll have my assistant write to your parents."

"No need for a letter," said Tommy. "I can tell them everything you said."

"Indeed, I suppose you can," said Dr. Price, settling back down in his chair and disappearing into the obscurity again.

"I'll be going then," replied Tommy, standing and then turning to go out the door.

"Don't forget," said Dr. Price. "But then, of course, you won't," he added sardonically.

As he backed out of the office, Tommy felt the strange sensation of vindication at his inability (or unwillingness) to define himself by the expectations of Dr. Price and the other teachers at Normal. He refused to believe that his gift of memory was some sort of failing. So many times he had rescued the fumbled recall of a family member or friend. He loved telling his stories, even if some might call them distractions. He felt the past to be a warm and pleasant place where he could always be secure, certain, and solid. Faced with a future of unknowns, he would never be anything but shy and unsure. He relished the thought of returning to Marion and the familiarity of its vivid and living memories. He could only be happy there.

When Tommy reappeared that late spring on the bright, expanding horizon of the coming summer in Marion, he decided he would never stray again from the quiet circumference of the life to which he was accustomed. For a short time, his parents were disappointed at his absence of ambition, but seemed satisfied that he seemed content to remain at home.

After several weeks of prodding, he finally applied for

a position with the Post Office as clerk, relying on his acquaintance with Ada's father for the recommendation. After a week in this slot, standing behind the wooden counter, fetching packages and selling stamps, he was demoted to letter carrier because he insisted upon chatting with each customer, telling them long and complicated stories or questioning them about their affairs. He seemed not to notice the accumulating line of nervous and anxious patrons shuffling their feet and clearing their throats, waiting for attention. However, if the Postmaster believed Tommy would simply traipse in silent service from one house to the next, he was mistaken. No matter how hard he tried, he strayed into one distraction after another, chatting with anyone along his path about the weather (this year and last), the chances of a good harvest, the coming Christmas holidays and all the Christmases past. As he made his rounds, he gathered more information for the tabloid of his memory: family histories, marriages, births, illnesses, the whole complex warp and weft of the town's living history. Somehow, in the midst of his incessant talking, he discovered the secrets of his listeners. Perhaps they told him gossip simply to fend him off, to interrupt his chatter, and force an escape from the thrall of his conversation. If he sometimes failed to complete his rounds for the day, he volunteered to deliver on Saturday afternoons. He decided this was the perfect position for him, and he rejoiced in his ability to be the peripatetic historian of the community, the bard with a mailbag.

Apart from his work, Tommy had a meager life. Although he liked girls well enough, he knew he bored them with stories about the past, for they were, he realized, looking for excitement in the new sheet music songs that came from New York and St. Louis and the latest dance craze like the Cakewalk. They attended the new nickelodeon theater, and dreamed the romance of leaving Marion for the promise of some big city. In fact, he decided that the secret to successful courtship must be to arouse the false hope of escape from the very place he loved the most, but he was unable and unwilling to encourage such empty ambitions. Even if most of the girls he knew eventually settled down with some sturdy farm boy or an ambitious young lawyer or clerk, none wanted a romance and courtship defined by admitting to such compromised endings. Inevitably, Tommy remained a bachelor, the odd man out, only invited to family events and then only rarely really included in them. As these occasions became fewer, especially when his aging parents finally passed, he found himself unable to resist the temptation to talk endlessly in a stream of historical consciousness. When his audience began to move away or tried to interrupt, he only spoke louder and more precisely, scattering more details. More than once, some newcomer might challenge his ability to remember with such precision. Such a contradiction merely drove him deeper into the thick folds of memory, unable sometimes even to rescue the point of the story he had initiated—even if he recalled all the particulars. He could not help himself: he had become an eccentric, someone whose cheerful hello sounded to others like a warning bell.

After a few years passed, Tommy became slower and slower on his delivery rounds even though, as the ripples of expansion spread across the placid surface of Marion and out into the surrounding corn fields, his route became longer and more arduous. He noticed, but was not affronted, when he approached a house to see the front door close or a curtain shift as the occupant pretended to be absent. Regardless: he had a few regulars who enjoyed his tales, and there were always enough newcomers in town, who knew nothing of the history of Marion, to satisfy his yearning to explain.

Still living in his parents' old house on West Frankfort Street, he left everything as it had been when they passed, gently dusting old photographs and pictures on the wall, and repairing and restoring, with loving attention to the details he remembered. When senility crept into his life, well before his time, he welcomed it. Soon, he could no longer work because of a painful stoop in his back and a faltering step, so he simply announced his retirement to the new Postmaster. He never hesitated about how he would spend his last days. Each morning after breakfast, he made his way to the Williamson County Courthouse on Illinois Square. Sitting on a bench next to the steep steps that he could no longer climb, he greeted every visitor with a knowing smile, because he recognized most of them and could guess what brought them to the building whether it was a rare lawsuit, a search for documents, a marriage license or a trial. Even if they failed to stop, or notice him with anything more than a slight, dismissive wave of the hand, he could still recall their histories, the story of their families, and speculate about their purpose. Sometimes he caught himself saying these things aloud, and then he realized why some patrons gave him a wider berth than usual. Nonetheless, he thought himself the friend of everyone in this bustling town center, and he judged no one, for he reasoned that to know everything about a person was the beginning of forgiveness and understanding. There were also more frequent moments when, as he sat and sensed the time revolving around him, that he became dizzy with his memories. Past events became less connected until the narratives that held them together began to slip away leaving only details: the precise details of something he was sure had great importance even if he could no longer quite grasp the meaning.

When he became too ill to maintain his daily vigil and too disoriented to know where the present and past separated, he took to his bed. His dreams and recollections receded even further, until he could recall nothing much more than a few childhood events. When even the details of those happy days were dimmed by confusion, he knew that the end had come. Someone said—probably it was Doc Watson—that in his last moment of consciousness he mumbled: "there's no way to carry on if you can't remember."

The Heiress

Vera knew she was sitting several pews behind. She could almost feel Lucille's eyes on her back, measuring and evaluating the shabby coat she had hastily thrown over her housedress. If eyes could burn! She wanted to turn around and stare back, but it would be a horrible mistake, as bad as her failure to dress for church. She had anticipated only a small group at the early service, but not Lucille. Now she had to resist the temptation to turn back. She had planned everything so carefully: the meal for Earl, topics for conversation, even a list of questions she needed to ask him. But not this! It never occurred to her that his daughter would be sitting here, judging, evaluating, weighing, and ready to spoil everything.

That Sunday morning of her special dinner, she had attended early service at the little Baptist chapel, knowing that she needed several hours to prepare for Earl's arrival at 2:00. She took very little care for her appearance—that would come later—and simply pulled her old green cloth coat over a housedress freckled with faded stripes, and then walked the few short blocks to church. This service was not her habitual one, but she was not surprised to see the pews only half full. In the pale morning light, the chapel revealed its studied simplicity. The clear glass arched windows and the pulpit to the left of the plain wooden alter, set with a bright red velvet runner were the only gestures to traditional church architecture. She imagined it could be a schoolroom or even an office, except for the hymnals wedged into the slots on the back of each wooden chair. She looked to the front where Reverend Lawson had posted the hymns on the wall in a black framed box with white, moveable numbers. She reached for the book in front of her, found the first hymn, and placed a finger in the spine to mark the place.

At that moment, Mrs. Greeley, the pianist, entered from the side and wiggled as she sat down on the bench, fussing until she found a comfortable position. Then in place, she struck a sudden loud chord. The meager congregation rose clumsily, and began to sing as ten or so members of the choir entered from the back and swayed in jumbled, rhythmic steps in their home-sewn robes up the center aisle to the front row where they would sit until just before the sermon. When Vera turned to watch the procession, she caught another glimpse of Earl's daughter. She was standing across and two rows back, gripping her hymnal in both hands like hefting a heavy weight. Her mean eyes were fixed in Vera's direction. Vera blushed slightly and turned away quickly, hoping that her notice had not been remarked.

After the hymn, she sat numb during the service that appeared to ramble on interminably. The minister's words, his singsong quotations of familiar Bible passages and then his homey translations and explications, seemed wholly inappropriate to the mounting anxiety and excitement that she felt. She yearned to turn toward Lucille again, to read some expression on her face, but didn't dare.

When the choir finally marched out to the recessional, Vera held back, hoping to avoid Lucille. What a terrible mistake it had been to throw on an old and ill-fitting housedress. Sunday Meeting was always a time when the town dressed up, and she had simply hoped to slip away with a brief greeting to the minister who always stood at the entrance shaking hands with each of his congregants. Now, as she approached him, she realized she must pause to chat. There would be no escaping the inevitable questions about her parents.

"Sunday blessings, Sister," he said as she approached. She almost laughed at this because he always addressed parishioners as "sister" and "brother," to save learning their names.

"Hello, Reverend Lawson. Interesting sermon this morning."

"Well, I do my utmost." He then frowned and lowered his voice. "And how is your father today? We surely do miss him."

"Not well. Not well at all."

"Then perhaps I should come to call. I don't want to set him to fright. But there are certain assurances..."

"Oh, he won't frighten. In fact he probably won't know you at all," she continued, suddenly struck with the thought that the odd word "assurance" had a double edge to it: his soul, of course, but maybe also a bequest to the church. "However, not today. But do come tomorrow morning if you can. It won't be long now I'm afraid."

Just then, Vera noticed that Lucille had edged up to the other side of the minister.

"Good morning, Sister," she exclaimed brightly.

"Hello, Lucille," Vera replied, pulling her coat closed around her unbecoming dress. "Well, I must be off now. Good day to you both."

"Yes, good day."

"And expect me tomorrow," called the minister after her.

Even if she had carefully prepared her dress, Vera could not deny that she looked "country," although she had never lived on a farm. She was short with a solid frame, thickened by the heavy household chores she performed. She even dressed "country." After a while, she stopped wearing any makeup or other feminine frills other than an occasional church hat and gloves to hide her rough hands. "Folks need to take me for how I be," she sometimes said in explanation, relishing the emphasis with bad grammar. There was nothing in her ordinary appearance anymore to betray her long forgotten dream of a romantic wedding or her desire to be swept away by a handsome young man. In Marion, the possibilities of love for a middle aged—although not officially yet spinster—and unmarried daughter living with elderly parents were daunting. True enough, some younger folk managed to find romance, or at least seemed to, but most left for St. Louis or Chicago thereafter. She sometimes thought she had been born with her feet in the wrong century, and now that she had reached the age of 35, there was nothing left for her but the society of single ladies, all marking the long wait for old age.

Her mother and father, still living in the earth-colored brick family home on East Hickory Street, always had pretensions to wealth although nothing was on display in their parsimonious and mean life to show for it. She had been raised to consider deprivation and hard savings to be a sure sign of status and secret affluence. Of course, Vera knew of rumors that her father, now a retired pharmacist, was hoarding a small fortune, with a treasure hiding somewhere in the house or stuffed in a deposit box at the Williamson County Savings Bank. If ever asked, Mr. Smithson, the head teller, was secretive on the subject even though he sometimes made an obscure joke about rich citizens who never spent for show.

Vera suffered gravely for this unseen fortune. When she was younger, the possibility of wealth drew suitors of every sort to call, sitting in the living room, listening to the old Victrola scratching out melodies on records, thick as black plates. Sometimes the pair would peer through the stereograph at the set of pictures from the St. Louis World's Fair her parents had purchased. But somehow, this intimacy never progressed beyond an accidental touch as the youngsters sat on the love seat and passed the viewer back and forth between them under the watchful eye of one or the other parent. Stepping out unchaperoned or dancing was out of the question for such folk steeped in the strictures of religion. Most important, the possibility of inherited wealth gave her father an absolute power over her future, which he exercised time and again, finding some grievous fault or rapacious purpose in a young caller. Before too long, the futility of courtship became a kind of public reputation that foreclosed Vera's future, and, although she never knew exactly what was said about her, she realized that her contemporaries began to treat her as if she had skipped forward a generation into premature middle age.

The misfortune of being an only daughter gradually dawned on her. Possessing no special education, and therefore ill-suited to be a schoolteacher or librarian or even a postal clerk, she understood that her existence was more and more at the whim of her aging parents. On occasion, she even suspected that they were keeping her unmarried and plain for their own purposes: to do the housework and be a servant-daughter for their old age. That left her only with imaginings of herself: the happy mother of a brood of handsome children, the envy of her neighbors, and a respected member of the Shiloh Baptist Church. She knew these were not greedy ambitions. She wanted nothing more than any other woman in town possessed. It set her to wonder why she must only dream in vain for a life that for others was simply ordinary.

On the day Vera turned 30, when she decided to give up celebrating birthdays except to record her thoughts with greater care than usual in her memory book on that day, she looked at herself carefully in the mirror in her room, and realized that age had transformed her. The once-bright skin of her face had lost its glow, leaving behind a rough geography of lines and ridges. Her neck was soft and loose, already missing the tautness of youth. Her figure had shifted perceptibly, with a waistline expanding upward to encroach on what had once been a tidy silhouette. Observing herself dressed in a cotton frock, with tiny, faded flowerets, a plain collar and short sleeves, she turned to the side and pulled her hair back, but seeing no improvement or the possibility of it, shut her eyes and sobbed.

"Why had they?" she ventured aloud, surprised at hearing her words. "Why do I have to be a drudge with no future other than to be their housemaid?" She thought she had even begun to look like the hired help.

She knew it was uncharitable to think of her parents this way, and sometimes wondered if her failures could be her own fault. She asked herself what good was it to be the daughter of a rich father if his wealth had destroyed her prospects and turned her...yes, she thought...made her a servant girl, a rough country cousin waiting on her parents? She surprised herself with a thought that shook her like the onset of fear. Almost trembling with shame, she knew what it was, without letting the full idea escape fully into her consciousness: "If they only died..."

Five years later, she could still remember that moment with absolute clarity and the dangerous emotions it let loose. Now, her father, who had retired only a year earlier, had begun a steep decline into dementia, a condition about which she could muster no sympathy. If honest with herself, she even welcomed it as the signal of his approaching end. Old Doc Watson had said it might just be a natural waning, but most probably the result of a stroke. He held out no hope of recovery, and advised Vera and her mother to suffer his bouts of anger and frustration as best they could.

"No need to seek special treatment," he advised. "And a trip to some expensive hospital in St. Louis like the Missouri Baptist Medical Center, will simply waste money."

Nothing else could be done, he continued, and institutional treatments for his condition were often casual and heartless.

"Best to keep him at home."

Vera understood that this meant in her keeping and care...her task was to restrain his temper, and dress and feed him, for her mother was unable to cope with his rages, and retired to her room for most of the day claiming indisposition or a terrible headache: one of her "spells" as she put it.

Thus, Vera became the nurse to his decline and guardian of his retreat into madness, and it forced her to be strong and commanding with him but soft-spoken with her mother and considerate of her untimely illnesses. She decided this was the most terrible situation: caught between such conflicting moods and demands on her patience. Something else changed however, something surprising about this new circumstance at home. It occurred first in church, when an elderly member, who had lost his wife several years passing, stopped to talk with her, tipping his hat ceremoniously and inquiring about the health of her parents. Then again, it happened when one of the town's confirmed bachelors asked her in plain view and in a loud voice so that any passersby could hear:

"Was you planning to attend the church social on Saturday afternoon at the Chautauqua Grounds?"

From such incidents, she realized that her father's severe illness had restored her status as an eligible wife, with a supposed large fortune in the offing. From then on, she decided she might allow herself to fantasize again.

One man, Earl Steadman, in particular, caught her fancy. He was a widower with three children, two of whom had moved to Chicago. His wife had died many years before, in childbirth, and the surviving daughter,

Lucille, almost her own age now, lived at home and worked as a nurse in Doc Watson's practice. This being so, the daughter had undoubtedly mentioned the rapid decline of Vera's father. Steadman, himself, was a retired railroad agent and like her father the subject of town speculation about a hidden, if more modest, fortune.

In the weeks that followed her insight, Vera realized that Earl's frequent inquiries about her father's health had become a form of shy courtship, and so she decided to invite him to dinner one Sunday afternoon. If this attention came from his anticipation that she would soon be a lady of means, she fully intended to exploit it. Of all of her possible new suitors, Earl was probably the most distinguished. Of course, she did not love him; she could scarcely imagine anything more than a gentle affection to grow up between them...if even that eventually. But the opportunity excited her, and she planned to make the most of it.

Certainly her mother would remark on Earl's age and his ordinary looks. Vera also had her doubts about the daughter. Would she move out if they married? At that thought, she caught herself and intentionally stopped such considerations from racing too far ahead. It was enough to contemplate marriage again and to feel the flush of excitement course through her body, without planning for every possibility.

The following Sunday after church, when Earl had paused to utter his usual solicitations about her father, she responded in a voice that croaked with excitement.

"But why don't you stop next Sunday for supper?"

Earl looked as if he had anticipated the invitation.

"Of course, I would be honored. Please don't go to too

much trouble. I understand the burdens you bear."

"It won't be a trouble a'tall, but a welcome change to have some company. Both of my parents abide mostly in their rooms, and the house is particularly still and lonely on Sundays when the town is still at prayer."

"It won't be a bother," she repeated, knowing that it would be both a bother and a test. She needed to think long and hard about the menu, and how she could keep her parents from interfering. She had pointedly not invited Earl's daughter, hoping to avoid any comparisons of their ages and looks. No doubt, it was calculating but then she realized she was testing the tepid waters of a middle-aged romance with an unpracticed foot.

All week she worried about what to cook for dinner. Her only experience with the male palate was the list of her father's curious likes and dislikes—a ledger that grew longer on the side of distaste as his health declined. She had long since ceased to defend herself when he angrily pushed aside a dish that had once been a favorite, claiming that he had never once enjoyed a steak or roast chicken. His capriciousness was like a condiment that he dished out at the beginning of each meal, and his temper made his wife cower and sometimes retreat behind the kitchen door, leaving Vera to coax him to eat.

There was no possibility her father could join them, and as for her mother, she might present a problem. Above all, Vera wanted to give the impression of a pleasant family afternoon. That was not entirely possible, she knew, but perhaps Earl would admire her effort. At least she could demonstrate what she was best at doing: taming anger and feigning concern.

So on the Sunday morning of her dinner, she attended

early service at the little Baptist chapel to give herself adequate time to prepare. After hastily leaving Reverend Lawson and Lucille standing, Vera scurried down the street, away from the church and her embarrassment. She passed quickly across the windswept main square with its two banks tightly shuttered. The other stores were also closed. Without the usual bustle of the few automobiles, and wagons, horses, and foot traffic, the town looked shabby and run-down, a reminder of its limited economic fortunes. She paused to look into the window of the shoe store and noticed that a faint rim of dust had accumulated on the pair of black and white men's wing-tipped special, displayed prominently. No one in Marion would ever buy such a fashionable item, she thought, but she understood that Mr. Irving tried to keep up with trends, if only to prevent the few well-off families from traveling to St. Louis for their purchases. She wondered about the man who might wear such shoes, and if he would take her dancing. She felt a momentary quickening in her chest, imagining she had run out of breath from swirling around a polished floor to the bittersweet sounds of violins.

But who would ever ask to waltz with a frumpy old maid from Marion, she corrected herself. There would probably be no dancing anymore, anyway. Indeed, Reverend Lawson had recently preached several sermons against the practice and its evil mate, the Demon rum.

These corruptions of city life were slowly spreading out even into our blessed small community, he warned.

"And the very worst contagion is the lure of the movies. All those foreign ideas!" "The window of temptation," he called the local nickelodeon, and often railed against the crime, seduction and fast living pictured in its flickering dark. And then, Vera reminded herself that hers were only local dreams. Her horizon was already fixed, low and steady on the figure of Earl, the solitary figure in the lonely landscape of her possibilities.

She turned and hurried on up the street to her house to begin work on dinner. She had planned a meal around a roast beef—her father's favorite once, with mashed potatoes, green beans with vinegar and bacon and a cherry pie with a latticework of dough strips woven across the top. She realized this was heavy fare, but there was an advantage to the drowsiness induced by so much starch. It would set Earl in a mood of contentment that would help ease him along in thinking about the contented state of marriage.

Hanging her coat carefully in the closet, but leaving a large space for whatever outer apparel her guest might wear, she glanced into the sitting room. It was tidy and straight, with the faint smell of polish she had used to oil the furniture the previous evening. All the pictures were plumb and the windows sparkling. Despite her care, however, it also seemed empty and plain with faded old furniture that had worn threadbare from age and use. What would Earl think about courting an old maid who seemed the living counterpart of such dilapidated surroundings? She shuddered at this idea but quickly left off thinking about her condition. After all, she was only approaching middle age...and there was her father's money that wouldn't buy youth, but perhaps entice a husband. She walked into the kitchen, picked out a fresh apron, tied the strings behind her back and set to work. As she did so, her mother came into the room, still wearing her nightdress, with her hair hastily pinned back into a grey, wispy ball.

"I think I won't be able to dine with you today, I have this premonition of a headache coming on. You'll give my excuses to Earl. But you shouldn't neglect your father. He was asking for you in the last hour. There wasn't anything I could do for him."

"Yes, Mama. Just make yourself a cup of tea and I'll see to Papa right now. Do you think he'll want to come down to dinner?"

"Oh no, certainly not, Vera. He's much worse this morning, which you would have known had you not left us alone earlier. Just a faint gleam in his eye and the rustle of the covers now and again. You'd think his time was coming on. It will be a blessing I dare say."

"The minister will be visiting tomorrow morning. I told him to. And there's the rest of the family to notify, if you think it's right."

"Yes, they will all be here soon, whether we want them or not. Looking out for their interests."

"Is that kind, Mama? Are they only after Papa's money? And isn't there a will anyway? What could he change at this late moment and in his condition?"

"Yes, there's a will. But you know lawyers and the power of hope and greed. They'll all have their hands stretched out, just like your new suitor. Strike while the iron's hot and marry an aging heiress with her head turned by the unexpected attention."

"Mama!" Vera almost shouted. "That's not it. Earl isn't like that, and besides, he has his own money. You are being very unkind."

"Then why this sudden interest in a middle-aged spinster whose fanciest dress is an apron? Do you think it's suddenly ruttin' season for old stags? Does he really want you, or does he...? But, I'm sorry. I just don't want to see you get up your false hopes."

Vera turned away from these sharp words, hurt by the truth of them. She pressed her hands against the sides of her dress, smoothing the soft loose flesh underneath, her body almost as pliable as bread dough that could be kneaded into any shape.

"You and Papa! You've never encouraged me to marry. Sometimes I think you just wanted a servant girl and not a daughter. Now that I have prospects, yes, I admit it's because of the money, you want to step in an' spoil it again. This time, I won't let you...I'll fight you and I'll leave. Papa has always said he would will me the money and give you the house. That's only fair, isn't it? Like a kind of belated dowry. If it makes me attractive to men, well that's the truth of it!"

"You may be surprised," her mother cautioned, as she turned to leave. "And please bring me a cup of tea and something sweet. Don't bother to call me when Earl comes. I'm going to look in on your father now."

Vera slid a metal chair out from under the kitchen table and sat down heavily, her elbows on the table, her head in her hands. She felt ready to sob, but her anger at her mother's cruelty, and the strangeness of her words, caught the sound, half-expressed, in her throat.

"I won't give them the satisfaction," she said aloud. "I'll take my life back with compound interest!"

The dinner with Earl that afternoon passed quietly. He seemed attentive, but cautious, and after she had answered a few questions about her mother and father, and when they had exchanged the tidbits of gossip that they could compare, there was not much else but a comfortable silence, the quiet ticking of the corner clock, and his occasional sigh of contentment. Nonetheless, Vera felt jittery because there was one delicate subject she wished to discuss. Finally, she asked gingerly, pretending that the question had suddenly occurred to her. It was forward of her to inquire, but she wanted to know.

"Does Lucille have any plans? She's such an attractive girl. It's a wonder she hasn't married yet."

"You know, Vera," he began, "what the war done. The boys who come back home alive most generally left Marion if they had a head on their shoulders. But I can answer now that Lucille has a beau and they're fixing to be married up this summer. After that, I'll be alone. It's not right for a man to live by himself, you know."

Vera looked carefully at him, wondering if this was a proposal. He was nearly the age of her father and had, she must admit, a small town look about him. He appeared uncomfortable in his Sunday suit, a shiny blue-black uniform, slightly used at the elbows, a somber blue tie, and a yellowed white shirt. What remained of his red hair had slid down to his temples and, in the back, almost to his collar, leaving only a fuzzy remnant on the top. Like most redheads, his skin had suffered damage from the sun. He had curious deep blue eyes that gave him an intensity that she thought might have passed for good looks in a younger man. He was sturdy with broad shoulders and large, soft hands that belied the physical labor he had performed earlier as a railroad worker and then as the station master. Vera wondered if she could bring herself to feel any romance for this elderly suitor. Perhaps. It was a curiosity, she thought, that as she aged, older men, who had never been attractive to her, now set off a stir of emotion that felt almost like a shiver...something she used to feel when she saw a handsome younger boy. It appeared that her tastes had aged to match her years.

She looked again at his satisfied and expressionless face. She thought she had passed some sort of test; perhaps beyond the quality of her steak and peas, the lightness of her yeast rolls. It occurred to her that the tolerable silence between them might represent the most important quality of a good marriage which was the ability to sit quietly and comfortably in each other's presence.

"Getting back to your father? I understand from Lucille—I don't mean to pry—but I am concerned..." He let his voice trail off waiting for an interruption.

"I'm obliged that you asked, Earl. Yes, I...we...are all prepared for the worst. Mama's not much help at present. He's miserable when he has a clear patch, and makes us all miserable when he falls into his angry ways. Doc Watson warned us it will be soon."

"I dare say, and no one would blame you for saying right out that it's for the best." He paused and folded his napkin nervously by the side of his plate. "And what will you do...I mean when he's gone and there's just your mother?"

Vera looked into his inquiring eyes, thinking for a moment that she saw the flicker of something animal, the anxious tension that suggested the moment for flight or attack. Something about this look jolted her. She realized that she knew nothing of this man or his life. This very ignorance dared her to suggest an idea, something she only half-recognized as a plan.

"Mama is to get the house, and I'm sure she will sell it. She's always talked about moving to Mt. Vernon to live with Sister Ellen when the time comes. I think it would be good for her. They aren't great friends, of course, but they're kin, and they can take care of each other. Mama's frail and needs minding, and a change might restore her."

"Well, yes, Vera, of course, that sounds real sensible. But what will you do? You have your whole life..."

"Yes, I've thought on it a great deal."

She paused and studied his face to see if he suspected the untruth of what she was about to say:

"I've always dreamed...you might think me childish...dreamed of traveling and living elsewhere. I want to see New England and maybe the West. There's always England, too. I've read so much about London and I think there are tours; on a ship, a week at sea, and then so much to take in. Maybe even Venice. Maybe move to St. Louis or Chicago. Papa would never approve but then it wouldn't be his money anymore would it?"

She certainly wasn't asking for his approval, just raising the possibility she planned to spend her fortune foolishly.

She was sure that her words surprised him because he flushed slightly. Vera remained apprehensive about her recitation. Had she gone too far too fast?

No doubt he would consider her odd for such frivolous thoughts. For a moment she felt ashamed that she had revealed to him...to anyone...the fragile fantasy world that she invented to fill the loneliness of a life without any real purpose or prospects. At the same time, she realized that she had spoken with another purpose: to make him jealous of her possible escape, and to force him to a decision. With a man of his sort, she guessed, there were two strong motivations: the desire for money and the need for someone to cook, and clean, and tend him, especially since his daughter was leaving. Without a prior thought, she had blurted out an impossible dream that baited a trap. And now she would have to bear the consequences, right or wrong. All along, he must have thought her weak and vulnerable, a low-hanging, over-ripe fruit ready to be plucked just before it turned. But instead, he had become the prey. She realized that everything that transpired between them, every word she spoke, came from the plan that she had formed without realizing it.

"Some of us would be very unhappy if you acted in haste. Could you really leave all your friends here, your life, and your family?"

"Of course, Earl, you're right. But sometimes a person has to act rashly, step out of the past and take chances. I think I'm ready to do that now and with all that money of Papa's..."

"And some folks will be mighty unhappy if you left Marion."

Was he edging up to the sentence and words she hoped would follow on?

"I don't know. There's just Mama and some aunts and uncles around about. They don't care much. Although Mama will miss my cooking...and if she moves, well, then, I'll be free of this old house."

"And you are a wonderful cook." Earl gestured to his empty plate.

"But that's hardly a reason, is it, to spend the rest of my life in this small town?"

"And some who aren't in your family might care a

good deal," Earl continued, his voice suddenly lower and very serious. "I care."

"Why Earl! That's so very nice of you. Very neighborly to say."

"More than just nice. I thought we might come to some understanding. I thought you already suspected..."

"My goodness, Earl, you surprise me. Is that a proposal? Because if it is, I'll want to think about it for a piece."

"Yes, you think about it, and then you'll say yes. Before you go off and make other plans that everyone including yourself is going to regret deeply."

Vera stood up to clear the plates. "I promise I'll think seriously on it, Earl. And I assure you I won't wait too long. No, this is a decision-making time. So many changes are coming on quickly now. I'll have to study my own mind. Give me a few days and I'll have an answer for you."

"I'm countin' on it in the affirmative."

Looking at his face, Vera thought she saw a look of pleasure, the sort of expression of someone who had just concluded the purchase of something he coveted and bought at a bargain price. She decided to tell him in a day or two...but hoped the wait would merely increase the momentum and resolve of his proposal. Moreover, there were appearances and customs to observe, even if both of them were rushing toward a final commitment. They would need to appear slow and certain of their decision.

When Earl had left, Vera cleared the table and carried the dishes into the kitchen. As she stacked them in the sink and put wash water to boil on the stove, her mother appeared, almost noiselessly, and settled into a chair without offering to help.

"You're quiet as a shadow, Mama. I scarcely know sometimes when you come into a room."

"It's my headache; walking softly is necessary. I have to because the slightest jolt sends the pain shooting through my brain like a nail. You wouldn't imagine."

"No, I certainly can't." She stopped herself. Was she too harsh? She wanted to believe in her mother's illnesses, but she could not help wondering if all her symptoms were just excuses for unhappiness. Did she recite this litany of indisposition to keep Vera close? Guilt, she thought suddenly, was the only emotion that had ever bound this family together and it all fell on her.

"I think sometimes you don't have any feelings, Vera. You never have. You're just waitin' for your father to die quick so you can run off with one of your gentleman friends. Is it Earl you're thinking of?"

"I don't see why you say such horrible things, Mama. I've never even had a real beau, and I never threatened to run off with anyone. You wouldn't let me!"

"But this time is different isn't it, Vera. It's your last chance. What sort of story have you invented to entice him on? Why he's old enough to be your father."

Vera's mother said this waving her hands in the air. Her pale countenance brightened as her soft, puffy cheeks reddened. Her eyes flashed for a moment, reminding Vera of the slender girl in the framed photographs in the living room when she was younger and full of energy. Then just as suddenly, her face twisted up. She gripped the cotton robe tightly around her throat and coughed.

"I suppose you intend to abandon me too when your father passes. Is that your plan? To run off with Earl to St. Louie. Well, I can tell you a thing or two you might want to consider before your scheme advances on. You always had a powerful imagination for such a plain girl. It appears you haven't outgrow'd that yet."

"What are you trying to tell me, Mama? You're being very mysterious. What's your secret you're holding close?"

"Will tell; you'll find out soon enough. And then you'll see what your Earl has to say about your steak and yeast roll dinners!"

Vera thought she saw triumph on her mother's face and determined that she had to pry the secret from her now, even if it would destroy her hopes. Then suddenly she guessed.

"It's Papa's will, isn't it? He changed it and left you everything. That's why you think Earl will drop me. It's the money."

"No, Vera, the will hasn't been changed. It's still upstairs in your father's dresser drawer. And I know the lawyer's got a copy—for all it will do you or anyone any good."

Vera waited because she knew her mother wouldn't stop once she had begun to pour out a hurtful revelation. She obviously relished Vera's perplexed look.

"But it is the will anyway, isn't it. You haven't denied that."

"Yes, yes, indeed. Just that there's just nothing in it, that's all. Just this old house and all the old, broken-down things inside it. And that there comes to me. As for the rest, your father always exaggerated...no, that's not the right word...lied. He's wanted everyone to believe that he was hiding a fortune. But there's nothin' else for you or for me. Don't you see that's why I never objected when you suggested I should live with Ellen? I really have no choice.

And you...will you be able to find a job somewhere? No one will want to marry a penniless old maid even if her yeast rolls is light."

"Mama! That's so cruel!"

"Maybe, but it's as true as I sit here. I'm even a bit sorry for you, Vera. You never had much of a chance and that's to be pitied. But that's that. Now make me a cup of tea. I'm feeling a bit better. I think I'll stay downstairs for a sit."

Vera glared at her mother and then reached to put the kettle on the old gas range. As she turned back something occurred to her and she said.

"It will be a terrible shame on all of us, isn't that true, Mama? On poor Papa especially if anyone should find out our misfortune before he dies. We mustn't say a word. Just go living as we do and let everyone think what they want to think about a fortune. It'll be soon enough to face the rest of the town with the news of our poverty."

"Perhaps you're right, Vera. Right now, I couldn't face the other ladies at the church. We'll just go on as we always were...won't we? When your father passes. And no one will ever know."

Vera's heart raced because she realized she had drawn her mother into her confidence. When the teakettle began to whistle, she poured enough water into the pot for two cups. As it steeped, she took off her apron and sat down across from her mother, taking her thin hand in her own wet grip. She had decided she would not tell Earl a word about it. Let him think whatever he wanted. In the next few days she would agree to his hasty scheme of marriage. Then, well, then, there would be a whole lifetime left for admitting the truth.

Sheriff Bennington

Sheriff Bennington walked with a determined gait, swinging his long legs in front of him as if the purpose of each motion was to measure every stride. Some called his step a swagger; others thought he loped like a wounded animal. Those who knew him best understood that it was the influence of drink and the need to steady himself. A man of moderate height, heavyset, with a beard that darkened his face by mid-day and long arms that never quite moved in unison with his ungainly pace, he used his unusual presence to good effect. There were times when his mere appearance could quell a disturbance, a saloon fight, or a gathering mob with murderous intent. As sheriff of Williamson County, he divided the town of Marion into three groups. There were teetotal ladies led by the Reverend Mrs. Turnbull and their genteel male consorts who clucked about crime and drink and looked at him with suspicion. The next group comprised hardworking souls, among them a contingent of foreigners, who rarely made trouble except when riled up seeking to settle an affront with group violence. The sort below them were the tramps and petty criminals, vagabonds and swindlers who were his regular clients. He knew this last group best, having learned their ruses and excuses through long experience. Underneath the placid surface of commerce, community, and church, he understood that a few dark roots of Marion sank deep into the dank and noisome soil of accident, petty crime and, on occasion, deadly passion.

Of those rare occasions when he thought about it, he worried that he had become too acquainted with the lure of irrational ambition and foolhardiness that led to the commission of crime. Sometimes he wondered if consorting with misdeeds had changed him. Mostly, however, he considered it accidental happenstance and bad choices that led men to act in ways which when sober or feeling content, they would never consider. Anger, ignorance, and temptation were the enemies of right living, and he believed that no preacher's exhortations could stop a murder if it was fated to happen. He was reluctant to share these conclusions with anyone, but not because he feared some misunderstanding. The explanation lay in the recognition of such dark impulses in himself, or at least he understood them well enough to feel how the coming on of anger and unthinking reflex could end in violence. He never considered himself a criminal, but ever since the county had voted Dry, he had frequent commerce with illegal bootleggers. It was something of a town scandal that the sheriff often appeared to be tipsy and was rumored to favor a political alliance with Catholics, foreigners, and upstate Democratic Party Wets.

Sometimes he concluded that knowledge and

acquaintance with low life had led him to drink. It was an open secret in Marion that on nights when the sheriff was "indisposed," only his deputy would be available. In spite of these infrequent absences he managed to maintain his office, although, on occasion, some anonymous person (he had his suspicions) slipped a "demon rum" tract or the announcement of the next Men's Temperance Meeting at the Methodist Church under his door. He vowed never to let this private indulgence compromise his ability to enforce the law, except, of course, when it came down to closing illegal speakeasies.

Bennington occupied a small apartment over the law office building that faced the courthouse. Twice when he was younger, he had ventured on serious courtships, but somehow neither developed beyond a passing fancy, and he decided that living alone not only suited his temperament, but the inconvenient hours and dubious companions of his profession. "It comes out that being the law ain't much different from being outside the law," he sometimes confessed to his few close friends. "Enforcing the law means you only make acquaintance with the underside of things." It was difficult, he thought, when he began this sort of talk, to explain the effects of constant intercourse with roughs, murderers, liars, and cheats, knowing that he had had to teach himself to think and react and speak like them in order to comprehend—and apprehend them. In his experience, most of the culpable left an incriminating trace or were foolish enough to brag about their crimes, or even regretted and confessed their actions after a few hours of consideration. He found that an evening spent in jail was a wonderful motivation for truth telling. The only truly difficult part of his job was deflecting the vengeance of lynch mobs that sometimes gathered to demand immediate justice. Of course, Illinois was not Mississippi or Missouri. He knew this from reading the news that reached the Marion newspapers. Nevertheless, impetuous justice smoldered just beneath the surface in Little Egypt, and even if it rarely burst forth to burn hot and destructive, it was a constant worry, particularly for the black citizens and foreigners who came to work in the fields and mines.

Sheriff Bennington's deputy, Aaron Longstreet, was a lazy, slovenly but good-natured assistant, dependable in a crisis but with little talent for solving even the simplest crimes. He often had to be restrained from a snap judgment that might mar a case or contaminate the evidence. He had a tendency to jump upon the obvious, which in nine times out of ten led to a correct resolution, but Bennington had to restrain him from "solving a case before its due," as he put it. Longstreet had the habit of fitting whatever crime they encountered into three or four distinctive stories, as if criminals were unable to invent new motivations and could only enact well-worn narratives of greed, jealousy, anger, and temptation. Complexity was not his greatest strength, but he was loyal, and more important, available when the sheriff was ill or feeling poorly.

Unlike Bennington, Longstreet was tall and lanky, and as a young man had earned the name "Long Feet" which he suffered without comment, just shrugging his shoulders as if to say that being noticed was all that mattered. He was ten years younger than the sheriff and married to a strong-willed and outspoken woman who thoroughly disapproved of his chosen profession and criticized the prolonged absences of his superior. The two had a single daughter who inherited her father's physique and her mother's temperament, which she displayed even at an early age. Theirs was a pleasant, if sometimes cantankerous family and the sheriff enjoyed their company, sitting on their front porch, sipping lemonade and listening to the easy banter between the deputy and his wife. At times such as these, he thought he might have liked such an arrangement. But he also knew he already shared his life with a bottle, and an intruder, in the shape of a wife, would probably make him a project for reform, perhaps even—intolerably—the object of prayer.

One of Sheriff Bennington's deepest beliefs was that crime had its seasons and he often remarked to Longstreet that fall was the very worst of times:

"When the crops are gathered, the canning is done, the fields turn fallow, and the hands are flush with money, the boredom sets in. October and November are the most worrisome months."

"Yes, sir, I reckon we'll see some autumn violence come 'round again this year," Longstreet always affirmed.

"Boredom and a dollar is always a fatal combination."

Yet what happened in the fall of 1910 was a surprise, even by Sheriff Bennington's dark expectations. Sitting in his office one dreary late October afternoon, feet up on his desk and a small flask of whisky sitting in the open drawer on his right side, within reach, he took an occasional swig, thinking about the coming evening. A knock at the door broke this pleasant atmosphere. He pushed the drawer shut, and shouted, "Come on in."

"It's me, Sheriff," said his deputy rushing into the room out of breath.

"Yes, I can see who it is, Longstreet. Sit and tell me what's took the air out of you."

"There's been a murder, sir, out of town near Carterville. You're to come quick. They say it's a most gruesome sight."

"All right, Aaron," said the sheriff, swinging his legs off the desk and glancing at the closed drawer. "Give me a minute. You can wait outside."

Longstreet stood, giving the sheriff a curious look, and rushed to open the door.

"And close that. I won't be a minute."

When the room was quiet again, Bennington reached into the drawer and pulled out the flask. He took two long drinks and then wiped his mouth with the back of his hand. Fortified, he reached into the opposite drawer, pulled out a Colt pistol and holster, and buckled it on his waist. Picking up the jacket that hung on a peg on the wall, he strode out of the room and into the hall where Longstreet was pacing back and forth, anxiously.

"Calm down and tell me what you know."

"It's the Elmore farm out of town. Mrs. Elmore is murdered and her husband all covered up with blood. Len Oldfield, the near neighbor is holding him in the house with two Elmore sons 'til we can arrive. No doubt he did it. That's all I know as yet exceptin' that the third boy come to town and he's waiting outside. That's how's I found out what I know."

"All right, Aaron. We'll see when we get there. Did you bring the buggy ' round?"

"Yes, sir, it's in the front. And a very short ride. We should be there by a half hour."

"And the boy told you all this? He saw what

happened?"

"Yes, sir, you can ask him yourself. He's standing right there on the steps."

"All right, Deputy. I'll join you in a minute."

The deputy turned and walked out of the building, and, without instruction, deliberately closed the door behind him. Retreating into his office, the sheriff leaned over and opened the desk drawer again, pulled out the bottle and took two more deep draws of whisky. Wiping his mouth, he put the bottle away, but took out a small flask and put it in his pocket for later if the night got long. He stood, exited the office, and walked down the brick staircase, across the sidewalk to the buggy. The one-horse, black carriage stood empty, but Longstreet and a boy of about twelve sat on the step, his face streaked with tears.

"Sheriff," he shouted. "You got to come now. It's Mama!"

"Yes, Son, you can tell me all about it on the way back to your farm. Now hop up and we'll be off."

The three climbed up and sat on a leather-covered bench. The sheriff pulled a long whip from the metal sleeve and flicked the rump of the horse. Almost immediately, it began a quick walk, heading west out of town along a road that abruptly became a broad, dirt pathway with deep ruts. The horse slowed as the buggy jerked and slid over the rough surface, and Sheriff Bennington shouted encouraging words to keep up the pace.

"Alright, tell me, Son, what happened; only what you saw. But first your name."

The boy looked anxiously at the sheriff and then started a rapid account that was so confused that

Bennington stopped him.

"Name first, boy."

"I'm Bobby Williams. I'm the youngest son."

"But why ain't your name Elmore? Ain't James Elmore your daddy?" asked the deputy.

"No, Bert Williams is, but yeah, Mr. Elmore, he's also kinda my father. He married my Mama, but my real daddy died two years now."

"Well," broke in the sheriff, "I guess it's a complicated story you're living in the middle of, what with your second father marrying your mother and you the stepsons–at least that's what I heard."

At that moment, the carriage jostled over a particularly deep rut and shook and swayed, banging the occupants against each other. When he could recover, the deputy said in amazement, "How come they was each twice married?"

The sheriff steadied himself and, keeping his eyes fixed on the sweating rump of the horse and the road in front, explained:

"It's a mighty complicated story about James Elmore and not a happy one. He and the first Mrs. Elmore, Emily–she was the daughter of Ida and Wilmer Stanforth, they got married about 30 years ago, when the Elmores settled in Marion after the Civil War. Bought themselfs a small farm and lived on dirt and varmints until they made a go of it. After his first wife passed, James Elmore, he met up with Sarah Williams several years after her husband, Mr. Williams–that's Bobby here's daddy–run off somewhere's, maybe dead. So James and Sarah got married. She brung along her three sons but with him contributing nothin' but trouble. Second misfortune for Mrs. Elmore it seems from all the woe she's had with him.

Don't know what it is with these marrying and hitchin' up folks. Don't seem quite smart to me."

"That's a confusing tale, Sheriff!" exclaimed his deputy. "Can't conjure what gets into folks! Or how those boys keep their names straight."

"Well, it's a true story and now it's come to this. James Elmore never was quite right. You'd a' thought she'd a' seen it before now. Don't mean to criticize, boy," he stopped, putting his hand on Bobby's shoulder. "It don't merit a killing no matter what," he said as if to reassure him.

As they drove on, a grey, unpainted farmhouse and out buildings emerged against the flat horizon. The house was set at some distance from the barn and a large fenced area, where barbed wire penned in several cows. Closer up, the house looked untidy, with a sprawling elm on the south side and low bushes under the left front window. An open porch up two steps held several spindly rocking chairs. The only color was a red rose bush right next to the side of the porch, indicating the effort that someone made to brighten the drab property. As they approached, they could see two men sitting on the porch, one in a derby hat and work clothes; the other, in denim overalls with a shotgun across his lap.

Sheriff Bennington pulled on the reins and the buggy stopped in front of the house. He and the deputy climbed down.

"You sit awhile there, Bobby. Don't come into the house." He turned and walked onto the porch.

"Well, you got yourself in a pickle, ain't you, Elmore," he said as he walked up the steps. "And thank you for holding him," he said to the man with the gun. "You are?"

"I live just over the edge of that field," he said, indicating with his head. "Heard the shots and come running. Knew it weren't no good. I'm Len Oldfield. Been expecting trouble all along. We all were. He's no good, that one," he slightly raised the rifle pointing at Elmore. "She was most feared of him. Has a terrible temper except soft and gentle as a lamb when he wants a favor. And has a way with women."

Elmore looked up at the sheriff briefly and then bowed his head down again as if he were studying the rough planks of the porch floor.

"Why don't you tell us what happened, then, slow and easy," said Bennington, pulling the only remaining chair to face Elmore. "You go inside, Aaron, and check the body. But don't you move anything."

Elmore looked up again, took off his hat as if in apology, and then placed it back carefully on his head. His face was red and damp with tears and his right hand shook slightly as if it were the guilty member.

"Wanted to see my wife today, and rode out this morning. Horse is still in the barn. I come up to the door, and Sarah, she wouldn't answer when I knocked. But I could hear voices inside—her and them three boys of hers. I knocked again and I guess I shouted something, but she still wouldn't open up."

"But you know you weren't supposed to come here anymore, Elmore," interrupted the sheriff. "I know about the 'Peace Bond' she swore out against you a couple of months ago. Got a court order and threatened a fine if you bothered her again. What made you want to come out here anyway?"

"But she's my wife. She don't have no right to keep me

away. I didn't mean no harm."

Oldfield, who was listening intently, caught the sheriff's eye and shook his head in disbelief.

"So I just knocked and then had to kick the door in. I don't know what I intended, but I went in."

"And you were carrying a pistol? But you didn't have any intention of using it?"

"Don't know why, as I said. And there she was, yellin' at me. Telling me to get away, and the three boys shouting and cursing. Her Williams' boys and not even mine. They never did take to me. I got confused and angry. One of them threatened to run to the neighbor's and the biggest one came at me with a kitchen pot. I guess I lost my temper and I fired a shot just to calm him down, but it hit my wife, somehow. Don't know why...maybe to calm her down...but I fired again at her and she screamed and fell down. I tried to pick her up; got myself all bloody; but I could tell she was dyin'. Didn't mean it; told her so." He began to sob, putting his hands across his eyes as if to erase the memory. "Didn't mean none of it. Told her I was sorry!" He stopped suddenly and jerked his head so violently that his derby hat toppled to the floor.

"That's when Tom Williams run out to fetch me," said Oldfield. "I come right away and then sent the other boy into town to fetch you, Sheriff. That's pretty much the story. I could tell she was dead. Other boys are back at my place. Told them to stay with my wife. No place here for youngsters to hang about."

The sheriff nodded, stood up carefully and walked into the house. Just behind the door, so it could barely swing free, lay the body of Mrs. Elmore, sprawled on the bare floor in a pool of dark blood.

"She must've fell right where she was shot," said the deputy, who was standing off to one side.

"No, I think not. See here is a streak of blood, where Elmore dragged her. Just as he said, he must've tried to pick her up. She would have gone down back a few paces. See, behind you, there's blood there too."

Bennington knelt down and grabbed her wrist and then let it drop. "Cold already. But we'll send Doc Watson out to look just to get the story straight and then they'll be wantin' to bury her. The boys...and whatever family is elsewise round abouts. You know of anyone, Longstreet? Think maybe there's an elderly aunt somewhere."

"Yes, I think so. A Miss Carter or something. I'll ask around and let her know."

"All right then; you go on outside and put some irons on Elmore so we can take him back to town. He's pretty quiet now, but he's a bad one and I don't want him running off and committin' more mischief."

The deputy went outside. Bennington leaned against the entrance wall, looked at the body, and shook his head in disbelief and disgust. He reached into the pocket of his coat and pulled out the flask. He took a long drink of whisky and then another. "Folks," he said quietly. "Trouble 'n folks." He put the flask away, stepped around the body and then outside.

"Put him in the buggy, Deputy. And thanks to you, Mr. Oldfield. Do you think you could keep this boy for a while, too? All them Williams boys? Can you keep them until we find someone wants to claim them?"

"Sure, Sheriff. I can always find some work for them. Need a new fence put up, and digging fence posts is just the thing for these lads. Yep. I'll keep 'em."

On the way back to town, the three sat quietly. There was no call to talk among them. Elmore had confessed and the sheriff had no words for him. By the time they reached Marion it was dusk, but there were still people walking in the streets. Almost everyone noticed the trio: two law officers and a manacled prisoner seated between them. One man even shouted at them when he recognized Elmore. "Damn you, Elmore! What you gone and done this time?"

Elmore looked at the sheriff with frightened eyes, but said nothing, dropping his head as if this could disguise him. When they arrived at the courthouse jail, Bennington led the prisoner inside. As the two entered the doorway, the sheriff turned back and called to the deputy.

"Go tell Doc Watson. And don't tarry and be gossiping about this case. Elmore ain't popular in town and I don't want trouble."

"Yes, Sheriff," mumbled Longstreet as he shuffled off toward the doctor's house.

The sheriff guided Elmore inside and down the stairs into the basement that held a single cell. The iron bars were rusted and the stone walls glistened with damp. A single, high grated window let in the diminishing light of the late afternoon.

"You'll be here 'til your trial is set. Don't know yet when that will be. But you'll be wantin' it over soon I expect."

He opened the door and pushed Elmore gently inside.

"Turn around and I'll take off those irons. Can't escape from here and you might as well have the use of your hands. I'll have someone bring you supper later."

Bennington removed the cuffs, slammed and locked the cell door, and went back up the stairs to his office. He sat down at his desk and leaned back, hands behind his head. Then suddenly he started, as if he remembered something. He reached down, slid open the drawer and pulled out the whisky bottle. It was half empty, enough for the evening, but he knew he would need to buy another one for tomorrow. He put it back, shut the drawer and closed his eyes.

What came to his mind at that moment was a case only last year that almost ended in a lynching. Trouble in the mines. He pulled out the middle drawer of his desk and retrieved a clipping from the *Cairo Evening Citizen* November 11, 1909. He had kept the paper to remind himself of the nearby danger. Two men, Will (Froggie) James, a black man, and Henry Salzner, a white man, had been lynched on the same night in Cairo, just a day's journey south. The paper gave a detailed and gruesome account of the mob: its fury only died when the state militia appeared.

"Damned newspapers," he said aloud. "Seems they want to stir things up."

Sheriff Bennington shook his head. "Not here in Marion! By golly! Not here!" He knew the danger, what with the opening of the mines and foreigners brought in, and then black workers imported from the South to do farming. He had to be careful that the mixture didn't combust. He knew other sheriffs, especially in Missouri, looked the other way when a crowd with a noose appeared, but he was determined that would not come to his town.

The sheriff did not remember much else from that

evening. He realized that the deputy had returned; Elmore had a meal. Beyond that, he wasn't sure when or how he returned to his room on the square. When he woke from shouting and banging at his door, he discovered that he had slept in his clothes and boots. His head was a misery and the noise hurt like spikes being driven in.

"All right," he said, struggling to sit up. "I'm coming. Hold your horses!" He stumbled to the door, smoothing his hair back as he walked. He noticed the sharp rays of sun streaming through the open window, like a sundial indicating the late hour.

"It's me: Longstreet!" shouted the deputy through the door. "Come quick. There's a crowd at the jail."

Bennington pulled open the door and stepped outside.

"Calm down, Aaron," he said. "Doesn't help when you get excited. Now tell me."

"There is about 40 or 50 men and boys and even some women folk outside the jail calling for Elmore. A couple of them is carryin' a rope."

"And how did they know what happened?" said the sheriff angrily. "Did you say something?"

The deputy looked away and spoke as if consulting an anonymous person at his side. "Only told what had happened to the boy who brought in Elmore his food last night. He wanted to know how long he'd be in there and I guess I explained a bit."

Bennington looked at him, his eyes fixed in disbelief.

"I wish you hadn't been..." continued the deputy, "been so...'indisposed.'"

"Go on, say it. You shift the blame to me just because I had a drink or two."

"But Sheriff, you know when you're like that, we can't

even wake you up sometimes. Don't put it off on me."

Bennington started to speak, but caught himself. He knew he should have been more careful, and understood now what he had to do. He picked up his step, trying to shake the fuzziness out of his brain and focus on the task ahead. It would not be easy to stop a lynch mob once it got up a head. The only way to save Elmore was to sneak him out the back way and out of town to Harrisburg. The deputy could take him while he talked down the crowd.

The two entered the jail through the back. They walked quickly down the stairs to the cell where Elmore stood, his back to them, on tiptoes peering out the high window.

"You'll be wantin' to leave now, Elmore," said the sheriff. "The deputy will take you out the back to the train station for a ride to Harrisburg. I reckon you can hear the crowd out front. Probably friends of your wife; her neighbors. There's talk of a rope."

"Let me at them," snarled Elmore. "Just give me a gun and I'll put a couple of them down. Then you'll see what your mob is made of: a bunch of scared rabbits!"

"There'll be none of that. It's my duty to save your neck for an official rope. None of that vigilante justice on my watch."

Elmore glowered at him, turned and spat.

"Put the cuffs back on him, Longstreet, and get yourselves to the train station. I'll deal with them that's out front."

The deputy did as he was told, locking Elmore's wrists behind him, and guiding him up the stairs and then out the back door after looking to see that the alleyway was deserted.

"Maybe not so serious," said the sheriff to himself, as he pulled a large rifle out of a rack, "if they didn't even put a watch on the back door."

He walked to the front of the office and swung open the door. It smashed against the wall like a gunshot. The sheriff stood in the doorframe and looked out over the crowd. He estimated about fifty or so grim-faced farmers, some young boys, and a few women. He recognized almost no one and so he surmised they had come from Centerville, near the Williams farm. That explained why they milled around the front of the courthouse neglecting the rear.

Bennington strode out onto the landing at the top of the steps, the sun catching him in the face, its bright penetrating light reminding him suddenly of the terrible headache and thirst that afflicted him. He remained silent, immobile, looking over the crowd, holding the rifle in two hands by the barrel and stock. The crowd began to move uneasily until someone from the back shouted, "Let us have Elmore...a rope's too damn good for him, but it'll do."

"I think you good folks need to go back home now," Bennington called out. "We won't be having no lynching here! The state will do its duty and put him on trial. I won't have this disorder in Marion. Now go on back to your farms and your chores. We all got work to do and mine is justice."

"How 'bouts justice now!" shouted a man in front. "String him up! Lots of nice big elm trees here in Marion just waitin' to do their duty!"

The crowd laughed at this sarcastic joke and began to move toward the sheriff, shouting. Bennington hefted his rifle in his right hand, pointing it down at the ground, but in the direction of the crowd.

"Stop right now," he commanded. "I'll shoot the first man who tries to enter here. Now go on home! All of you!"

The men in front hesitated for a moment and then pressed forward again. Bennington sensed that there was no leader among them, no one giving orders or willing to stand out from the rest. He also realized that the menace was empty unless someone took charge, and he determined that it would be him.

"All right, then. You need to be off. We have Elmore safe and secure. He'll stand before a judge for his deeds. You'll have to kill me to get at him and that will just lead to a string of hangings. Where's the justice in that?"

A woman cried out at him: "But you'll let him off. Poor Mrs. Elmore. Never did no harm!" The crowd murmured.

"No, ma'am," Bennington said sharply. "This here is also a crime against the great State of Illinois and we'll do this the right way. Now go on home! Nothin' more for you to do or say here!"

With that, the sheriff turned his back to the crowd, went up the step to the door, entered, and slammed it behind him. Visibly sweating now, from the tension of the encounter and the night of drink, he walked back into his office. He knew the crowd could move one way or the other: disperse or break into the courthouse, but he believed that his confidence and nonchalance had persuaded them. He sat down at his desk and pulled open the drawer. Reaching in, he found only an empty bottle and realized he would have to go out. Just as soon as the mob broke up, his life could go on.

Hyacinth

Some mornings, and especially today, as Hyacinth Jefferson began her long struggle to tame the tangles and knots in her hair, she thought of her mother. "Mama," she said aloud, looking at her image in the mirror and shaking her head. She was never sure if it was loneliness or vexation that made her recall her mother so often, but she did know there was still a deep emotion that came with the memory and the likeness she saw in her own face. "Mama," she would say and shake her head again.

Her strongest early memories of Nannie Jefferson had been the struggle before the tarnished and cracked mirror in the bedroom as her mother pulled the rough comb through her kinky hair, stretching the curls tight into plaits that she tied with small pink ribbons. There were times when Hyacinth felt that her whole scalp would come off from the tearing snag of the black comb. Finally, when all her plaits where tied and in place, she saw they were pulled so tight that it gave her a surprised, quizzical look, her eyes wide with amazement.

It wasn't just the brisk tidiness of her mother that she remembered most vividly on this particular morning before she set off to the Turnbull residence to begin her daily duties of cleaning and cooking. There were the "talks" between the two of them. Mother and daughter, which meant simply, a stream of one-way advice. Nannie would always begin by telling out her story. She had grown up in Kentucky, the daughter of a free farmer from the hardscrabble, stubborn, and exhausted farmland in Hickman County not far from the Tennessee border. Her father loved to joke about her: "Such a slim beauty of a girl with large friendly eyes and a laugh that rung like a bell. You'll capture a fine man, sure as anythin'."

Although Nannie knew her parents watched over her, she began to meet boys who ventured just to the edge of the farm, fearing to come any further.

"I wasn't no prisoner to my chores, and when they was done...well I guess I was a wild one! No matter what they warned me, I run off with the first han'some man that came courtin'. And oh my, he was a han'some man! I knows what I was doin' sure. But couldn't stand no more farm work. Wasn't gonna tend chickens and chilins' on some farm for all my days."

As she told Hyacinth later, she knew what she was doing and the price she might pay when her parents discovered her wandering. That was why they traveled north to Marion in Little Egypt where her handsome young lover took a job building roads and then hiring out as a gardener, and where she gave birth to Hyacinth, her only daughter. After he left, she stayed behind, doing maid work, to wait his return.

"Do you remember him much, Mama? Why did he

leave us?" Hyacinth would often ask.

"Don't you be startin' up with your silly questions," was the usual reply, but sometimes she caught a dreamy look in her mother's eye as if some distant memory flickered bright in her mind. "Sometimes," Nannie would reply, "I remember most his hands. He got the most beautiful, big soft hands, copper-colored from wear, but gentle...so gentle." Then Hyacinth knew she might ask to hear her favorite story, about the time Nannie first met him.

"Tell it, Mama, 'the story.'" An absent look would pass over her and the music would come into her voice. She often began low, like the beginning of a sorrow song: "I never expected to see the like. But there he was, one time at the fence near the grove of trees that the creek run through. As soon as I 'served his laughing eyes, I knew he had been awatchin' me. He just standin' there, hands on his slim hips, chewin' a long stem of grass and just as forward as he could be. I knew it then; I could never resist a tall, thin man like that."

"Will he ever come back, Mama?" Hyacinth would ask.

"Oh yes, he will I s'ppose, but even if he don't, I still got you and you're the best piece of him."

There were other times when Hyacinth's mother just yanked her hair even tighter and laughed. "Don't you go on then; I ain't tellin' nothin'."

Saddest of all, Hyacinth remembered these morning talks for the warnings her mother imparted afterwards, and looking back on them, she realized how bewildered she had been at first.

"I want you to practice to be 'visible; don't let no one see you observin'," she would often begin. "And never look a white person direct in the eye, and then most times they just won't bother to see you," she explained. "Because if you be 'visible then you can occupy places where no one's gonna notice you, even where you're not s'posed to be. Just never look no one in the face unless you got to, and you'll be safe."

"Yes, Mama," Hyacinth would answer dutifully at first, without the slightest idea of what she meant. Sometimes, afterwards, she would sneak into the bedroom and sit before the mirror to practice, turning away her face and then looking back quickly to see if she had, for one instant, been absent from the glass. She never succeeded. Her dark face always returned, dangling plaits with their pink ties, and her large surprised eyes. Never once could she make herself disappear. Later, of course, she began to understand exactly what her mother meant, and she became adept at occupying space without calling much attention to herself. Sometimes she even imagined herself to be a ghost or a spirit, or a night bird, hovering close over the world, but never touching it, and observing and listening to the conversations and complaints of those who could not see her. She even wondered what it might be like to float into the open window of one of the grand houses in Marion where she cleaned and listen to the talk of folks who would never think to speak to her, to attend their dinners and their parties as an unseen, all-seeing guest.

In a fashion, her wish was fulfilled, but not quite in the way her dream had plotted it. Like her mother, she became a maid, and instead of flying through windows, she came through the back doors of the houses she had once so desired to enter. At first, when she was only eleven or twelve, and had almost finished attending the broken-down school at the east edge of town where they lived, she went with her mother to help. She learned to polish silver, clean and trim lamp wicks, wax floors, shine windows, and do the endless laundry that seemed miraculously to accumulate in piles of a size and variety that astounded her. When she was still at this young age, and wearing her plaits and ribbons, not yet covering her head in a scarf like her mother, the lady of the house might speak to her kindly, even offer her a cookie or a glass of milk in the kitchen. However, as she grew older and into herself, these kindnesses vanished to be replaced by orders and lists and sometimes, a scolding for a job not done to a person's liking.

She left school around this time and reluctantly so because she enjoyed it. A bright student, quick in reading and geography, her intelligence pleased and surprised her teachers once they had mastered their bewilderment. Their approval seemed infectious. One or two of the poor girls from the white side of her class said hello and even looked at her full on. At such moments, she wondered about her mother's advice to study the ground in front of her and never lift her eyes in curiosity, never to inquire of another soul's thoughts and intentions if they were white. "Not to look is not to be seen," was her mother's frequent caution. To Hyacinth, this seemed to deny herself, and she puzzled at the fear it carried.

She might have remained with her class; that is, until the 'incident' after school in November that changed her life and determined her to forever finish with learning. On November 20, 1909, a day she later calculated backward, she remembered she packed up her schoolbooks in the calico bag her mother had sewn up for her and pulled on her coat against the wind that had begun blowing the night before. Although the hour was still early, the bloodshot sun had already sunk down near the afternoon horizon, just visible in a narrow band of brilliant blue that cut through the heavy lid of clouds scudding across the sky from the south. As she walked quickly down the rickety, unpainted wooden steps and out into the bare schoolyard leading to the street, it seemed that the wind was whistling around her ears. Clutching her coat tighter, she hurried on and then heard the whistle again. This time she realized it was not the wind but a voice calling to her.

"What's your hurry, little black girl?" she heard, or thought she heard. "Wait up a minute, won't you?"

Hyacinth thought she recognized the voice, one of the older boys from school, but she forced herself not to look around. She knew someone was behind her, and even thought she heard the sound of steps on the rough carpet of leaves and broken branches that littered the path.

"Let it be the wind," she said fiercely to herself. "Please let it be the wind!" She walked even faster, but the sounds behind her gained, as if her shadow was catching up to her. She thought, as she walked on, that she heard a laugh and then she realized there were two following her, and the laugh was some sort of communication between them.

"Little girl," said a voice very close behind her. "What's your hurry? Where you goin' so fast? Why don't you stop a piece? Don't mean no harm to you."

These words of false assurance made her shiver like a cold wind, but she refused to turn; she would not stop.

"Don't be unfriendly now," said a different voice, with an edge of threat.

For a moment, Hyacinth tried to put a name and face

to the voices. But she refused to believe that they could be students from a higher class, boys she might see every day. She didn't want to know anything more than they sounded white, older and dangerous.

For a moment, she thought to flee, but fear had drained the energy from her body and her legs felt heavy and dead. She looked from side to side, but this stretch of her path was desolate, just an empty field of withered and frosted grass on one side, and a dark, closed-up house on the other. Suddenly she felt a hand on her shoulder, pulling her to an abrupt halt.

"Now let's get a better look at you," said one voice. "Can't hardly make out your black face against the dark that's comin' on," he laughed.

The other voice, now in front of her, commanded, "Look up, girl. Let me see them wide open eyes!"

Hyacinth shook her head violently, and kept her gaze on the ground. She knew—her mother had told her, hadn't she—that if she looked them full-square, the trouble would never end. She didn't want either voice to possess a face or a body; that was her only protection: to refuse to let either of them be real.

"Now don't be peevish," said the younger voice. "We don't aim to hurt you unless..."

Then, strangely, the older boy began to sing, softly at first, and then louder.

"Down in the jungle lived a maid,

"Of royal blood though dusky shade."

He stopped: "Can't recollect the rest of it."

And then the other voice joined in: "But I reckon I know it:

"If I love-a you 'n you love-a me

"We'll live as two

"Under the bamboo tree."

Both boys laughed loud. Hyacinth could hear one of them slapping his knee in rhythm.

"And don't you love me, little Nigra girl? Don't you want to lie under that there bamboo tree with me?"

Hyacinth couldn't speak, even if she had tried. She was trembling all over and her shudders shook tears out of her eyes. Still she refused to look up.

"Thought all of you little black girls might like to have your own big, white Zulu Prince," said the older boy, laughing at his own joke. "Now you just raise your head up and look this way."

With that, he grabbed her chin roughly and jerked her head back. Hyacinth sobbed, but squeezed her eyes shut as tight as she could: "I'm not here," she said to herself. "Please let me not be here."

"That's not po-lite little girl! Don't you mama teach you no manners? When a white man talks to you, you're 'spose to answer: 'Yes, sir; no, sir; if you please, sir.' Now how about a little dance, Zulu girl. You got to know the Cakewalk. All's you people round about here knows it, I'm sure."

Hyacinth said nothing, her chest heaving as she struggled to hold back her sobs.

"OK, Bill," said the younger voice. "I'm gettin' cold and this ain't no fun no more. Besides, she's too young for sport. Just a scrawny kid. Let's go."

"All right," said the older boy. "Just one last thing I gotta do."

He dropped her chin from his grip, but at the same time slapped her sharply on her cheek. "You just learn how to be treatin' white folks, now, 'n let this be your first lesson. Next time, you speak up when spoken to."

He slapped her again, hard, and then shoved her along the path, almost making her trip. She stumbled, but refused to fall or even run away. She raised her head up again, cheeks burning, and headed toward home. She had survived.

Right away, she knew she would never tell anyone, especially not Mama. She would blame her—tell her that it was her fault and Hyacinth knew she would never understand. But her mother had been right; she had experienced the lesson that her mother cautioned her with. They had let her go. She knew that if she tried with every taut muscle of her body, she could make herself invisible to danger.

When she reached home, Hyacinth hung up her coat in the hallway and entered the meager living room of the small cottage her mother rented. She carefully placed her calico bag on the table near the sofa, which also served as a work place, and was about to enter their shared bedroom when her mother emerged from the kitchen. Catching her eye for a long moment, Hyacinth thought that she could almost see inside her.

"What is it girl?" her mother demanded. "What's happened to you? You been cryin'?"

Hyacinth paused to answer, considering in one confused moment what it would have meant to answer truthfully, even to accuse the two boys whose voices she probably knew. There would never be any costs for them. White men lived in a world without consequences; she understood that already. The truth would fall heavy on her and she knew she could not bear it.

"No, Mama," she said as calmly as she could. "The wind; it's blowing mighty cold, and it made the tears come on."

"Seems to be," replied Nannie, and said nothing more, although Hyacinth could sense that she knew there was a story wanting to be told.

She kept her promise and told no one, especially her mother, and there was no friend close enough to reveal her thoughts to. Her mother continued to quiz her at first, but Hyacinth just hung her head and wouldn't answer. Finally the decision to quit school when the term ended seemed like a natural thing and her mother finally accepted it. Later, Hyacinth decided that 'the event' separated her life into two unequal halves: a short and happy child's world and the adulthood that came upon her suddenly that day and snatched her future away from her. Looking back on it, she saw a clear dividing line between light and dark, between bright memories and the dull drudgery of living a life whose course, ever unknown to her, was determined by the whims of others, and into a future where she had ceased to dream.

Looking back on the 'incident,' or the 'lesson,' as she sometimes later thought of it, she remembered the voices of the two men: kind at first, but changeable and then angry, and then the words of that terrible song they sang. She asked her mother several weeks later about it.

"What's a Zulu, Mama?" she inquired one day, trying to be very casual.

"What you want to know such a strange thing for?" was Nannie's retort.

"Just wondering," said Hyacinth. "I heard the word in school one day and I been puzzling over it ever since."

"Then you should go back to school and ask your teacher," was her mother's quick response.

A few weeks later, she raised her hand during a quiet moment and asked Miss Edna. Before she could answer, two boys across from her in the white section began to snicker and drummed on their desks: "Zulu Chief, Zulu Chief," they cried.

"Quiet now," said the teacher angrily. "Where did you learn that word Miss?"

"Just heard it somewhere, I s'pose," answered Hyacinth quietly.

"Well then, you don't need to know much about it do you?...Just means an African man: a dark, uncivilized man, without the blessings of God or civilization."

This made little sense to Hyacinth, but she averted her eyes to signal that she was satisfied. She got very little else from her mother when she asked the meaning of "cakewalk."

"You sure are enough full of questions, young lady," was her answer. Then her mother laughed and continued: "It's a dance, and a song that they do up in the big city like St. Louie. I expect you'll never see it. But what," she paused, "what makes you such a curious child? First Zulu and now Cakewalk. What they been teaching you at that school? Can't think such is any use to folks like us. Nothin' we need to know 'bout or understand."

This much was all that Hyacinth ever learned about the strange words of taunt she had heard, but she knew enough about what had happened, and what had not happened with the two boys, and she understood she had saved herself by her silence, by her ability to disappear in front of white people.

As she grew older, she took on more of her mother's cleaning rounds, and often, when Nannie complained of swollen legs, she went alone to the big houses near the Square. She understood that as far as the ladies she worked for, one pair of black hands was worth as much as any other so long as they were quick and willing. Sometimes she began to feel like a silent part of these families. At first, she was curious and even taken aback at how casually they spoke in front of her, carrying on their lives, talking, arguing, and revealing themselves as if she was only a portrait on the wall, or a chair set up in a corner. Almost from the first, she learned more than she ever wanted to know about them, and on many occasions, had to answer back: "Don't you think, Hyacinth?" "Isn't it true, Hyacinth?" "I just don't know what to do or say; do you?"

Her silent presence seemed to draw out these words of inclusion although she never let on any curiosity. There were even moments of intimacy that she witnessed when husband and wife would embrace or argue bitterly. At such times, she tried to slip out of the room, but it gradually dawned on her that—so she thought—they actually wanted an audience, that their lives were, to some small degree, enacted for her, as if her presence would confirm their status or the significance of their emotions. If this made her uncomfortable—and on occasion it did—the knowledge she gained and the casual closeness she experienced was even more unsettling, although she never let on.

Then there were the children who treated her as a confidant when they were angry and frustrated with their parents, or like some pet with a wagging tail to whom they could pour out streams of resentment and tears of unhappiness. She knew that by being an almost inanimate object, a ghost, a fixture, a half-shadow, or unremarked presence, she learned everyone's secrets because they told her things without even realizing that they were talking to someone.

At the same time, there was a danger in her close connection with these families, a threshold that she could see clearly never to step across, but which the others, in their familiarity with her often failed to detect. One time, when she just began to accompany her mother to work at the Ceciles, the boy there, about her age, Ralph, followed her around while she carried buckets of water and rung out mops and polishing rags, chattering away as if they were the best of friends. He even asked her if she would like to see the bird's nest in the back of the holly bush. She would surely have accepted, but her mother, who seemed to anticipate all possible transgressions even before they happened, called to her at that very moment to help in the kitchen.

That evening, Hyacinth knew she was in for a lecture. Her mother, to amplify the effect of what both knew was coming, made their simple dinner without comment except to criticize, in her impatient tone, the sloppy way Hyacinth had cut up the vegetables. Only when they were washing up, did she finally begin.

"You got to know, child, that they'll turn on you, no matter what you think. Take advantage of you."

"Yes, Mama," Hyacinth replied, "but Ralph is such a nice boy. Didn't mean nothin' by it I'm sure. He's told me all about hisself. Tried once to run away with the circus and all. Could we go next summer, please, Mama? And look at the lions?" she asked, purposely changing the subject.

"You sure do talk a piece of jumble," Nannie laughed. "We'll just see about that circus if'n they let colored folks in. You never knew what be the rules."

"But he said he'd take me."

"Well, we won't have none a that. No, no, no! Never know what might come off 'a that."

"Why are you so afraid, Mama?" cried Hyacinth. "You always tell me what I can't do, can't say, can't look at! Why?"

"And is I ever wrong?" replied her mother, softly. "Have I ever lied to you or directed you wrong?"

"No, Mama," said Hyacinth, suddenly remembering "the event."

"You got to be afraid, cause fear will keep you safer than anything else."

As if this lesson needed another demonstration and an affirmation, shortly afterwards, when Hyacinth and her mother were trudging home after a cleaning job that took them past the courthouse square, they saw a large crowd of angry men and boys gathered in front of the entrance to the building. This strange and unfocused mob, made up of small groups, came together quickly and broke apart again, like a boiling stew. Nannie grabbed Hyacinth's hand roughly and pulled her away, but Hyacinth said, "No Mama, I want to see what's happening."

"No you don't, child. This is no place for us. You hear that word they shoutin': 'lynch him.' We got to run. Nothin' but danger here. And I never thought ... here ... again ... thought that was all over and left behind down south."

With this, Nannie started to walk faster, pulling Hyacinth behind her. Before they reached the edge of the square, two large white men stepped in front of them.

"What you be afraid of then, Misses?" shouted one of them, grabbing Nannie roughly by her sleeve. "We ain't stringin' up no Nigras today. Got a murderin' white man holed up in the jail just wanted to get his neck stretched. Yes, sir, a neck stretching is about to happens. You want maybe to watch? Ain't your turn yet. I recognize you, sure enough. But it'll come. Maybe we'll find that man of yours what run away...Don't you fret. We got a nice friendly rope here for him."

The other man took of his cap and threw it up and caught it in one quick motion as if he were celebrating. "Yippee," he cried. "Why Edgar, you do talk fine? Ain't it a grand day for a lynchin'?" Both men laughed and hurried off toward the courthouse door.

Nannie seized Hyacinth by the hand and they started to run together, past the dry goods store and the shuttered shop next door where some prankster had circumcised the name plate to read "old...Jew." All the way down East Main they hurried until South Calumet where they finally slowed. Only then, as the town began to recede behind them, did they slow to a fast walk. Hyacinth could see that her mother was crying, silently, with tears streaming down her face. When they reached home and shut the door, Hyacinth felt enormous relief, as if they had escaped some terrible danger. She knew better than to ask immediately about what had happened. Her mother would tell in her own time, without any prompting. She always did explain her strange moods when they came on, even if the reasons made no sense to Hyacinth.

That evening, when the night hovered over their small house like the wings of a dark bird, Nannie surprised her by asking, "Do you know, girl, what we just saw?"

"No, Mama, I don't know that word 'lynchin' and why they was a crowd, and why those men yelled at us. Why was you so afraid and drug me away so quick. I been puzzling."

"What a mess of questions," cried Nannie. "But I s'ppose you're old enough now to know. So I'll tell you the story I've been waitin' to 'splain. Come sit here and I'll tell you, but you got to keep your questions to yourself. Don't stop me 'til I'm done or maybe I just won't finish. It ain't easy for me, with you interruptin' me and making me 'splain what's plain as your eyes and ears will tell you if you just hold on."

"OK, Mama, yes, please tell me, and I'll sit on my tongue."

"Better still, you set right in the middle of that sofa couch there, and I'll sit myself down right here in this chair. Now, no interruptin' me."

Hyacinth sat down on the couch, settling into a space between the lumps made by protruding springs. Her mother drew up the only other chair in the room and sat right in front of her. As if an afterthought, she placed her warm hand on Hyacinth's forehead and pushed back a curl of hair. Then she took Hyacinth's hand in her own and covered it with the other.

"Your daddy and I come here to Marion 'bout fifteen years past and found this little house where we are just now. We was mighty happy to be gone from Kentucky and dirt-farming and we had nothing but a life of happiness spread out before us. Then I was gettin' big with child, with you, Hyacinth, and you was born to the proudest mama and papa that ever lived. Your daddy love to pick you up and hold you way up in the air: 'So God could observe you better,' he always said. He'd sing to you in his sweet, sweet voice. He was the gentlest man alive and I never saw the like."

"I knew it!" cried Hyacinth. "I was sure I knew him!"

"Yes you did, child, yes you did."

"But where did he go then? Why ain't he here? Where is he?"

"Now you just hush up and let me tell it my way. You promised and a promise is always meant to be kept."

"Yes, Mama. Tell it."

"Like I say," Nannie resumed, sighing, "We had this little house here and your daddy found hisself a fine job working at some of the big houses downtown in Marion as a gardener. He had a kind'a magic touch 'bout green things. You know that's why we named you after some flower. Oh, how he loved them flowers! And he trimmed and edged and planted the gardens of Mr. and Mrs. Turnbull and old Doc Watson, and then the Pinkneys...you don't know 'bout them 'cause they departed the town a long time ago. He made their gardens glow bright in the summer with flowers and trees and then he delivered wood chop and tended coal furnace in winter. Sometimes he come home covered with good black dirt or coal ash and we'd laugh and laugh about how he had become so dark he wasn't no more than a shadow at night, creepin' about followin' the light of the moon."

"But Mama!"

"Hush, I say," repeated Nannie and she stopped and fell silent.

Hyacinth could see the sadness that had suddenly come over her as she prepared to resume. She knew the hard part was coming on.

"You was 'bout two years old one warm spring day...but wait. Let me go back a piece. It was late winter when your daddy was just beginnin' to plan for the summer gardens when he came home one day actin' very strange. He told that Miss Elizabeth Pinkney...they lived, as I recollect, up on North Vicksburg Street...you know, where the cemetery be. Anyway, he says that young Miss Elizabeth had started up to follow him 'round when he worked. Lots a young ones want to watch you work. I know that and so do you, I 'pect, already. But he said there was something strange goin' on and he didn't like it. She had took to teasing him, and he said that once she asted him why he didn't take his shirt off in the heat of the day when the sun got so bright. I didn't like that, none at all, and I told him right then: 'You be careful now. You know that folks is as changeable and fierce as a summer storm comin' up. One day all sunny and the next full of rumblin', high black clouds.' You know that yourself, Hyacinth, don't you? You seen that when we are cleaning. One day Miss Sunny; the next, Miss Stormy and never satisfied.

"Anyways, your daddy promised to be careful and look out for young Miss Pinkney, but he couldn't hardly order her away or speak to her mother 'bout anything other than where to place the petunia bed or how high up to trim them bushes. So I reckoned it was just gonna happen no matter. And it did. One hot afternoon shortly after, he come runnin' home, sweat pouring off him like from a rain shower, and he took me by the hand and says: 'Lovely Nannie...' I remembered his sweet hurried words. 'Nannie,

I got to be leavin' right now. Help me pack up a knapsack and a bit of food. I'm goin' to head over to the river and try to get across to Missouri. I'll only travel at night. Help me, darlin.'

"'What happened?' I asked, 'What you done?'

"'Nothin, except bein' a black man what works in the garden. But that young Miss Pinkney. She followed me 'round today askin' all sorts of questions. Then she ask sudden if I'd be wantin' to kiss her. 'Just to see,' she said. But I said no, and I told her to go find her mama in the house and leave me be to my work. So she starts gettin' angry, and stamps the ground with her fine, little leather shoes and say, 'If you don't, I'll tell.' Nannie, what was I to do? So I leaned over so she could kiss my check, and then she slapped me hard on the face.'

"'Don't you dare!' she cried out, and run off into the house. So I just set my tools down right there and left, sayin' not one word and not even lookin' back. I walked slow, 'cause a black man runnin' is bound to capture attention and here I am. They'll be comin' for me soon and I got to leave.'

"'But what if she didn't tell,' I asked him, knowing all along that it was dangerous even to think that.

"'Don't matter. They'll be here with a rope, sure as I'm standin' in this house. So help me Nannie.'

"And that," said her mother, "was the last I ever seen him. About eight years gone now, and he said he'd send for us. But I'm still waitin', always waitin' and hopin'."

"Did they come for him? Did they chase him? Did he let her kiss him, really?"

"Now Hyacinth, there you go wantin' to know everything there is that I can't tell you. But I just don't know what happen'. Didn't have time to contemplate it.

"But the next day," she resumed, "that sheriff man done come by and asked for your daddy. Told me that he had stole somethin' out from the Pinkney house. So I figured, little Miss Pinkney just told her mama a lie, or maybe it was a trick to catch him up; don't know. But he was right to leave. They would've strung him up; I know that in my heart, although it make me sad when I recollects. And walkin' in town today, seein' all them menfolk with faces full of hate. They would be happy as not to lynch him up for no reason at all. Yes, they would 'a done it."

"But why don't he just come back now, Mama? After so long? Why don't he send for us?"

"I don't rightly know, Hyacinth, but 'til that day, you and I will just wait for him. We does our work and keeps our eyes on the ground in front of us and still we'll see and know everything goin' on in this town and pass invisible so as when he do come back—and he will—we just all disappear together and nobody knows we is gone. I guess, Hyacinth, that's how us folks have got ta live: always wantin' and wishin' and starin' down. And the past always circlin' round to catch you up. But I sure have done me a portion of wishin' and I'm blessed tired with that."

Poor Mama! When these thoughts of her mother came on strongest Hyacinth could almost hear her say: "all that waitin' and still nothin' ever comin'." And Hyacinth wondered if she would be like Mama and just wait and wait "'til nothin' comin'." Would she be waiting like that? Or did she have the strength to be different?

Three Women

Hyacinth had no training as a nurse and no special knowledge of anything medical except always to approach a sick person from his left side (as her mother cautioned her) and a natural kindness toward those too ill to care for themselves. When old Doc Watson called on her that warm summer evening, it was a surprise, because very few white men with good intentions had ever approached the cabin on the edge of town, where she lived. Most surely never at night. When he knocked at the door, Hyacinth still wore a bright bandana around her head and was putting up the broom from sweeping the kitchen. The sound stirred her for a moment until she realized it was just a neutral rapping, indicating no special enthusiasm or anticipation: just someone wanting her attention.

She walked slowly toward the door that opened into the living room, but paused before raising up the latch. There was no glass around the entrance and the joined slat-wood with two crossbeams had no peephole like the one in the fancy house where she cleaned regularly. More than once when she was alone, she had stood, squinting out through the strange glass eye, pretending to be the lady of the house, deciding if she should answer, and calculating if the man she imagined standing impatiently outside should be admitted. Whoever it was here, tonight, at the edge of the darkened town was insisting that she open the door.

Doc Watson stood on the wooden landing outside, hat in hand. When the door opened slightly, Hyacinth made no gesture of invitation, and the two stood for a moment in an uncomfortable embrace of silence. Light from the single gas lamp in the living room cast a yellow shaft on his face but only etched her figure as a dark shadow.

When she made no movement to allow him to enter, he spoke:

"Very sorry to bother you, it being nighttime, Miss Hyacinth, but I'm in sharp need of someone to help me out."

Hyacinth was quiet for a moment while she tried to read the message behind his words and then she replied, opening the door a bit wider but still standing squarely across it:

"Oh, it be you, sir," she exclaimed, and then paused. "But I don't see how's I could help much seeing that I got full-up daily work already."

"It's not that, Hyacinth. It's for the evenings. Nights in fact. You know the Murphys on Franklin Avenue up near Main St. You might'a heard tell of them: old Ben Murphy, Harriet his wife and that daughter Ellen. Kinda strange family, but Ben is mighty sick and is taken to his bed most of the time. Needs tending to and the women seem to be able to manage during the day. But they also need their sleep. So I was thinking you could come ’round after your duties elsewhere and cook dinner and then watch him during the night. They’ll set up a bed for you in his room and you can be there when he needs assistance getting up and so.”

Watson shifted his weight from side to side as if he were standing on the unsteady bridge of a rocking boat.

“The pay would be OK too,” he added.

Hyacinth looked at him with curiosity, but said nothing.

“It wouldn’t be for too long, I expect,” he continued. “Maybe a month or two. He ain’t got more time in him than that.”

Still she was silent.

“And one more thing. Nothing to cause a worry for you, but you’ll notice right off, and so I’ll tell you up front that those two women don’t talk to each other much. In fact, not a single word passes between them as far as I can figure. No need for me to spell out the reasons, not even sure myself. But it would be a help to have someone there to break up the silence.”

Finally, Hyacinth replied: “I ’spose I could do it. If you say only a month or two.” She opened the door just a bit wider, not to let him in, but as a gesture of accepting. She wasn’t embarrassed about the modest interior. It was clean and always neat. The rag rug she and Mama had hooked out of old clothes sat exactly at the center of the small living room. Every other piece of furniture sat in its expected place: the spindle table and gas lamp, the walnut rocking chair with the woven cane seat, the small, faded purple couch. She just preferred to conclude their business there at the doorway.

"I could do it," she repeated.

"That's just fine, Hyacinth. I thank you. You can start tomorrow evening if that suits. You just go up to the house. It's number 25. You'll remember, won't you? I'll let them know you're comin'. And thank you again."

He turned and walked down the single wooden plank step and onto the hard mud path that led out to the street.

Hyacinth remained at the open door, watching him disappear into the shadows. For a moment or two, she wondered what kept the two women who lived together from speaking to each other. She knew there had been times of stillness with Mama, when they just sat together after a meal or worked to tidy the house. However, these were the silences of love, when nothing needed saying. To keep quiet for some other reason; never to speak? That was a puzzle, and Hyacinth wondered for a moment if this was how white folks acted when you wasn't around them. Maybe they just couldn't feel love like she felt toward Mama.

The next afternoon, after she had finished cleaning at the Turnbulls house and Mrs. Turnbull had walked her through each room, casting a critical eye to catch out some oversight of her work, some speck of dust or unplumbed picture frame, she walked the several blocks over to Franklin St. and the Murphy house. Like several other structures on the block, the house was set back from the street with a lawn in front, a curved brick walkway, and a three steps-up landing to the front door. The house itself was two stories, covered in white clapboard, with blue shutters aside the windows. Two large elm trees, like sentinels in green uniform, stood at either side of the house. Because of the width of the lot, Hyacinth could see around back to a large garden with several sheds. As she approached, she wondered if she should walk to the rear entrance, the way that most of her ladies insisted. But the doctor had told her to go to the front, and so she walked carefully up the steps and took the hinged knocker, shaped like a hand, and rapped it against the metal plate embedded in the door. A deep thud echoed inside. She waited.

After half a minute or so, there was a slight commotion and the door swung inward. Standing in front of her was an elderly woman, with carefully done-up white hair, wearing a tight, flowered housedress, something that might have fit her figure better several years previous. In the gloom of the hallway, her face seemed almost featureless, her skin pale and shiny. Her blue eyes were the shade of a humid summer sky and her eyebrows just wisps of bleached white tufts.

"You must be Hyacinth," she said loudly, reaching out her hand and then letting it fall, heavily.

"Yes, Miss Murphy?"

"It's Mrs. Murphy, if you please. Come in, girl. Don't just stand in the doorway."

"Doc Watson asked me to come 'round after work to be helping you and Miss Murphy. Should I be goin' round the back next time I come? Maybe you'd want that."

"Might be for the best, yes. Door's always open there, so you can just let yourself into the kitchen. But for now, please come in."

She retreated into the hallway and Hyacinth closed the door behind herself.

"Kitchen's in the back. You're to make supper. You'll see what's to cook when you look around. Just make three separate trays: one for Mr. Murphy—although he hasn't got much appetite—one for me; I eat in the dining room; and one for Sister Ellen who'll be eating in the kitchen with you. You're welcome to take some of what you cook for yourself. Come on back now and I'll show you."

Mrs. Murphy led the way through the hall and toward the open doorway at the end. Light spilled out from it onto the dark wood floor and in the reach of its glare revealed green and white wallpaper, with baskets of flowers and swirls of garlands.

Hyacinth followed behind, past an archway that opened into a parlor, a door ajar on the other side leading into a dining room, and then past a staircase. Taking in all this geography, she wondered at the accent of the woman who walked in front of her. It did not seem to be from Marion, but much deeper and thicker from somewhere south where the vowels ran together in lazy rivulets of sound and the words ended before they were supposed to. In fact, it was more like her Mama's, but not as friendly.

The kitchen was bright in the late afternoon sun that streamed into the window behind the sink. The room was large. A big Sears icebox with several wooden doors and brass handles stood in the corner. A wide black cook stove with a curved exhaust pipe leading to the wall behind it, and a bucket of coal alongside sat opposite. There was a small round table and two chairs in the corner near the icebox and a larger worktable in the center of the room. A cupboard with twin doors stood next to a sink. Despite the hour, the stove radiated heat. It would just require stoking and a fresh supply of fuel to heat up the surfaces.

"I'll leave you then to get busy, Hyacinth. You'll find anything you need. Fresh-killed chicken in the icebox and some peas to be shelled. My husband does like his peas! I'm not sure he'll eat much else. You can try, however. The rest of us..."

Saying this, she walked back into the hallway and disappeared.

Hyacinth sat down at the table for a moment to rest. Her long day at the Turnbulls—the longest and most demanding in her week—had exhausted her, and she usually just meandered home to a light meal and then to bed. For a moment, she closed her eyes and then opened them when she heard a sudden rustling. Standing before her and staring down at her was a middle-aged woman, dressed in a brown skirt and a white blouse. Her posture was erect, suggesting that she wore a tight corset. Her face was set in an expression of incipient disapproval, prepared to utter some correction. Her most striking feature was her hair: bright red curls, so tightly rounded and sparsely scattered across her head that her shiny scalp showed through.

"You are Hyacinth, then? I'm Ellen Murphy. I presume, since you are here, that Mrs. Murphy let you in. Did she explain your duties to you?"

"Yes, ma'am," Hyacinth responded. "I'm to make three separate dinners and then go up to tend your father."

"Exactly. And did she tell you anything about Mr. Murphy?"

"Not really. Doc Watson, he..."

"Just like her, of course, to assume!" Ellen interrupted. "I work all day at school, teaching those rascals and stubborn no-goods to read and write, and then I come home and have to pick up all the loose ends she leaves untied. What does that woman do during the day, I ask you?"

Hyacinth remained silent, knowing that the question required no answer.

"The doctor must have told you that my father is very ill. He has the wasting disease. Deadly for anyone who worked at the mines as long as he did. Not that he ever went underground. Just sat at the entrance all day, weighing the wagonloads that came out of the pit. Putting down notes in a big record book like Lucifer himself. But he always came home with the grime all over him, black as an imp."

She stopped abruptly. "It's made him sick. He needs help particularly at night. That's why you're here. For now, I'll let you get on with your work. I'm in my bedroom grading essays. Just call me when my dinner is ready."

She turned and left the kitchen. Hyacinth stood up and thought about the two women. They were very different. The wife was slow and southern, and Ellen more a daughter of Illinois. Whatever the wall raised up between them, it must be something high, she thought. Hyacinth warned herself to be careful.

Walking over to the icebox, she peered into the top compartment and affirmed the presence of a large cake of ice, and then opened the door below it where she found the chicken, bristling with pinfeathers and set on a plate. She took it out, along with a tub of lard, and placed both on the worktable next to the bowl of shell peas. She found that the cupboard held flour and corn meal and leavening and so she decided to bake a passel of biscuits with gravy from the chicken drippings.

She worked steadily but stopped every few minutes to listen. There was no noise in the house; at least none she could hear. It was strange to be in a house full of people and no one but herself making any sound. A house, she thought, should always be filled with the clamor of people talking, making a commotion with their feet, releasing a sigh of pleasure or relief or just a plain sigh like talking to yourself, knowing you were alive, and maybe a door slamming shut: noises regular or sudden, but always noises. This was a curiously silent house, except, she learned later, when the wind came up and it creaked and moaned.

Toward seven, with the red sun settling down into a nest of bushes in the back garden and the light dimming in the kitchen, Hyacinth finished her cooking and arranged three plates of chicken and peas and biscuits and flour gravy. She set one onto the kitchen table for Miss Murphy and carried the other, down the hall, into the dining room, placing it on the table. Returning to the kitchen, she laid the third plate on a tray and walked with it back into the hall. Stopping for a moment, she had no idea what to do. Should she search for the two women? Should she shout out?

"Miss Murphy, Mrs. Murphy," she called, loudly. "Dinner be set." Hearing nothing, she climbed up the steps to a landing on the second floor. All the doors remained closed except one. She walked toward it.

Inside the large bedroom, in the dim light, she could see a form propped up on a pillow lying on a four-poster bed.

"Mr. Murphy," she said softly, "it's Hyacinth here wit' your dinner."

The figure emitted a moan and then slurred a few words that sounded like, "Not hungry."

Hyacinth approached the bed (from the left side) and looked at the man who was lying as if he had been sunk into the same position for days. He was wearing a pajama shirt, wide open at the collar, revealing a patchwork of mottled reddish skin covered with fine white hair. His face was expressionless except that his mouth was open slightly with a thin ribbon of drool that had oozed onto his chin. He was mostly bald, although there were grey clumps that covered the tops of his ears. His eyes were sharp and mean, and when Hyacinth looked into them, she had to turn away.

"I'll just set you food down right next to the bed," she said, still not looking full-on into his face. "I 'spect you'll be hungry soon. I made you a nice chicken dinner wit' peas and all. Don't know if they told you, but I'm here to help you out during the night."

She set the tray down onto the small table next to the bed and then reached over and pulled up the pillows that had cramped down around his waist.

"Can't eat if you ain't properly upright," she said.

He said nothing for a moment and then, in a weak voice, asked, "Where are they? Why isn't it one of them here?"

Hyacinth thought for a moment, and then replied, "I think eating their dinner which I set out for them. Just like they told me."

He said nothing, but leaned over to stare at the food on the table.

Hyacinth waited for a minute and then picked up a spoon and carefully slid a number of peas onto it. Placing her left hand on his forehead, she advanced the spoon toward his mouth. He took the bite, chewed slowly, and then swallowed.

"I'm dying, you know. So what's the point of eating? They're just waiting for me to be gone. Then they can tussle over who gets this room."

Hyacinth placed a piece of chicken on a fork and advanced it toward his mouth. He shook his head.

"What are you doin', girl?" he said, slowly leaning back, and shaking his head. "Looks like if I don't eat it'll come on sooner, won't it?"

Hyacinth puzzled whether to try to get him to eat, but in the end, she just took the plate down to the kitchen. Mrs. Murphy was just placing her dish in the sink.

"I see he didn't eat," she exclaimed, looking at the dish Hyacinth was carrying. "No surprise. I guess he just refused."

"Yes, ma'am."

"We tried, or at least I did. Can't speak for that dried-up old daughter of his, looking like some old piece of fruit left on the tree to wither in the sun. As if she could help! Just imagine. Never left home; never had a beau. Why when I met him and we were married, it was like I was coming to move in with his first wife still living. It's not healthy. No, indeed, it's not healthy. You got to try to get out in the world. After a bit she just never said another word to me. Just moved over an inch and made me squeeze into a tiny space, like she couldn't stand me to share—even the waitin' on him. I asked him about it, but he refused to send her out. Said he needed her to be near; needed both of us. Mind you, girl, I'm the one you answer to here. Not her." She hesitated for a moment: "I suppose I shouldn't be telling you all this, except to explain what you're going to find out anyway, I guess."

Hyacinth said nothing, trying to appear busy with putting up the leftover food. Harriet followed her with an intense look for a moment, and then turned and walked out of the kitchen.

Hyacinth put the remaining portion of food in the icebox and stacked the plates in the sink. Before she finished the washing up, she wanted to sit down and think. Mrs. Murphy's words troubled her, and not just because they were burdened with so much anger and hatred. She wasn't sure she wanted to know what conflicted the two women. Instead, there was something else: the words that seemed to describe herself: "never had a beau." Was that also her? Would she be that apple hanging on the tree that someone forgot to pick? She had loved Mama and worked hard to ease her into old age. Was that all she was good for...that and work? It made her puzzle about the future.

When she finished her work and a brief meal of the leftovers, she went back upstairs to the bedroom, lit the lamp, and arranged Mr. Murphy's covers. When he asked for water, she went back down and fetched a pitcher and a glass. This time, when she entered the room, she found Mrs. Murphy sitting on the corner of the bed, holding her husband's hand.

"You sleep now, Ben Murphy. If you want something, just ask that colored girl; she's here to help you all night."

He mumbled something but the sounds didn't fit together into proper words.

"Her name's Hyacinth. You'll remember that! Strange name for a girl like that."

Standing up, she left the room, but paused to smile at Hyacinth.

About a half hour later, Ellen walked quietly into the

room.

"Asleep yet, Papa?" she asked, sitting down on the bed in exactly the same spot, and touching the frail hand that rested atop the quilt covering him. He scarcely opened his eyes when she placed the palm of her hand on his forehead. Shaking her head, as if in confirmation or, maybe, concern, she stood up and walked out carefully to make no noise.

Hyacinth returned every evening, walking into the open kitchen door to prepare three separate plates for each of the Murphys and then spent a troubled night tending to the fitful sleep of her patient. Over the next several weeks, Mr. Murphy sank further into unconsciousness, with only a few, sudden lucid moments when he was sure to demand his wife or his daughter.

More and more during this time, Hyacinth had learned of the strange rituals in the house that kept the two women apart in their pattern of separation. Piece by piece, she learned more about the two and the bonds that held them in thrall to this weak, dying man. Each of them occupied her own special place and routine, punctuated with the same nightly rituals. After dinner in the dining room, Mrs. Murphy often sat in the parlor, reading by the dim light of a lamp or sewing. If ever someone called—and that was rare—she answered the door, never Ellen. The latter, after the school day and following dinner in the kitchen, retired to her bedroom and only emerged to say goodnight to her father. If the two ever met in the hall or accidentally entered the kitchen at the same time, they never spoke but passed with a sudden stiffness that was the only sign of mutual recognition.

Hyacinth learned Ellen's story, related as if it were a tidbit of current gossip from Mrs. Murphy. Once there had been a boy, whose courtship ended abruptly. Maybe Mr. Murphy disapproved of the lad and made her break it off, she speculated. After this one chance slipped away for whatever the reason—although Mrs. Murphy's voice lowered when she recounted it implying something improper—this turned out to be her only chance. Ellen remained at home, first the aging daughter to her two parents and then, when her mother passed, the companion and housekeep of her father.

"Yes," Harriet Murphy exclaimed when recounting this story. "She's a jealous daughter that wanted to keep her father entirely to herself. I never understood it," she continued. "And when her father and I married, and we two met for the first time, it was about the last time she purposefully spoke to me. I tried to get Mr. Murphy to say something to her, but he just shrugged it off as a spite that women folks allow themselves. Sometimes I even detected his pleasure—being the center of a scuffle between two women. If I ever brought up her leaving again—and I did it sometimes at first—he just said he needed her close by. So I've lived with it. With her here haunting our years. When he goes, I don't know what will happen. Don't even know if he's made a will or who the house will go to. But I'm not the one to leave...you understand me, don't you, Hyacinth? I'm his wife after all!...It's so nice to have someone to talk to: to listen to me."

Gradually, in bitter drops, Ellen recounted her story, just a few bits each time, as if the sour taste of the words stopped her cold. Slowly it became clear to Hyacinth what had transpired. In the beginning, after Ben Murphy's first wife passed, he had stepped out with several widows in town: "only those broken-in fillies—not broken down, mind you" he'd always joke to Ellen. Perhaps he was trying them out, she suggested. Would they make a good wife, he wanted to know. How would they treat him? Then along came Harriet, a Kentucky woman whose husband brought her up to Marion. He died suddenly in an accident.

"She was quick to be looking around to get married again and as soon as possible," Ellen recounted. "Oh, you could see the need in her eyes—hungry and greedy for a man. You can still see it! She played him. Pretended to be a perfect wife, to wait on him hand and foot. No doubt she thought he had money, looking at this big house we have. But there isn't anything else. When she found out that still didn't stop her. She married him, and moved in with us and tried to push me aside. Away from my own father! But I wouldn't let go. I couldn't move out and leave her alone with him. You can appreciate that, can't you, Hyacinth. A person has to fight for what belongs to them. He needs me as much as her. Maybe more."

Hyacinth tried to understand both women, and she could see the justice on each side, but she refused to judge them; it wasn't her place to do so. For that reason, Harriet and Ellen became friendlier, treating her less as a servant and more as a confidant; both of them seemed to have stored-up conversations and feelings that had nowhere else to go. More and more, they sought her out and established a pattern of talks that seemed to occur at regular and distinct times, as if they had agreed on a schedule to parcel out their solitary time with her.

None of them expected Mr. Murphy to hold onto life so long. However, he finally fell into permanent unconsciousness so that it was difficult to say if he still lived. When Doc Watson came to call the last time, he warned that the end was approaching fast. His prediction proved to be accurate. Ben Murphy died quietly, without protest, in the middle of the night two days later. Attuned to every creak and moan of the house and the motions of its dwellers, the absence of his shallow breathing stirred Hyacinth from her watchful sleep that night, and she knew he was gone. She rose from her cot and lit the gas lamp by his bedside. He lay, rigid with the effort of his last gasp of air, mouth and eyes wide open in astonishment at his own death. She gently shut his eyes and pushed up his slack jaw. Taking his hands out from beneath the quilts, she laid them across his chest and then walked carefully out of the room to waken his wife and daughter.

She did not wish to return to the bedroom to listen to the strange duet of their grieving. Instead, she went down to the kitchen and busied herself with coffee and breakfast. By the time she finished, both women, still in their nightshirts and with tear-stained, stark white faces, descended from upstairs. "So same-like," Hyacinth said to herself, "like two sister spirits." She had placed two plates on the dining room table, and set bread and bacon and scrambled eggs on platters. Instead of sitting down, however, Ellen seized a plate, served herself, and retreated to the kitchen, leaving Harriet to eat alone.

Over the next days, Hyacinth stayed on to work at the big house on Franklin Street, cooking, washing up, and helping prepare for the small wake that followed the service at the new funeral home up on North Market Street where they had taken the body. Late one afternoon, when she had returned to her own house, Doc Watson appeared at the door. Hyacinth answered his knock and as before stood square in the frame.

"I need to come in," he exclaimed. "Need to explain some things to you, Hyacinth."

She backed up and allowed him to enter.

"You want something?" she asked. "A glass o' water? I could make coffee if you got a mind."

"No, Hyacinth. Nothing thanks. Just sit down. I want to talk to you. Ask you something."

She waited for him to sit and then eased herself onto the couch.

"I suppose the lawyer could have come and explained better, but Mrs. Murphy insisted that I talk to you."

He leaned forward, closer to her in the small room.

"You see, they read the will and old Mr. Murphy left the house and everything in it to them both. The legal words are 'joint tenancy,' but you don't need to bother yourself with understanding that. It just means that they both own the house together, equal parts outright. There's something else. If one of them decides to leave...even just to move out, then the other gets the share. Do you understand?"

"Oh yes, sir, I understand, yes sir. It mean that both of them got to stay there 'til one be gone. Seems like he's wantin' to make trouble from down in the grave. That's what I think."

"I dare say you're right, Hyacinth...but there's something else. Not in the will, but it concerns you. Both of those women want you to come live with them. I don't know what you did, but they both think highly of you. Seems as if they need you."

Hyacinth smiled and then shook her head. "Probably it me being quiet all the time, just listening. Could just as like been a dog or a pet cat, I think."

"No, Hyacinth. Not at all. They really want you to stay. You could keep your day jobs and just make dinner and spend the nights."

"Don't think I'd like that much. And you promised, first off, didn't you, that it would be a month or two."

"I know that's what I said, but things have changed."

"I don't think I ken do it, sir. I got to stay here where Mama lived. That there is a bad house, full o' night noises and angry spirits, and them two dividing up the territory like two fightin' men. I'd always be in the middle of somethin' where I didn't want to be. Both waitin' for the other one to go. No, sir, I got to get on with my own life. I seen enough of them already. I got my memories of Mama, and then I got me."

Saying this, she stood up. It shocked her that she could almost be firm with a white man, to realize that she had that strength to end the conversation so bluntly. Doc Watson didn't seem to notice and he stood too.

"I'm not surprised, Hyacinth. In fact, I warned them both that you had your own mind. That you was yourself and wouldn't answer to nobody. I wish you luck, for it. I really do."

He walked toward the door and pulled it open. Turning around, he said again: "Good luck to you, Miss Hyacinth. Excepting I don't suppose you're gonna' need it."

Orly Blair

The *Egyptian-Press Semi-Weekly* appeared first in 1872, published out of an old brick townhouse on Public Square until it moved in 1907 to a large new building with a modern linotype machine on West Franklin Avenue just a block away. Shortly after this repositioning, Orly (short for Orville) Blair, a young and impatient dropout from the Normal School in Carbondale, signed on as reporter, writer, telegraph operator and general printer's devil for the publication. As one of only three employees besides the editor-publisher, who made all the large decisions about design and content, Orly clipped stories from the Chicago and St. Louis papers that arrived daily by fast train, took in advertising copy and often wrote squibs about the latest women's tonics or the price of coal or special store sales from favored retailers. Often during the morning, he received notices of town events from owners of the opera house or the titles of church sermons or mention of their endless catalog of moral suasion events and abstinence meetings. He wrote small stories about relatives visiting the town's important families and minor mishaps and accidents that struck the nearby coal mines in Herrin, if the seriousness of casualties merited mention. Almost every night he helped set print and even, once, drew a cartoon that appeared on the front page. He wrote the words for advertisers to promote sales and helped clothing stores choose among the many formatted pictures available for ladies' and gentlemen's wear that were on offer. In other words, he was an indispensable reporter and the main source of the official news that Marion knew about itself.

Orly was the only son among four children and the youngest, being a surprise gift to his parents after an interlude of many barren years. While his parents had invested considerable energy to make good marriages for his sisters, as a late-comer and a boy, he shone in his father's eyes and felt the weight of anxious expectations.

"A ripe apple never falls far from the tree," his father loved to say proudly. At first Orly was puzzled by this adage until he finally realized that his father wanted him to be a court clerk like himself. Unfortunately, Orly didn't have the mind or patience for legal matters. Nor did he ever take to learning Latin phrases, nor interest himself much in the nature of contracts and wills. Instead, he was an excitable, curious boy, who loved to contemplate what he later called "human nature." He even sat sometimes alongside old Mr. Patterson, down by the courthouse, listening to him go on with his long-winded stories of the town's history.

In all other ways, Orly was a middling sort. Not of extreme height or particular good looks, his presence was often overlooked, but his absence always subtracted a feeling of comfort and completeness from the group of his chums. He made friends easily because he demanded little, spoke well, but listened even better, and for these reasons, he was always included in conversation and asked on social outings. Acquaintance came easily to him and he was as comfortable among the oldest families in town as well as the new foreigners who increasingly came into Marion to shop or attend school. As for the church things that meant so much to other members of his family—two of his sisters were prominent in the local Presbyterian Anti-Saloon League—he could take some religion, but leave most of it. Exhortations about sin and salvation meant little to him for they seemed to be mere words that failed to describe the real things that people did or believed in, and he preferred reality in all its odd and unexpected quirks to the all-purpose advice of proverbs and sermons. He was, as his mother once said of him, "Too interested in people to make judgments." He knew that she meant this as a mild rebuke, but for him it was a compliment of a higher order.

Orly could divide his childhood by an indecision to choose between his two great loves: reading and sports, and so he followed both avidly as long as he could. He devoured the newest American novels by Stephen Crane and Theodore Dreiser, although his high school teacher forewarned him of the scandalous and prurient interest of modern authors who wanted only to peer behind the curtains of propriety to search for the hidden dirt of human folly. He also read and marveled at Edward Bellamy's Utopian novel, *Looking Backward*, and for a time, he attended the local Bellamy club, sitting in the back row and listening to the grandiloquent optimism of the speakers who sought to make something called Nationalism into a new American political calling. Yet he was just as happy playing a scruffy game of baseball. Most of all, he enjoyed centerfield, where, with his keen eyes, he could chase the towering flies that often floated his way.

Until he was seventeen or so, he never thought much, if anything, about what might tie these two favorite pastimes together until one day he concluded that the unity lay in character: the odd fictional inventions of writers and the real flesh and bones, the sweating and swearing companions of the baseball diamond. He liked them all for the curiosity they aroused, and not knowing quite why they acted as they did, fictional or real, he was endlessly fascinated to figure out both. Around this time, as he was learning more about himself and his aptitudes, he realized he wanted to write. Not novels, of course, or poetry, although he enjoyed thinking up the doggerel rhymes for limericks, but perhaps for a newspaper where he could monitor unfolding events and meet the men and women who were building not just Marion, but also Illinois and the nation itself. This ambition persuaded him to try out for one of the local newspapers, perhaps to work his way into reporting the stories about the people who were making the "news," or the "new" as he sometimes put it.

However, first things first. Thinking he should know more of the world before he embarked upon this adventure, he persuaded his parents to send him to Carbondale to take classes for a year. He planned to specialize in history and the new field of political economy where his knowledge was scant. Upon his return, he would begin a trial position with the *Egyptian Semi-*

Weekly. The editor, Mr. Foley, had made a sly and non-committal promise to Orly on condition that he finished a year of study. Orly wasn't entirely convinced of the trustworthiness of this promise, but thought to pursue it anyway. The other promise he extracted was from Hattie Worth. The two had been courting for over a year, and Orly was truly attracted to the slight daughter of the foreman at the Peabody mine who had been a classmate through the last few years of high school. The company brought Hattie's father to town to superintend the mine after several strikes had threatened to cripple production and burst into chronic violence. Orly wasn't quite certain what he felt about the brisk, even brutal way that Mr. Worth treated his employees, nor was he entirely convinced that the workers lacked cause, but he was fascinated by the quiet, shy way Hattie smiled and pronounced his name and looked at him with a sincerity that melted something inside him. He promised, upon his return, that he would court her seriously. Her response was a light laugh, a smile, and an almost imperceptible touch of her fingers on his wrist that he took to be an assent.

With this future settled, Orly set off to Carbondale and his year of preparation. He found lodgings quite near the school in a boarding house with several other students, all first year and, like him, "wet behind the ears" when it came to the ways of college life. What that phrase meant, when he heard it applied to them, was a self-effacing shyness in class, a frequent loss for words, and a general timidity. Outside, however, this pent-up reticence burst into endless chatter around Mrs. Dermott's dinner table usually ending on the relative prospects of the St. Louis and Chicago baseball teams.

For Orly, his studies were interesting enough, but he could not see in them the progress toward the knowledge that a newspaperman required. By Christmas time, when the winter had closed around Carbondale, when even here, in the south part of Illinois, the snow had piled up several inches, studded with tiny black diamonds of coal dust, Orly decided that he would not return to school, but ask for his job at the paper immediately, and learn to write on his own. He had long carried out a nightly regimen of copying sentences that caught his fancy from the big parlor Bible at home and from the old copy of Lamb's *Tales of Shakespeare* that he found next to it. Although the latter was a much-simplified version of the complicated plots of the Bard, Orly loved the clean prose style and tried committing some of the author's elegant phrases to heart. He also thought, upon his return, he might buy a book of speeches by Abraham Lincoln and memorize their cadences.

Almost to the day that he made the decision to return, he received an agitated letter from Mr. Foley, the owner of the *Egyptian*, begging him to return to Marion as soon as possible. The only reporter for the paper had suddenly left town "on account of marital inconveniences," and the paper was without a writer. Orly could only chuckle at the odd phrase that Foley used, but he was delighted that his return now had a purpose, or rather, two significant reasons: a real opportunity at the *Egyptian*, and a chance to see Hattie again and take up, with utter seriousness, where he had left off.

Back in Marion at the beginning of 1911, Orly commenced his new duties at the paper, rewriting stories he copied from out-of-town newspapers and penning original pieces about church doings and the social life of the town. He followed the dangerous rumblings and rumors of trouble at the mines and threats of strikes, and described the deadly accidents that seemed always to plague the railroads. He closely measured the growing tension and political struggles between Wets and Drys as townships and counties throughout Illinois gradually passed local ordinances that shut down the sale of liquor. The state law that allowed this local option had passed a reluctant and divided legislature just a few years back, and Orly understood that total prohibition failed only because big cities like Chicago and Springfield and Joliet opposed a statewide ban. But no matter where, the new law seriously circumscribed the sale of liquor: never on Sundays; not near old folks' homes; and ended ownership of taverns by giant brewers like the Busch family in St. Louis. Orly had hoped to determine who was Wet and Dry in Marion, and he wanted Mr. Foley to allow him to write political commentary on the Democrat and Republican split over the issue, but he refused. Orly thought this might be because the heavy influence of the Anti-Saloon League in the local churches had made the editor timid about the issue. When Williamson County voted itself dry later that year ("wrung out the Wets" as Mr. Foley once commented), his hesitation proved astute.

During his first days back in Marion, one other story fascinated Orly and he persuaded the editor to allow him to report on the trial of James Elmore, who had murdered his wife. He knew of the near riot when the suspect first appeared at the jailhouse, and he fully expected more trouble at the trial. Once he had finished writing copy about sermons by the editor's favorite preachers, setting type and running errands for Mr. Foley, and composing a series of articles about cures for female ailments, Orly turned to thinking about the trial that was set to begin in the spring.

When that day finally came, the *Egyptian's* new (and only) reporter was early waiting for the courthouse doors to open and the proceedings to begin. By the time the guard parted the double doors to the visitor's gallery, a crowd of thirty or so of the curious, perhaps—Orly guessed—including some of the neighbors of Elmore come to see the inevitable justice meted out with a judge's benediction and a hangman's rope. Once inside, he took a seat on the front row of benches in a raised gallery, looking down into the courtroom. The jury sat stoically: twelve stern-looking, nervous men, eyes avoiding the noisy crowd that was jostling for places to watch the proceedings. The bailiff stood guarding the wooden half-door that enclosed the jury box. Next to him there was a high, stiff-backed, raised chair for witnesses and above this sat the judge's podium with its invisible chair or stool behind it. Set off in back of the judge's stand, and against the wall were two flagpoles, one with the Stars and Stripes, and the other the old Illinois flag with its eagle and a message of union, both furled, but distinct. Around three quarters of the room were transom windows, far too high for anyone outside to peer in, but large enough to let in ample light or air if need be. With wood paneling on the walls, benches and chairs and the shiny slat-oak floor, Orly briefly imagined the inside of a ship's hull. The room was sure to echo and clatter with the words of the judge and witnesses and the long-winded speeches of the prosecutor and defense attorney. Nothing had been expended to furnish the room with anything but cheap utility, and Orly wondered if this was a visualization of simple justice or merely the stinginess of the county government.

After five minutes or so of waiting, the crowd became animated and the jurors looked around with increasing anxiety and impatience. Finally, the bailiff shouted, "Quiet in the courtroom!" From a hidden door behind the podium, Judge Pynchon emerged, untidy black robe gathered up in his fist in front, scowling at the crowd of spectators. He stepped up to his podium and seized a large wooden mallet, which he rapped sharply on the wood, making a noise like the report of a rifle.

"Order in my courtroom!" he said, and the crowd immediately fell silent. "Anyone who speaks out of turn will be expelled by the bailiff. I'll tolerate no disorder or reaction of any sort to these proceedings. Bailiff, bring in the prisoner."

The bailiff walked to the side door next to the jury box and opened it wide onto a black void. After twenty seconds or so, Deputy Longstreet emerged, followed by Elmore in handcuffs and then the sheriff. The latter looked slightly unsteady and grabbed the jury box railing to balance himself. The deputy delivered Elmore to the prisoner's table and his seated lawyer, and then he and Bennington sat slightly behind them against the wall below the spectators' gallery.

The judge smacked his gavel again to squelch the slight murmur that had arisen.

"The prisoner will stand while the bailiff reads the charge."

Elmore remained standing, and Orly pulled out his

notebook and wrote the single word: "defiant."

"James Elmore," began the bailiff, "you are accused of willfully murdering your wife on October 13, 1910, after you intentionally broke the 'Peace Bond' sworn out against you and unlawfully intruded onto her farm. You then, with malicious intent, fired two shots into your wife's body, killing her immediately. The crime of which you are accused is nothing more or less than first-degree murder. How do you, James Elmore, respond?"

Elmore looked hesitantly at the crowd of spectators as if he understood there would be no friendly or encouraging face among them. Orly wrote down the word "audience" in his notebook.

"It weren't my intent to kill her and I'm mighty sorry for the shootin', but she was yellin' something terrible, and that older boy looked to be fixing to broke my head in. Warn't first-degree nothin' like it," he repeated.

"Then you plead not guilty," said the judge.

"If you say so, I guess I do; if you want me to say it like that."

The crowd began to mutter and the judge again rapped his gavel. "Silence!" he said sternly and the crowd was quiet again. "One more hint of an outburst and I'll expel all of you!"

Satisfied that order would prevail, the judge allowed the day to proceed. It passed slowly, with the statements of the prosecution and defense consuming most of the morning. Elmore's counsel, a large man with a florid face that almost glowed red when he emphasized a point, fascinated Orly. He wore a shirt, ruffled down the front, and a black string tie, and a suit that gave him a jaunty look. Hailing from West Frankfort where he had a flourishing practice, Andrew Scott—his full name was Andrew Jackson Winfield Scott (named for the President and the General)—had a reputation for delivering murderers from the noose and persuading juries of the contribution of victims to their own demise. Elmore could only have managed to hire him by selling off all his worldly goods: his horse and saddle, boots, and whatever else he had accumulated from his sorry life of bad marriages, gambling, and roustabout labor. Whatever the verdict—a hanging or a life in the State Penitentiary—he would have no further need for such things.

After lunch, when the court reconvened, Orly took his seat up front again in the spectators' gallery, pencil and paper in hand. He had written down his reaction to the first hours and sketched the main characters in cartoon impressions: an oversized judge leaning over his podium; Elmore looking on the verge of speaking angrily; the sheriff, bleary-eyed (even more so after lunch); Scott, the lawyer, gesticulating; and the prosecutor pointing his finger. Orly was no artist and his quick outlines were merely to remind him of impressions for later use in writing his story for the paper. The one, unmistakable feeling he got, which he could not easily capture in a drawing, was the ominous tone of his fellow spectators, whose whispered comments, particularly in reaction to defense assertions, appeared touched up with threats and rage.

The intensity of this hostility to Elmore puzzled Orly so he had taken the occasion of the midday break to ask about the accused's reputation. To a person, the response was the same. Despite his naïve demeanor, Elmore was a well-known scoundrel, a part-time bootlegger, a ladies' man who had cheated two of his wives out of their property, a gambler, and a spinner of lies and perpetrator of crooked schemes. Not only the better families of Marion and the ministers and Anti-Saloon Leaguers, but even petty criminals distrusted his slippery reputation. It was quite an accomplishment, thought Orly, to alienate both sorts.

In the afternoon, Doc Watson testified that Mrs. Elmore had died almost instantly from two bullet wounds to the torso. Try as he might, Andrew Scott could not persuade him to speculate that some of the shots might have been accidental. Watson was firm about his conclusion: "I've seen and treated hundreds of bullet wounds in my day." he answered. "Sometimes if you see a shoulder wound or even a head wound, you think it could come from a stray bullet or ricochet. In this case, the shots to the stomach and chest could only come from purposeful intent. From the angle, you can see plainly that they were done up close. No accident, you can be sure."

The next witness was Mrs. Elmore's son, Matthew Williams, the only actual eyewitness to the murder. The prosecution asked him to recount the events as he remembered them.

"I just come up into the house after doing my outdoor chores. We was in the kitchen, and Mama made me a cup of coffee and I was eating a biscuit, when we heard a terrible loud knockin' at the front door. Mama said, 'You sit. I'll go. I know who it is.' And she picked up a broom what with to...I should'a gone myself, but I was tired. Should'a gone. Anyways, I heard the door bein' smashed open, and Mama began to shout and cry, and I figured it must be Elmore comin' 'round again, botherin' us. I ran to the front just as I heard a shot and then several more...don't know how many as in the confusion I couldn't count, and then Mama screamin' once. I saw Elmore then."

He pointed to his stepfather, and continued: "He was holdin' a smokin' gun. 'Get back boy,' he shouts to me, and then turns and runs outside. I could see Mama was hurt and dyin', so I ran to the neighbor's just over the hill. That's the next farm, and Mr. Oldfield come and then my brother got the sheriff. No doubt who done it."

As the boy spoke, he turned progressively paler, as if his own words, as they flowed out, were bleeding the quick out of him. He paused at the end of his account and wiped his eyes with the sleeve of his work shirt.

Andrew Scott stood and waited for Williams to collect himself. "It's a sorry thing you must have witnessed, son," he began. "A mighty rush of events and a shock. I'm sure anyone will excuse you for being confused."

"I ain't confused," said the boy softly. "I know what's I seen."

"I'm sure you think so," said Scott encouragingly. "But just let me get a few things clearer for the jury. You said Mrs. Elmore went to the front door and you only came into the hall after the shots were fired."

"Yes, sir."

"And you said your mother had picked up a broom. Did you think she might have done that to protect herself?"

"Yes, sir. She knew it to be Elmore comin' round."

"Then why did the sheriff find that cast-iron skillet lying near the body. Did your mother carry that too?"

"No, sir."

"Could it be, boy, that you picked up the skillet and

followed your mother to the door, and when you saw Elmore, maybe you threatened him with it? Wasn't that what the shooting was about?"

"But he weren't suppose' to be there. She swore out that Bond on him and he was to keep away. He had no business com' back, snoopin' 'round."

"So you admit that you threatened him."

"I don't remember right off," Williams answered quickly. "I might have been carryin' a pan. But he was pointin' his gun. Mama stepped right up to him and then he fired."

"And then what happened?" asked Scott, looking from the boy's stricken countenance to the jury and then back.

"He run out the door."

"But is that all? Didn't he thrown down the gun and grab your mother in his arms and say he was sorry...that he didn't mean it? Isn't that how he got all bloody?"

"Yes, I reckon that could'a happened. But he still had no call to shoot her. No reason at all to come by totin' a gun like that."

"Thank you," said Scott, turning away from the witness and addressing the jury. "You see things are always more complicated than they seem at first. Looks like self-defense to me, and a terrible, hurtful accident." He sat down slowly, and as he did, someone behind Orly shouted, "Damn you murderin' Elmore. Don't you think you can get off with your fancy-pants lawyer!"

Judge Pynchon leaped up and shouted to the bailiff, "Clear out those spectators right now! We'll have a recess for an hour. Jury, you are to return to the jury room. We'll have no more outbursts in this trial."

The bailiff walked toward the crowd and motioned to

the sheriff who stood uneasily and advanced with him toward the gallery. Freed from the constraint to be silent and protesting their expulsion, several spectators exited noisily through the back door spilling out in angry clots into the hallway. Following them, Orly could catch bits of furious comments: "Blaming the son! A rope is too good for him! Killed her and then he'll be gettin' off; you'll see!" Though still a small huddle of men, the group could swell quickly into a mob, and Orly feared that the idea of rough justice had already seized it. Just to measure the extent of the mood, he asked a few of the better-dressed observers, as they walked along the corridor toward the front exit, for a comment. No one would talk to him, and he took this to be another ominous sign. He knew about other instances of direct justice in the nearby area like the case six years previous when Thomas Sellers had been murdered in the mine at Herrin and then his house robbed. Orly had looked up the story in the *Twice-a-Week Williamson County News*, partly for comparison, because he knew that Elmore had already escaped lynching once. The *News* story, he commented to Mr. Foley, had read almost like encouragement. There was also the double lynching in Cairo. He wondered if some sheriffs, in neighboring counties, allowed mobs to deliver justice without interference. He was sure this would not be the case with Bennington—if he remained sober enough to quiet the crowd. However, nothing was certain.

After a quick cup of coffee at the café across the square, he went back inside the courthouse, pacing up and down the hall in front of the locked trial room until the crowd gathered again and the door finally swung open. He pushed ahead of the others and found his front row place where he could lean over and survey the whole room.

Seated again, each member of the jury looked forward, eyes seemingly unfocused, as if they had been instructed to avoid noticing each other or the crowd of spectators above them. Orly wondered if they even talked in private while sequestered for lunch. He had never served on a panel himself, and the whole trial procedure had the aura of a mysterious play in which half the characters were mimes, selected to watch in silence, knowing that they could only speak amongst themselves offstage while the other half performed a ritual of questions and answers before an audience.

When the bailiff and lawyers entered, the crowd began to comment excitedly. Only the appearance of the judge, who stared angrily at them, quieted the conversation. Then the door leading to the holding cell opened, and Elmore, followed by the deputy, emerged from the gloom that encased the frame. The sheriff was missing, and Orly wondered if he was already "indisposed."

The trial resumed immediately, and only one witness remained, Elmore himself. Orly wondered at the wisdom of his testimony, but he guessed that the defendant had insisted...out of arrogance, self-righteousness, or foolhardiness.

Elmore climbed into the witness chair, swore on the Bible, and then sat back as if he thoroughly enjoyed the attention. Jackson Scott began the questioning:

"Tell us in your own words, Mr. Elmore, what transpired on the afternoon of October 10."

"You mean the day my wife died, I guess."

"Yes."

"Well, I was hankerin' to see her and also to pick up

some property that belonged to me, seein' as how that Peace Bond had deprived me of goin' anywheres near my own house. So I went to the farm, 'bout early afternoon and knocked at the door. She took her time, and then opened up, shakin' that broom at me and tellin' me to be off. I tried to explain why I come, but she starts to yellin' somethin' awful and cussin' in a way that ought to burn a real lady's tongue. So I was about to leave, when that young Williams boy come runnin' at me with a big cast iron skillet, bigger than a plate, and was about to swing it at me. So I took up my gun to protect myself and fired out a warning shot. But just then my wife stepped up in front and must've took the bullet. Don't know what happened next. The boy starts screamin' and I guess I fired again, and then he run off. Seein' my wife fallin' down, I grabbed her and told her I didn't meant it; it was a terrible accident, and I got my shirt all bloody as she fell against me. Wasn't nothin' I could do then."

"Thank you," said the lawyer, and addressing the jury, "It's pretty clear he didn't mean it. Just a terrible accident like he says."

"Scoundrel," shouted someone from behind Orly. "Liar!"

Orly could almost feel the rising temper of the crowd as several stood and shook their fists, pushing toward the railing of the gallery and shoving him to the side. The judge smacked the podium with his gavel, and the crowd quieted just as suddenly as it erupted.

"One more outburst and you'll all go," he shouted, his face reddening with anger. After a long minute, where he sought and fixed the eyes of every spectator, he looked down to the prosecutor.

"You may begin," he said.

"I have only one question to ask this witness now that he has admitted to gunning down his own wife in a frenzy of rage. Only one question, and you'll see why."

Turning to Elmore, who was gripping the arms of the wooden witness chair as if to hoist himself higher, he asked:

"When you were fixing to break the Peace Bond that your wife swore out on you to protect herself, and when you were planning to go to the farm in spite of the sanction placed on you...and you were planning it, I'm sure the jury knows that...why did you take along with you a loaded gun? Why, if not to shoot your wife in cold blood? Tell the jury why!"

Elmore suddenly looked shocked and began to shake his head. Orly thought he heard a low moan of protest start to emerge from his mouth, but he went quiet again and just looked at the floor as if he were studying how the planks were joined.

"You have to answer," insisted the prosecutor.

"Well, I ain't gonna," said Elmore quietly. "And you can't make me. I got rights just like you does and what I told you is true and I'm through talkin', no matter what you want. Can't force a man against his will."

There was a moment of surprised silence in the courtroom, and then suddenly, someone from the gallery shouted, "Hang him up!" Other shouts followed, and Judge Pynchon jumped up, waving his hands.

"Bailiff, sheriff," he cried, "clear all those spectators out, every last one of them. Get them out of the courthouse, now! Trial will resume tomorrow!"

The bailiff and the deputy waved for the crowd to exit, and herded them into the hall and then outside to the courthouse steps. Orly followed, pushing to the middle of this group for a moment to hear what they were saying. Two black women passed by on the sidewalk looking curiously at the group, and then hurried on as if anticipating some sort of trouble. Only Thomas Patterson, seated on his customary bench seemed curious about what was happening, and he stood up slowly and edged closer to catch the conversation. Orly knew he would linger and then piece together everything he heard; perhaps he might check back with Patterson, just to get the facts in order, before he filed his story with the *Egyptian*.

It was not an evening, however, to delay long outside, as dark clouds were gathering in the west. The crowd dispersed with all but a few stragglers, who remained on the sidewalk, unaware or uninterested in the coming storm. Eventually, even Patterson seemed daunted by the threat of stormy weather, and after listening carefully, shuffled off toward home. Orly was also among the last to leave, even though he knew nothing more would transpire that day. Testimony was over and only the closing arguments remained for tomorrow. He anticipated that there would be a sharp exchange the next morning, but at the same time, he thought that the real story lay with the angry crowd, which he knew would reassemble to hear, and perhaps act on the verdict. Before the storm could blow in, he made his way back across the Square to West Main and then two blocks beyond to South Granite Street where he had his room at Widow Bickley's. The arrangement was not perfect and only temporary until he and Hattie set a date for their wedding. Still, it served him well to be close to his work and near the courthouse and large downtown churches and stores where so much of the recordable life of Marion took place.

The next morning, after a heavy breakfast—he had asked Mrs. Bickley for extra biscuits, red eye gravy and ham—he picked up an umbrella as he left, thinking that some of the most significant events of the trial might occur outside. He reached the courthouse around 10 o'clock, when the proceedings were set to begin, but he was surprised that the spectators' gallery door was already open. He entered and saw that it was almost full of men and boys with only a few women. Pushing his way to the front, he spotted the bailiff who motioned for him to approach.

"What's to happen today?" he asked.

The bailiff sidled up and said in a whisper: "You just missed the summing up. Didn't take but a minute or two each side. The jury's already deliberating and from the looks of it, it won't take much time. When the judge comes back in, you'll know they have a decision." He turned and walked back to stand next to the jury door. Then, as if by some simultaneous signal, all three doors opened. Judge Pynchon emerged slowly, his open black robe sweeping behind him. From the second door, the jury filed in and took their seats. Unlike the day before, their faces were animated, and several of them waved to friends in the gallery, as if the spell of serious deliberation had broken, and they had returned to being just ordinary folk. Elmore emerged from the last door, slowly and with difficulty, his arms still in handcuffs, followed by the deputy, his attorney and the prosecutor. Once in place, the din from the crowd, first whispering and then talking, grew louder and more excited. Everyone was present and ready, except, thought Orly, for the sheriff, and he had his suspicions about why he was late.

"Silence," cried the bailiff, just as the judge was reaching for his gavel. "All of you folks sit down and be quiet, except for Elmore here and his lawyer who got to stay put standing and face the judge."

The crowd hushed quickly in expectation, and Orly could feel the excitement pass through them as if they were watching some dangerous high-wire act of the circus. He thought for a moment that this was a perfect metaphor: the rope, a man swinging wildly—that is why they had caught their breath in collective expectation of the pronouncement of a hanging.

Judge Pynchon looked satisfied and turned to the jury.

"Have you reached a verdict?" he said slowly. "And if so, what is it?"

The well-dressed man at the end of the jury box rose and answered, his voice cracking slightly until he cleared his throat: "Yes, yes, we have."

"Well go on then, Foreman. Let us know," said the judge with impatience.

Again the foreman spoke: "We find James Elmore guilty of murdering his wife, and guilty by intent, and so, by the instructions you gave us, guilty of first-degree murder."

The crowd around Orly suddenly leaped up, some clapping, some shouting with clinched fists: "That's right! Hang him! Give him the rope!"

Judge Pynchon, fully expecting this unruly moment, let the crowd shout its approval and then suddenly banged his gavel again. There was immediate silence because no one wanted to miss the sentence.

The judge looked gravely at the crowd and then turned to Elmore: "James Elmore, by the power of the State of Illinois, I hereby sentence you to life in prison."

There was a moment of quiet. Even Elmore shook his head in disbelief. Then just as quickly, the crowd began to shout again. Orly could barely make out the words, but he knew they were threats and curses. The State of Illinois had sentenced him to life in the penitentiary, but the people of Marion were ready for death.

The judge rapped his gavel repeatedly, but now to no good effect. He then motioned to the bailiff to escort the prisoner back to his cell, and then turned and disappeared through the doorway behind the podium. With nothing left to see, and no one to berate, the crowd quickly dispersed into groups of gesticulating men, moving in angry groups into the hallway and then out the front door. It would not be long, Orly feared, before word spread and a bigger and more dangerous crowd gathered. Elmore was about to suffer his second threat of a lynching. The worst of it was the missing sheriff, although Orly thought he knew his whereabouts.

Looking back once more at the courthouse, he wondered if the heavy wooden door could be broken down easily. He turned and hurried down East Main to where dense settlement gave out into several large, dilapidated warehouses, set in helter-skelter fashion. From the chimney of one of them, thick smoke rose up in a cloud shaped like a question mark. Orly walked on the muddy path to the front door and pushed inside. The atmosphere was gloomy, but not dark, and he could make out several faces who turned inquisitively toward the open door. A rush of warm, boozy air, thick with cigar smoke and the stale smell of spilled beer and sweat, washed over him. He saw the sheriff, sitting by himself in one corner at a table. As he approached, Bennington looked up, straining to recognize the newcomer.

"You better come might quick, sheriff. There's a verdict in the Elmore case, life in prison, and it looks like there's gonna be trouble."

"What time is it? Who sent you?" was all Bennington could mumble.

"Don't matter none. It was my idea and it's real late. Just thought you might be here. I'll not let on where I found you if you come right off."

The sheriff stood up abruptly, pushing back his chair until it tipped backward and fell with a clatter. He put both hands on the table to steady himself.

"All right," he said, "fresh air won't do no harm, and I'll be obliged if you just keep silent about these premises."

"Yes, if you come now," said Orly, grabbing the sheriff's arm and escorting him out the door.

The clear air seemed to steady him, and he managed to keep up the rapid pace back to the courthouse that Orly set. By the time they reached the square, the flush on the sheriff's face had faded, and he was swinging his legs rapidly. They arrived just as a crowd of shouting men emerged from the west side of the street, walking rapidly toward the front door. In their midst, Orly caught a glimpse of a man with a long, coiled rope over his shoulder. The sheriff saw it too and quickly said to Orly, "Go round quietly to the back door and find the deputy. Tell him to take Elmore right now over to Chester where they can hold him. Go by train if you think it's safe. I'll deal with this mob of halfwits."

Orly walked on as if preoccupied, and then turned suddenly when he reached the corner of the building, not looking back to see if anyone was following. The sheriff climbed up the steps of the courthouse, almost stumbling once when he misjudged the distance. He turned, put his hands on his hips and faced the crowd. They quieted for a minute, and then someone shouted, "Give us Elmore! Can't get off this time!"

The sheriff raised his hand for quiet and said in a steady voice: "You go on home now. Verdict's in. Elmore ain't goin' nowhere but the penitentiary. Never comin' out and can't do no more harm. So go on home now!"

The crowd pressed closer to the steps and the shouting began again.

"No one gets by me," cried the sheriff. "I'll arrest anyone who tries and you'll be sharin' a cell with Elmore if you're not mindful."

"Give us Elmore! Hang him!" was the reply. Someone else shouted: "And hang the blasted judge too!"

The sheriff looked over the crowd, searching for familiar faces, until he found several that he knew. He held up his hand again.

"Wait a minute, all of you!" he shouted. "You, there, Tom Andrews...yes, I recognize you...who put you up to this mischief? Who's your leader?"

There was quiet as the men looked at each other, but no one stepped forward.

"Just as I thought," said Bennington. "You ain't got a leader and without it you're just a clutch of angry men who ought to be at work or home chattin' with your pretty wives. Go on now," he repeated. "Go on home." He turned, walked to the door and let himself in, betting that his confidence would disarm the crowd. It had worked once and it did again.

Nothing more than a brief and business-like nod passed between Orly and the sheriff over the next two months except when some story of a crime demanded confirmation. Neither one said anything about the near lynching of Elmore, or the drinking habits of the sheriff. Sometimes, Orly thought, the silence passing between the two men carried a hidden meaning. Nevertheless, he was too busy with wedding plans and his job to pay much attention.

For the time being, Orly remained at Mrs. Bickley's rooming house because of the convenience. He enjoyed the meals and listening to her peculiar speech, sprinkled with words like "precious," and "wicked," and "shocking." Gradually he had begun to take to the other long-time boarder, John Clarke, the biology teacher at the high school who had occupied the large second story front room for many years. Clarke was a middle-aged man, pleasant-looking and soft-spoken and almost as fussy as Mrs. Bickley. Sometimes, Orly thought the two were like elderly sisters, so familiar with each other that their usual communication consisted of half sentences finished by the other, and sometimes only with a nod. On rare occasions, John would talk about his childhood on the docks of Baltimore and the work of stevedores. He had to be persuaded to reveal these memories, because they invariably made him sad. Try as he might, Orly never convinced him to explain how he had come to Marion, especially after attending the Johns Hopkins University.

He only guessed that something large and terrifying in his past had suddenly sucked up his future and deposited him here in this backwater, as if he were in perpetual hiding. *From himself?* Orly wondered. Sometimes when he spoke, the regret was almost palpable. Orly also knew that Clarke, if not exactly shunned, was sometimes the subject of gossip, no matter how hard he tried to efface his presence in the town. He seemed to have no real social life, except Mrs. Bickley, and now Orly for these few months. It was altogether a sad existence.

Toward the beginning of summer, when Orly's wedding date was fast approaching and he and Hattie were preparing to purchase a small house on the south side of town, Clarke suddenly became sadder and more reticent in conversation. Orly wondered if it was the prospect of being alone at Mrs. Bickley's again, but he wasn't sure. Clarke seemed barely able to speak and looked down at his food and rarely at Orly, except with a kind of reproach that seemed to signal that he was about to lose his best and only friend.

Two days before Orly planned to depart, in the afternoon of a hot end-of-May day, when the spring winds had stopped blowing and the heavy damp was settling in, he returned from the *Egyptian* late in the afternoon and had finished washing the grime and ink from his hands, when Mrs. Bickley knocked excitedly at his door.

"Mr. Blair, oh, Mr. Blair! Open up quick!" she cried. The distress in her voice shocked him.

"It's Mr. Clarke. He didn't come to breakfast this morning and he won't answer when I knock. Please, would you look in? I'm fearful to enter his room."

Orly immediately put down the towel he was carrying

and walked to the door of the front bedroom. He knocked sharply, and when there was no answer, he guided Mrs. Bickley away, down the hall so she could not see in. He turned the handle and entered, closing the door behind him. Simultaneously he felt a wave of fear sweep over him, even before his eyes had a chance to focus on the scene. He wasn't sure if it was a feeling of foreboding or what he saw that registered first. There was Clarke, a belt strapped around his neck and fastened to the top of the four-poster bed. He had looped his hands together with a torn piece of cloth, and evidently jumped or strained against the ligature until it strangled him. Orly could only wonder that this grotesque suicide had left Clarke's face calm and placid, even peaceful. Nothing else in the room was out of place except for a piece of paper resting on the neatly made bed beside the body.

Orly quickly went to the door and called out:

"Don't come in, Mrs. Bickley. This is not a sight for you. You need to go find Sheriff Bennington and then Doc Watson."

"Is he...?"

"Yes, I'm sorry to say. I'll stay with him until you get back."

Mrs. Bickley looked faint, as if she might collapse, but she caught herself with a grip on the bannister, and scurried down the stairs. Orly returned to the room, looked at the body again, and then picked up the sheet. The note was short and written in a wavering hand, with several words crossed off as if Clarke had been searching for a better expression.

"Can't–(go on) continue as I am. Those names they call me; they (know I'm) know me better than myself.

Can't stand the loneliness again. It's (best) better to end it now before I die of the hurt and the shame or make a mistake with a student. (I don't) This is the only way to stop myself."

Orly clinched the paper and looked at Clarke's face. He had found peace, and Orly thought he knew what agonies had finally ended for him. He took the paper, folded it over, and put it in his shirt pocket. He continued sitting, staring at the simple, bare room, with its chintz curtains, tidy desk and bed, and round rag rug and then at Clarke's body. A few books and papers lay neatly on the desk. Orly noticed something partially visible under the bed and he stooped to see. He pulled out the half-hidden pile of magazines and on top was an issue of *All-Story* with the half-naked drawing of Tarzan on the cover. Orly shoved the magazines out of sight and stood up. The scene was the sparse summary and accumulation of a life that had scarcely been lived; that had probably ended many years before in Baltimore.

After a few more minutes, he heard voices downstairs and a door slamming shut. The sheriff bounded up the steps, his heavy boots thumping on the runner, and then echoing along the hall. He started to speak even before he entered the room.

"You still in there, Orly? Hope you didn't touch nothin'." He entered and walked immediately over to the body. "Yes, sir," he exclaimed after a brief look around, "a suicide for sure. Of course, Doc Watson will have to confirm it. Won't be long before he gets here. Sent the deputy to fetch him. And Mrs. Bickley's downstairs trembling with fear. Can't let her see this. Why don't you go down and sit with her?"

Orly stood up and was about to leave when the sheriff suddenly turned away from the body.

"Weren't there no note?" he asked. "Suicides always leave a note in my experience. And this weren't no murder. Anyone can see that."

"Well," said Orly hesitating for a minute, and then with decisiveness, he continued, "Yes, there is a note. I have it and I think I'll keep it."

"What's that, son?" Bennington answered sharply. "Won't do at all. Keeping evidence back like that. Let me see it."

"It's not evidence," replied Orly. "You can see with your own eyes what happened."

"It ain't right to withhold. Better hand it over."

"I think not, sheriff. I'll just keep it. You don't need it."

"Could run you in if I have a mind to."

"But I don't think you will, sheriff. You owe me, you know...for that time with Elmore and how I had to collect you from the speakeasy. Wouldn't want to start writing stories about a sheriff drunk on the job and breaking the law himself. Even if lots of townsfolk already know about it. I sure don't want a rumor to find its way into the *Egyptian*."

Bennington eyed him cautiously as if trying to weigh the costs.

"All right, son. No harm in a couple of secrets that don't change the course of history. The town's probably gonna be better for not knowin'. But we're even now. I'll forget and you'll forget, right."

"A true exchange, I guess. His last words won't bring him back, and at least I can put an end to what drove him to it. But it's an awful thing to think about Elmore and

Clarke: terrible the way the guilty manage to live on and the innocent find their way to the end of a rope."

Nature-Morte

Ruby Moore always dressed the part of her namesake, never venturing in public except in some shade of purple or lavender. Her wardrobe was legendary for its slight variations on the theme of these colors, all half tones clustered in a one-octave scale of minor harmonics. Her choice of hues ranged only as widely as the colors of flowers that thrived in the shade: pink impatiens, wine-colored asters, purple begonias, mauve hydrangeas, and violet clematis. The result was an impression of fragility when she stepped into the burning daylight of southern Illinois summers, as if the cruel sun would fade and dry her pale, freckled skin. In the usually dim lighting of her parlor, the blue rinse of her entirely white hair complemented the medley of pastels she wore and the blush of soft shadows on the walls.

The sitting room where she received her relatives for short formal visits was furnished with fine old mahogany pieces purchased at the Famous-Barr Department Store in St. Louis and procured over a lifetime of shopping trips to the bustling city on the Mississippi River that still served as a Mecca for Little Egypt. It took patience to wait for the train that hauled her items back to Marion and for the slow-handed deliverymen that she always tipped with a glass of iced tea when they finished their work. They were polite to her; thought of her as strange and touched their caps; but expected more. The house, which she inherited from her parents, was a sprawling wood frame structure, set back from the main street with a large open veranda in front and a sleeping porch on the north side, built to escape the steamy house in the misery of humid nights during August. There were rumors, however, that she never ventured into this dusty appendage, only allowing a thorough cleaning once a year to an area that had not been occupied or entered for years.

Sometimes, after sitting in stiff-backed chairs, answering questions about school, she invited Clarissa Tidewater, her favorite cousin, once removed, into the dining room for lemonade cookies and a glass of milk. Normally, this room was shut off, and when she pulled aside the heavy double doors, the dim light entering through the thick curtains scarcely revealed its features. The faint-hearted chandelier over the table only lighted the surface and just managed to push the gloom back against the walls. But the pool of light was still bright enough to reveal a tapestry tablecloth dyed in the manner of a Persian rug and on it, at the center, a cut glass crystal bowl in the shape of a basket, filled with fresh fruit and flowers.

From the first time she saw it, Clare had wanted to touch it and trace the diamond-like points that covered its exterior, to test their sharpness with the tips of her fingers.

All of the dim light in the room seemed to concentrate on it, refracting the crystal into muted colors of the rainbow that played in a pattern against the colorful cloth upon which it sat. It was almost hypnotic to watch as she sat politely eating her careful allotment of cookies and a small glass of milk. There were times when she hung back when her aunt made a gesture to leave the room, hoping to steal a forbidden touch, to move her hands around and over the bowl again to see if she could alter or interrupt the light, even pick it up to test its weight. Ruby never allowed such a diversion.

Clarissa's (Clare's) Great Aunt Ruby, with her blue tinted hair and purple suits smelled strongly of face powder, recalling the blossoms of the flowers whose colors she fancied. Ever since Clare was very young, she could recall languid visits to southern Illinois, driving from small town to small town, to sit in dingy parlors filled with ancient people identified as her forebears. In her imagination and recollection, she began to form images of aunts like cut-out dolls in ill-fitting paper house dresses held on by white, folded tabs, and a few surviving uncles sitting in faded shirts, who spoke only occasionally, while the "women folk" gossiped about absent relations: cousins and relations once and twice removed and departed. Later she imagined this was like a quilting bee, with each participant sewing into the muslin backing her piece of the story of this extended family, lengthening and broadening the textures of belonging, tying together and stitching up links with other families until the entire area seemed sewn together into one huge and extended relationship.

Among them, Ruby always seemed to have the greatest fund of knowledge and the quickest memory, and Clare suspected that the reason for this was her easy, friendly laugh, her openhearted acceptance that dismissed the most shocking revelations about the misdeeds of errant relations merely as new stories to be remembered. At the same time, she, herself, presented something of an enigma. Without a doubt, she had once been a beauty, for even now, as an elderly woman, from some angles and in a certain oblique light, her soft features and luminous and intelligent eyes hinted at youthful features that hid beneath the folds and wrinkles of old age. The only puzzle was her reticence to talk about herself, and often she just deflected questions with a smile and a wave of her hand. There was no confessional in her gossip nor was she ever the principal character in the stories she told, and no self-revelation about her past, except the occasional mention of her long career as a high school English teacher. She always prefaced the mention of this period of her life with a sigh of fatigue as if still exhausted by trying to correct the terrible grammar of the farm boys and coal miners' sons who troubled her classes.

Clare discovered later that her story was completely at odds with this impression. Ruby had been born just before the turn of the century and raised when southern Illinois was beginning to recover from the effects of the Civil War and the two hard depressions that followed it. The Peabody Coal mines had just brought in hundreds of foreign workers, and the small towns surrounding its spindly elevator towers had quickened with the appearance of strangers dressed in strange, shabby clothes and chattering in a gush of odd, rhythmic words. Ruby's family—her father was a banker—were local gentry which in this insignificant place included a thin layer of doctors, teachers, dentists, preachers, newspapermen, and lawyers that lay atop a heap of heavily mortgaged farms and small shops; a feed store, a grocery, and even, once, a jeweler. Inevitably, the eyes of these homespun gentry wandered away from small town preoccupations to the metropolis of St. Louis, which in 1904, in a burst of energy, held the largest World's Fair in history.

Ruby and her older sisters, dressed in their finest white starched dresses, and with her brother in his new knickerbockers, set out with her parents by train for the great show during that memorable summer. Ruby, only four or five at the time, had already caught the distemper of exoticism, although when she spoke of it later, she could only remember the ice cream scoops nestled in conical shaped waffles and the huge crowds: the bustling avenues of visitors walking slowly in the scorching sun, and the parades. There were soldiers, brass bands and circus animals, and sullen-looking Filipinos who glared at the gawking audience through the dust raised up by a thousand shuffling feet. This window into the outside world enticed the small girl who peered in timidly, clutching her mother's hand, to see and wish herself a part of this amazing variety of human kind. For many years afterwards, she would regularly take down the big souvenir book of paintings exhibited in the Fine Arts Building, and pour over the colored plates of the French countryside and the dashing soldiers in blue and red uniforms and their prancing horses. Her favorite paintings were the Dutch portraits of fruit, flowers, and the sad, lifeless ducks and geese or fish arranged on tapestry rugs so realistically reproduced that they had to be touched. For a long time she had puzzled over the French term given to these paintings—*Nature-morte*—until she found a definition in the dictionary: "still-life." But the English words didn't seem to capture the stark opposition of the foreign words which, she discovered, literally meant nature-in-death.

To her delight, a portion of the exotic world she observed in St. Louis had also streamed into southern Illinois in the guise of immigrant workers, recruited in New York, from the steamers banked along the docks of lower Manhattan: Italians, Bohemians, Poles, Irish, and Greeks. The Peabody contractors took only those men who claimed experience in the work of burrowing underground and blasting out the coal to fill the tenders of the transcontinental railroads and stoke the fires of the open hearths of Pittsburgh. What enticements they presented or lies they told could only be imagined, but they surely gave no accurate description of the meager and dangerous life on offer in the obscure backwater of Little Egypt.

Most of that "element"—as the elite of Marion called them—lived in a small shantytown of no particular name, adjoining the main Peabody property around Herrin just north. The unpainted houses, surrounded by yards of slag heaps in all shapes and sizes, immediately took on the streaked hues of coal dust. What children there were started to appear almost as soon as wives began mysteriously to show their faces at the local shops, carefully counting out unfamiliar coins to fill lists of items they could scarcely afford. Within a few years, the small grammar schools in the area overflowed with pasty-faced and ill-smelling children from the shantytown, wearing soiled and grimy shirts and short pants, but eager to learn a new language and to belong to the odd place where their parents had brought them.

Ruby's earliest grammar school class, which combined the first through third grades, was presided over by Miss Evelyn, who seemed to like nothing better than an unruly child she could discipline with her long oak pointer. Ruby was curious about the immigrant children...perhaps they reminded her of the wonderful world she had glimpsed in St. Louis...or maybe it was her natural inclination to eccentricity. She loved listening to their earnest struggles with English: the singsong addition of vowels and syllables at the ends of words that the Italian children tried to form, and the harsh gutturals of the Poles and Bohemians. As she watched them, she tried to imagine the strange villages their parents had fled, the dark woods where wolves roamed, where armies marched back and forth ravaging their lands. These children, she thought, should be welcome here; they should be her friends.

She particularly admired one boy in particular, Marco, short for Marc Antonio. He was a grade in advance of hers and unlike the slow farm boys and the other shy immigrant children, he seemed to catch on quickly and thrive even under the surprised and severe gaze of Miss Evelyn. Ruby loved to hear him read the Bible, which they did every morning, taking turns with the long, beautiful verses that she had never paid much mind to. When he spoke the words, they seemed to be clear, personal, and truthful even in the most obscure passages. When it came time for her to read a Psalm or one of Miss Evelyn's favorite parables, she would flush bright red, for she knew that Marco's eyes were fixed on her, encouraging her by pronouncing the words in silent unison.

Of course, her mother and father would never imagine inviting Marco to visit, even had she suggested it. "Foreigners have come to work, and not to appear in anyone's parlor," her mother announced once. In addition, there was already a bitter history strikes and a murder that condemned them in the eyes of the town's elite. Her parents insisted on selecting Ruby's friends from a small network of relatives and suitable families. Nor could she, herself, ever imagine someone like Marco in her parlor, sitting politely, or even attending the same Sunday school together. Those parts of acquaintance were inaccessible to them, and so they remained just schoolmates, subjected to the same daily schedule of memorizing, problem solving, reading aloud, and geography lessons.

In fact, before Ruby was eight or nine she could not remember speaking to Marco except for a polite "excuse me," or on occasion, a rare "hello." Then, in her third year, Marco disappeared. At first, she thought he might have abandoned school, like some of the other immigrant children who would simply vanish to work in the mines...much to the relief of Miss Evelyn. Then one day she saw him coming out of another classroom, taller, darker, laughing with the other boys, until he saw her and stopped to smile right at her.

Their shy mutual admiration continued through the rest of grade school, advanced by casual words and, occasionally, deep, lingering looks. But neither of them thought to brave the perilous social gulf between them, for to bridge that gap would invite the disapproval of both their separate communities whose histories and aspirations kept them at odds. Only in English novels and plays that were her addiction on summer vacations, reading in the hammock swaying in the shade of the hickory tree in the back yard or lying on a blanket on the porch propped up on her elbows were such thoughts possible. It seemed to her that all of English literature had been written expressly to excite her imagination. In one novel after another, rebellious young girls were tempted to look across the chasm of social inequality to find happiness or tragedy in marriage. She thought of herself as one of them: beautiful, rich, abiding in a stuffy family with its narrow circumference of plans for their future (about which they had little to say). Their parents tried to arrange a good marriage to an older, distant cousin, some bewhiskered lawyer or accountant whose life could be described in a few declarative sentences, and would never leave Hampshire...or she sighed...southern Illinois. She laughed sometimes to think herself as one of the heroines of Jane Austen or Emily Bronte novels, waiting for a chance encounter with a dashing, mysterious stranger on a bleak, wind-swept moor to whisk her into a new life. Except, of course, that southern Illinois had no moors and little fog, and no handsome gentlemen on horseback. There were only hot, endless summer days and nights as the corn stalks ripened to rustling skeletons, and the ruddy-faced, eager young men who increasingly stopped at her house for a casual conversation about school, a coming church picnic, and, very rarely, to chat about a book she was reading. Ruby became convinced at one point that her mother was encouraging these literary visits especially, by prompting a favored boy with the titles of the novels she was reading. It could not be by accident, she guessed, and only by design, that they too were spending their summers with Jane Austen and not fishing, bicycling, or helping their fathers with the businesses or farms they would soon inherit.

When Ruby finally finished her third year of high school, these visits became more like courtship, and she realized, at this point, that she needed to take them seriously, if only to put a stop to the plans being made for her by a collusion of adults. Like the heroine of her own novel, she confronted her mother in the kitchen after school one spring day. She waited until her mother was alone, so they could speak freely. Usually, on occasions like these, they talked about cousins who were planning to marry, or spring weddings, confirmation classes, graduation, and the excitement of the senior dance—at least her mother seemed excited about such things. This afternoon, Ruby guided the conversation to her senior year, about to begin a few months away. Her mother enthusiastically responded, because she imagined, finally, in Ruby, an interest that had always been missing from these talks. Perhaps she felt that her subtle prodding, her parade of suitable boys, her subtle talk of marriage, and the satisfactions of a settled life had finally taken hold of this strange, headstrong and romantic daughter, who seemed to be absent much of the time, wandering along imaginary hedgerows and moors.

However, Ruby was very much present that warm afternoon, as the house creaked and groaned in the harbinger wind that blew gusts of an early warmth to the low hills of Marion. She informed her mother, kindly, but firmly, that she did not intend to step out with the gangly, awkward boys that were invited to the house. She declared she would be a new sort of woman, the sort she had read about in the St. Louis and Chicago newspapers, and perhaps even like the women of Paris and London, who now seemed able to determine the course of their own lives. Henceforth, she would see anyone she pleased, and even planned to go to college. Of course, she welcomed her mother's sympathy and her approval, but she would tolerate no interference. Did this mean that she might not marry, was her mother's shocked response. No, just not marry well, Ruby had said, at least not well in the eyes of the local matchmakers.

Perhaps only at this moment, when her mother drew in her breath in an audible sign of defeat, did Ruby actually decide on a plan by which her daring words might actually lead to action. More than once in the past two years, she had stopped to talk to Marco, and after each one of these short conversations, she had come away with a light-headed, pleasantly confused feeling. He was unlike any of the other boys she knew. His handsome features had sharpened in maturity, and he seemed thoughtful where the other boys his age could only talk about summer baseball games. She imagined, but did not know, if the laughter in his eyes were directed at her. But she dared to hope that they expressed delight at her presence. He was serious about life–she had always sensed that–and she knew that his parents were proud and at the same time fearful of him. They had to be amazed that he had grown so tall and intelligent and distant from them. Were they also anxious that he might break all of the rules and codes of the society on whose outskirts they lived, looking in from the familiar misery of their shantytown? They had come to America for just this opportunity, not for themselves, of course, but for their children, but now that it might be happening, in such a dramatic form as a son who seemed to grow up and away from them simultaneously, the success of their ambitions bewildered them.

Marco was a solitary diamond discovered in the seam of black Peabody coal; the unexpected treasure brought up from beneath the ground, from days and years of grimy, backbreaking labor, a boy, chiseled out of hardship and polished by their sacrifice. And now they had no idea what to do with him and they scarcely understood his elegant speech, the cadences he picked up from the English Bible, the dreams that he gently confided to them, that seemed to speak of another world entirely. He was ambitious for himself and for his country and, indeed, he did not distinguish between the two. He was popular with the other boys and attracted the secret passions of almost all the girls in his class, but this would, he reckoned, never lead to a career in politics, nor a rich man's easy way with women. More than anything he wanted to study at the new University of Chicago that had just opened in the great grey city to the north, and then to travel, to teach ... and ... he dared to think, to marry Ruby.

Neither of them remembered when their courtship began because it seemed so inevitable, but suddenly Ruby and Marco were seeing each other after school, when he could get away from his part-time job. They met together in the local ice cream parlor and soda fountain, which was the only plausible rendezvous in her small town. Word of their meetings eventually reached her mother and father who made one half-hearted effort to break off the budding friendship and then decided they could do nothing to dissuade their headstrong daughter. Instead, they invited Marco to call, not of course, from any romantic motive they shared with Ruby, but from a self-congratulatory generosity, thinking themselves to be the authors of this democratic match: the banker's daughter and the miner's son. In fact, however, they understood that resistance would only have stoked the intensity of the friendship, and they hoped that out in the open air, as her mother put it, the implausibility would reveal itself. This generosity extended only so far, however. There was no question that his parents could ever appear at the big house on West Main Street. Should they by accident encounter each other in public, a polite nod of recognition was deemed more than sufficient. Small town democracy had its limits.

Marco began to call at Ruby's house on weekends the summer after her graduation. Sometimes he stayed for dinner. Other evenings they went to the new Bijou Theater on the square in front of the post office, a building that had formerly been a feed store now relocated to the edge of town. Sitting in the dark, on moveable wooden chairs, holding hands and watching the flickering screen in a room that still smelled faintly of leather and horses, they dreamed together of cities beyond the oceans of rustling cornfields and dreary small towns, of a life of adventure together in Chicago or New York or maybe London.

During one of these evenings in the stuffy theater, something exciting and dangerous strode into their lives. The program was a lengthy film, *The Man Without a Country*, and a Charlie Chaplin short, *The Adventurer*. An unannounced incident at intermission suddenly brought the real world into this inconsequential corner of Illinois. The lights went up after the opening Chaplin short and the pianist began to play the National Anthem. As the audience murmured in surprise, some of them standing in respect, the high school principal walked to the front of the room and stood before the assembly, motioning them to sit down. He held up his arms in a gesture of quiet and began to speak in a trembling and excited voice about the terrible war in France, the barbaric Germans, the rape of Belgium, and America's mission to set civilization back on course, to save Europe from the Huns and from their terrible long history of aggression. The war, he proclaimed, had even reached Marion, for the nation needed its sons to volunteer for the battle. Service was the duty of every able-bodied young American man, he explained, and no wife or sweetheart could be a patriot without sacrificing her momentary happiness to the cause. When he finished, there was no applause and no conversation, and as he walked off, the lights dimmed and Edward Everett Hale's famous story about the man who cursed his nation began. When it finished, Ruby and Marco sat still for a moment. He spoke first to say that, of course, he would go; indeed, he had planned for several months to join the Expeditionary Army, but had waited to tell her. With tears in her eyes, she replied that she knew, yes, of course. Since the declaration of war in April, she had known that he would have to go. As they walked slowly, hand in hand out the door and into the dark humid night, he promised that they would marry as soon as he returned, and she agreed that she would wait, no matter how long for that moment; for it only postponed the beginning of their great adventure together.

His departure happened quicker than either of them had imagined. Thus, in early 1918, after several weeks of training, Marco found himself in the company of hundreds of thousands of other boys culled from American farms and cities and small towns for deployment with the First American Army near the Front in the north of France. They had traveled by rail from the coast, through Paris and then north toward the great battlefield along the Marne River. He had written back to Ruby that this was not how he had intended to see France or the City of Light, not in its desperate, dark moment, against the distant boom of artillery, but he promised that someday they would return to walk its streets—once he and his comrades had chased the Germans away. War was no lark, he warned her, but there was no doubt now about victory. He understood it was a difficult, necessary job to do, something to finish before they could begin their lives.

When the second great battle of the Marne began in April, Marco was part of the 3rd U.S. Infantry that assaulted the German lines. The brash confidence of his unit had gradually worn off, and the inedible rations, the cold damp weather, the lice and rats, the stench of the open latrines, and the relentless boredom of waiting had soured their dispositions and deepened their anxiety. The battlefield itself was nothing like he had ever seen or imagined. The only visible landmarks above the trenches were the splintered trunks of trees, blackened by smoke and fire and the miles of barbed wire stretched in rows and guarded by sharpened pickets, with shreds of uniforms hanging from them like dead flowers in this garden of carnage. A deafening and a continuous barrage of artillery, aimed at the German trenches and the wire that protected them finally announced the battle. By the beginning of the actual assault, several hours later, the shells had fallen and exploded with such intensity that they opened cavernous, water-filled holes and reduced the ground itself to a friable black muck that clung to their boots and uniforms as they emerged into No-Man's Land between the two lines.

The artillery had done terrible damage, but as the Americans rose up out of their earthen trenches and began to stream across the broken ground, the Germans opened up with machine-gun fire, and launched a barrage of lethal gas bombs into their midst. Within a few minutes, a thick green cloud of chlorine gas hung over the battlefield. Marco and his comrades quickly reached for their gas masks, but he was slow in doing so because he paused to help the soldier struggling next to him. Before he could adjust his own mask, he felt the terrible, burning gas enter his nose and throat, scraping away the flesh like a metal rasp, and he fell, clutching his throat, into a steep hole where he lay for hours in a pool of dark water, mud and blood.

Later, he wrote to Ruby that the first thing he could remember was waking in a makeshift hospital behind the lines, the thunder of battle still breaking and roaring in the distance, and with an awful pain in his chest. At the time, he could scarcely speak a word to ask about his condition, but the anxious eyes of the nurse betrayed the seriousness of his condition. He thought he might live, but wondered if he would always carry a permanent wound carved out of his lungs, and if he would ever be delivered from the kind, but rough hands of doctors and orderlies, back to himself and to the innocent world of southern Illinois.

In June 1918, Marco finally shipped home to Marion, a wounded war hero, with no visible scars except the occasional involuntary twitch of his eye and a mouth that fell open as if to speak when he intended no words. He was still wearing his uniform when Ruby met him at the tiny train station, much thinner now, his black hair cropped short and his skin still stretched taut and translucent from the pain he suffered. When he talked, there was a delay in the coming of his words as if he spoke through a ventriloquist, for the sound seemed to come a beat too late, either from deep inside him or from somewhere behind. He walked slowly and deliberately now, like an exhausted long-distance runner just finishing a race and desperate to catch his breath. Ruby looked at him sadly, but he returned her grim smile with such a look of relief and joy that she scarcely could remember her anxious days of waiting.

Ruby also decided that they would marry as soon as a decent period of convalescence had passed. As he held her tightly, his mother and father, dressed in their Sunday best, advanced shyly to claim him, seeming almost reluctant to intrude upon this reunion. Ruby had already made arrangements. Marco would come to live in the big house on Main Street. He would have his own room and she would be his nurse until their late fall wedding. The autumn, she esteemed, perfectly matched the maturity of their love: the burnished gold and bronzes of the season would be the décor of their union. The dark mustards and violets of the chrysanthemums would transform her house, the church, with the entire small town glowing in sympathy. She promised herself she would travel to St. Louis to buy a special surprise present for him, something unusual, beautiful, and memorable that would reflect and display her feelings for him.

The days and weeks passed rapidly, and Marco seemed to improve gradually, as Ruby and his parents watched his progress with anxious encouragement. By the middle of

October, he was well enough to join Ruby in the plans for their wedding. Even his shiny black hair had grown back, and his fair complexion had lost the pallor of convalescence. The two began to make social calls together and to attend the happy reunions as well as funerals of the other young men who returned to town. In fact, he was feeling so much better that he proposed to return to live with his parents before the wedding. Ruby was unhappy about this decision, but understood the rules of propriety, and thought it would restore something of expectation and surprise to their wedding. It would recreate the moment before he had joined the Army, and erase the unhappy period of the war. No longer a nurse, she could imagine herself a bride again.

The evening before he planned to depart, Ruby cooked an elaborate meal in celebration, but Marco just sat quietly at the table, moving his food around his plate with the heavy silverware brought out of the smooth wood box and polished for the occasion. At first, Ruby only imagined it was sadness about leaving. Even if she refused to admit it at first, she noticed his flushed cheeks and chalk-white skin-tone. Finally, she allowed herself to acknowledge it consciously and asked him what had happened. Did he not feel well? Was he sad?

He replied that he felt feverish. Perhaps it was the Spanish flu mentioned in the newspaper, he said. The government speculated that soldiers returning home after their demobilization were spreading the contagion. How ironic, Marco commented, that so much joy and anticipation brought with it this plague of suffering.

That night the wind blew in from the west, bringing dark clouds and bursts of rain that caused the windows to rattle. By morning, the sky had cleared, but the temperature had fallen abruptly and Ruby's father predicted frost and ice by evening. Marco was very late in stirring from his bed, and when he entered the dining room, coughing painfully, Ruby rushed over to place her hand on his burning forehead, and immediately ordered him back to his room. All morning she brought him hot tea and sat by his bedside reading to him, watching his eyes focus and then blur as he passed in and out of a troubled sleep. By late afternoon, he seemed much worse, and Ruby's father insisted on calling old Doc Watson.

When he finally appeared, carrying a worn black leather case, and dressed against the cold, Ruby peered at him anxiously. She knew him well, but had no confidence in his ability to do anything other than set broken bones or prescribe the latest elixir. She wondered what he could he say other than confirm the gravity of Marco's illness; what could he advise other than give a name and a measure to his symptoms and then utter words of encouragement that had no plausible bearing on this particular case?

Ruby led Doc Watson down the hallway and then up the stairs, pausing once to see if the steps were too much for him. But he gamely managed, black bag of instruments in his left hand and boosting himself along the banister with his right. She turned at the landing and entered where Marco lay. Ruby's mother was sitting in the corner; she gave Watson an anxious nod as he entered the room and approached the bed. He recognized the familiar thick smell of sickness in the close atmosphere and observed the flush on the boy's face. There was no mystery; he knew immediately it was the Spanish influenza, which he had treated almost twenty times in the past week alone.

Opening his bag, he drew out a stethoscope and inserted the small pods in his ears.

"How are you feeling, son?" he asked, placing his hand on Marco's forehead to check the fever. "I'd like to listen to your heart and lungs if I might."

"Sure, Doctor," he said, coughing weakly.

Watson pulled down the damp sheet and unbuttoned his nightshirt.

"Breathe deep for me, son," he said, placing the circular metal resonator on his chest. He moved it around to several spots and then said again. "Now maybe you can cough; gentle, not too hard."

Marco complied, covering his mouth and wheezing once into his forearm.

Watson continued to move the stethoscope around Marco's bare chest and under the folds of his nightshirt, but it was unnecessary. He knew from the first that he would hear the sounds of the boy's breathing muffled through the liquid that was drowning his lungs. His actions were meant for the others; it was for Ruby and her mother that he performed this ritual of diagnosis.

In the prolonged moment of silence while he appeared to be considering what to tell them...in this short moment, the dreadful memory of the Civil War hospital came back to him: the sounds, the smell, and the violent throes of the dying. Just as surely as then, this case was another casualty of war and he knew, just as certainly, that he could no longer bear the arbitrary deaths it brought. Again. He remembered the sad, pleading face of the dying soldiers. Was it Elbert that he recalled? Was that his name?

"I'll be honest with you, Marco," he said, putting his

stethoscope back in his bag and pulling the covers back up over his chest. "It's what you probably thought: the Spanish Flu. Lots of cases around Marion these days and quite a few have already beat it. You'll need to drink lots of liquid. Water's best. Bring down that fever. And you need clean, fresh air. You shouldn't be breathing in the same sick air. I'll come round tomorrow to see how you're feeling."

He realized he was making this promise to give them hope; assurances for the living and the dying that he had made far too many times. He knew of nothing to be done.

His words were spoken out in front of the patient, but when the doctor reached the front door, he looked back solemnly at Ruby. Another problem, he warned, was the question of his weakened lungs—from the war. There was always the chance that the fever would not break. The sleeping porch, he repeated, was really the only remedy he knew to propose.

Ruby reluctantly agreed with her parents to move Marco immediately outside, into the clean, cold air of the blustery evening. As they prepared his bed and helped him into the mountain of comforters and quilts, Ruby could scarcely repress a sob that she tried unsuccessfully to swallow. She had to turn away from his bed, shivering in the cold so he would not hear. When she and her parents went back inside she suddenly begged her father to reconsider and bring him back in. It could not be good to lie in the cold, she argued, but he convinced her that the doctor knew best; the fever had to be broken.

All through the night, Ruby slipped out onto the frigid sleeping porch to hold Marco's hand, to feel his brow, to tuck him even more tightly against the falling temperature. She thought he seemed to be improving, and his breathing became less labored, and so toward morning, she allowed herself a couple of hours of sitting up sleep, until a pale sunlight lit up her bedroom. Still wearing her clothes from the night before, she ran anxiously to the door of the sleeping porch and shoved it open. Half buried in blankets, Marco's face looked relaxed and the flush had vanished. Immensely relieved, she walked to the bed and put the palm of her hand on his forehead. It was dry and cold and she knew instantly that he was dead.

Ruby's grief was so powerful and total that it followed her like a malevolent spirit, mocking her efforts to escape its presence. She rarely spoke about Marco after that, and only once referred to his dying when she told her mother that she had foresworn romance forever. She consigned her novels (and everything she had planned for) to the storm cellar to sit amongst dusty old jars of jams and jellies and sacks of potatoes and onions. She vowed henceforth to live her life differently. At the funeral in the small Catholic chapel, near the shantytown that no one ever seemed to notice before, she followed the mysterious and alien ceremony with dry eyes.

A week after the burial, she disappeared, without a word to her parents, taking the train alone to St. Louis to stay with a distant cousin in the city for two nights. When she returned, she carried a large parcel that she carefully unwrapped before her puzzled parents. It was a cut glass bowl bought from Tiffany's that she announced would be her belated wedding present to Marco. From a second, smaller package, she pulled out a large square of multi-colored cloth of thick brocade, designed in the pattern of a

Persian rug.

"This cloth goes under the bowl on the dining room table," she told them. "I will fill it with fresh fruit and nuts and flowers, just like the paintings in that book from the World's Fair. It's to be my still-life portrait, nature-morte—nature in death." She did not need to explain that this would be the constant reminder of Marco and a mute and permanent testimony to their love and lives forever frozen in anticipation.

Doc Watson

Doc Watson trudged home slowly from seeing his last patient. His right shoulder drooped as if the black bag of medical tools he carried was filled with stones. A malicious December wind swirled around him, nipping at his coat and trousers. Although it was still daylight, the sun appeared low in the sky, veiled, off and on by banks of rapidly moving, low clouds.

Delia opened the door as he approach the house.

"Let me have your coat and bag. You look terrible, David.

"No worse than I feel."

"It's not that flu coming on, I hope."

"No, just tired. Bone weary."

"Come and sit down, then. I'll get you a cup of tea. Or maybe you want an early dinner. Won't be long."

Watson walked into the living room, looked at his favorite chair near the fireplace, but chose the loveseat opposite.

"Come sit beside me for a minute, Delia. I got a few

things to say to you."

When she had settled next to him, he took her hand in his and studied it intently. With his finger, he traced the spaces between her knuckles made prominent and sharp by the arthritis that bent her joints.

"Where's it all gone, Delia? Where did we put the time?"

"I suppose into work. In just living. Watching our boys grow up. Helping the folks in this town make it a decent place to live."

"It wasn't what you wanted though, was it, Delia? I remember it so clearly as you opened the door to me when I first come to Marion way back so many years ago. I knew rightly then that all your expectations died, 'cause I wasn't who you expected to come calling. I could see it written across your face."

"No, David, you're wrong."

"So we made the best of things, I guess. Like most folks here, just getting by. Facing up to whatever gets tossed in their way. And dreams fadin' away like night shadows creepin' up."

"No, David, it's been much more than that. Of course, at first I had hoped to see my beau, but you've been something so much better than I could have hoped for...Everyone gives what they got to give. And you had so much to give. Can't ask for anything more."

"Didn't you want more, Delia...than this town, this life? Be honest."

"No. You're what I want...always wanted...Now you tell me why you're turning on yourself this way? Did something happen?"

"Yes. I suppose it did."

"Are you going to tell me?"

"It's that Marco kid, the soldier fiancé of Ruby Moore. You remember I talked about him. Died a few weeks ago and I can't help thinking about him. Nothing I could do for him or anybody else with that flu. Tried to tell him that he'd get better, but I couldn't lie anymore. Just couldn't speak the words."

He paused and looked away from her face because he knew he would see tears and he needed to go on.

"It's come full around, my life has. All that senseless dying and wars at either end. I grew up young with one and now I've grown old with another. I've run out of comforting words, Delia; they just won't come to me anymore, and I'm afraid of dyin' angry."

Delia reached over and turned his face toward hers.

"Look at me, David Watson, and let that sadness go. What you're saying, trying to say, is something I'm going to state for you plain out: it's time to stop. Let go of it. Let this town alone. You've helped it as best you can, as much as anyone could, but it's over and done now. You gave them your whole life so what else can you give? And if that means sitting on the front porch in an old rocking chair and listening for the train whistles and the wind stirring up in the trees or the voices of friends who might come calling, well that will be enough. I'll be right there rocking with you, David Watson, thinking about our two fine boys Ed and Cal and the life we made together. Now, you put your medical tools away somewhere safe so you won't meddle further with them, and come and have your supper and there's an end to it."

Author's Note

Living up North, Little Egypt was the destination of my childhood summers. I traveled there with my parents to sit in an endless parade of stuffy parlors in the presence of reclusive, white-haired aunts and silent uncles, handing around old sepia-colored photos and plates of lemonade cookies and listening to familiar stories. Only half paying attention to these, I have probably confused them in my imagination in writing these sketches. Are any of these tales based upon real people and names that lodged in my recollection? Are these family legends I heard recounted, but which I now presume to be original and of my own invention? Perhaps so. Among them, I can only say that one sketch reflects my own experience, and even that is true only in its vaguest outlines. As for the rest, I would simply suggest that remembered tales and recollected people, transformed by imagination and fantasy are among the strongest impulses of fiction itself. How could we ever deny the presence of memory in what we presume is our original creation?

About Atmosphere Press

Atmosphere Press is an independent, full-service publisher for excellent books in all genres and for all audiences. Learn more about what we do at atmospherepress.com.

We encourage you to check out some of Atmosphere's latest releases, which are available at Amazon.com and via order from your local bookstore:

Itsuki, a novel by Zach MacDonald
A Surprising Measure of Subliminal Sadness, short stories by Sue Powers
Saint Lazarus Day, short stories by R. Conrad Speer
My Father's Eyes, a novel by Michael Osborne
The Lower Canyons, a novel by John Manuel
Shiftless, a novel by Anthony C. Murphy
The Escapist, a novel by Karahn Washington
Gerbert's Book, a novel by Bob Mustin
Tree One, a novel by Fred Caron
Connie Undone, a novel by Kristine Brown
A Cage Called Freedom, a novel by Paul P.S. Berg
Shining in Infinity, a novel by Charles McIntyre
Buildings Without Murders, a novel by Dan Gutstein

About the Author

James Gilbert is a historian, educator, and novelist. While at the University of Maryland, he published ten books on Twentieth Century American culture, one of them, a *New York Times* Notable Book of the year. He has lived and taught abroad in Paris and then with year-long Fulbright Fellowships at universities in Sydney, Australia, Uppsala, Sweden (where he received an honorary Doctorate of Letters), Amsterdam, the Netherlands, and Tubingen and Erfurt in Germany. He was also a resident at the Rockefeller Center in Bellagio, Italy. Since turning to fiction writing, he has published a book of short stories and two novels, *The Key Party* and *Zona Romantica*. He currently lives in Silver Spring, Maryland.